S0-BCZ-452

IT WAS ALMOST THREE YEARS SINCE HE HAD TOUCHED A WOMAN, and when she fell against him he held her stiffly until she began to tremble and mutter his name over and over again. Then his arms tightened about her and he buried his face in her black shining hair, and there returned to him a feeling he hadn't known since the early days of his marriage. But the feeling was immediately punctured by the thought of his wife, and her moral point of view rose before him like a battlement through which a divorce would never penetrate.

For the first time in his life Harry knew for certain that his only hope for happiness lay in this woman he was embracing—that only she could heal the wounds of his past and quiet his aching need for love. . . .

The Husband

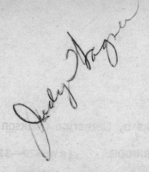

The Husband

(Formerly titled: The Nice Bloke)

by Catherine Cookson

A SIGNET BOOK from

NEW AMERICAN LIBRARY

TIMES MIRROR

NAL BOOKS ARE ALSO AVAILABLE AT DISCOUNTS IN BULK QUANTITY FOR INDUSTRIAL OR SALES-PROMOTIONAL USE. FOR DETAILS, WRITE TO PREMIUM MARKETING DIVISION, NEW AMERICAN LIBRARY, INC., 1301 AVENUE OF THE AMERICAS, NEW YORK, NEW YORK 10019.

First published in 1969 by Macdonald & Co. (Publishers), Ltd.

Published by arrangement with the author.

SIGNET TRADEMARK REG. U.S. PAT. OFF. AND FOREIGN COUNTRIES
REGISTERED TRADEMARK—MARCA REGISTRADA
HECHO EN CHICAGO, U.S.A.

SIGNET, SIGNET CLASSICS, MENTOR, PLUME AND MERIDIAN BOOKS are published by The New American Library, Inc., 1301 Avenue of the Americas, New York, New York 10019

FIRST SIGNET PRINTING, MAY, 1976

1 2 3 4 5 6 7 8 9

For Mr. R. G. Wilson
Another nice bloke

Contents

Dig in the soil of a quiet man and you unearth the savage.

BOOK ONE

HARRY BLENHEIM

The Nice Bloke

He sat encased in frozen terror aware of people passing him and the looks they cast on him as they went into the court. The terror had been rising in him since he awoke at four o'clock this morning. It had brought him out in sweats, hot and blush-making like a woman in the menopause; it had dropped him into baths of cold perspiration where his teeth chattered and he had to grip the bed head to steady himself. But now all his fear was at a standstill; it had frozen during this waiting period and he was grateful even for this respite because, gathering force as it had done since he entered the courthouse, he knew that if it rose just a little further he would go berserk.

His eyes unblinking, he stared before him and again asked himself why he was here, how had it come about? How had it happened to him, Harry Blenheim? He was a nice man, was Harry Blenheim. He didn't have to be bigheaded to know that was the general opinion of him. It had been his own opinion up till a few months ago, at which time he had been full of self-respect.

When he looked in the mirror he liked what he saw; not exactly a good-looking fellow, but, as his wife had once said in her far back loving, laughing days, his was a face full of character, with the kindest brown eyes God ever made. And then there was his voice, deep, what they called musical. And it was musical, because he could sing. It was the singing that had made him a successful businessman. It was odd when you came to think about it, but it was true. They had taken him out of the Sunday school and put him in the choir because of his voice, and in the choir he had chummed up with Tony Rippon, and that was something, because the Rippons were from the top end of Fellburn and he was from the bottom end.

When his voice broke, it broke well and he became a tenor. It was after he had sung solo with the church choir on television that Esther Rippon had singled him out. He hadn't taken to her very much at first and nothing might have come of it, but Tony died and she seemed inconsolable.

3

Mr. and Mrs. Rippon hadn't been elated when he and Esther became engaged. He was working then as a junior clerk in the rates department and his prospects, although secure, were very, very dull. And that was how Mr. Rippon saw them too, and, as he said, something would have to be done. And he did something; he got him set on in the firm of Peamarsh, of which he was then a junior director.

On the face of it Peamarsh's was a small wholesale chemists firm, but once Harry entered it he realized it had a finger in every pie in Fellburn. There were five directors, and they were all out to monopolize, most of all their youngest director, Mr. Rippon.

Harry had never really liked Mr. Rippon, even before he married his daughter. As for Mrs. Rippon, he wholeheartedly disliked her. He saw her as a psalm-singing, sanctimonious prig, and he only hoped Esther wouldn't take after her. Esther didn't—at least not altogether.

Esther was nineteen and he was twenty when they were married, and life, even with its pinpricks in the form of Mr. Rippon, promised good. And for sixteen years it kept its promise, more or less, until hell had opened and swallowed him. But the hell had been a private hell. The public had only got wind of it a month ago when he had tried to kill his father-in-law. He hadn't quite succeeded. He wished he had. Knowing what the consequences would be, he still wished he had.

He blinked once and looked around the wide corridor as if in search of a friendly face. Even at this moment he would have been glad to see Esther, but Esther was the last person he was likely to see. Nor would he be likely to see his sons, John and Terry. Then there was Gail. . . . Oh! Oh, Gail.

He hadn't seen his daughter for weeks. Esther had packed her off somewhere, and she said that if it lay with her he would never clap eyes on Gail again.

Esther blamed him; she blamed him for it all, not her father, oh no, not her father, that dirty old licentious beast. . . . But that was exactly what Esther had called him, himself, wasn't it? Not a dirty old licentious beast, just a dirty licentious beast. Well, he wouldn't have that. He told her he wouldn't have that; what he had done didn't deserve that title. He had made a mistake as many a man before him. He had been weak, and he had paid for his weakness. He was paying for his weakness at this moment as he waited for his

4

name to be called to be brought to justice for what, as one paper stated, was the worst case of its kind Fellburn had ever known.

"It shouldn't be long now."

He looked at his solicitor who had just moved away from the barrister. His face wasn't friendly. A month ago he had called him Peter and he had been Harry to him. They were both members of the Round Table; they played golf together, and it was they who saw to the organizing, each Christmas, of some stunt for bringing in money for parcels for the old folks. They had been buddies, Peter Thompson and he, yet when the balloon went up Peter had been reluctant to have anything to do with the case.

Nor had he any hope of leniency from the judge. Callow was one of the old school. He wasn't nicknamed Horsewhip Callow for nothing. At a talk he had given to the Round Table dinner he had indicated that a great deal of crime was due to people moving out of their class. "And don't let us forget it," he had said; "there is as much class distinction today as there ever was, and rightly so." As one member had remarked later, old Callow was a ghetto-minded old sod, and if he had his way, no one would be let out of his district.

Harry knew that he himself had been let out of his district, so to speak. Let out from the bottom end of the town and into the top end, and that people were remembering. It didn't do, you see; leopards didn't change their spots. And it wasn't only the people from the top end who were remembering, those from the bottom end were, too. That's what you got for being an upstart and trying to climb; they said, "But it wasn't really his fault, it was his grannie's. Mary O'Toole was a pusher. She had pushed him into the choir and then into the rates office, and he should have had the sense to be grateful and not try his luck."

But there were two from Bog's End who didn't think like this: Janet Dunn and her son, Robbie. And, as if his thoughts had conjured them up out of the air, he saw them standing before him. They said nothing, neither of them, they just stared at him. And he returned their stare, his gratitude for their presence making him speechless. When young Robbie put his hand out and touched his shoulder, he wanted to grab it and hold it, as he would have held John's or Terry's had they been with him at this moment, but he resisted the impulse and just continued to stare grate-

5

fully at Janet as her eyes asked, "How did this happen to you, how?" And as if she had spoken aloud, he shook his head slowly. He didn't know, he didn't know, it was just one of those things that started at an office party.

One

It was snowing heavily when he reached home. At the top of the drive the house greeted him with lights in all the downstairs windows. He could see the Christmas tree in the drawing room. It was bare yet; they would start decorating it tomorrow.

The snow excited him. He hoped it would lie over Christmas; it was some years since they had had a real white Christmas. He went to the boot and took out a largish parcel and wondered if he would get it into the house without Gail spotting him.

When he opened the front door he was met by warmth and the sound of voices coming from different directions, Janet's from the kitchen raised in protest against Terry—he must be pinching something again—John's voice from somewhere in the cellar, yelling, "Mother! Mother! I can't find them. What did you say they were in?" Then Esther coming from the morning room and looking toward him, and lifting her hand in greeting before she shouted down to the floor, "The old green box in the corner, the right-hand side of the boiler."

He was about to slip into the cloakroom and deposit the parcel until he could take it upstairs when a cry from the landing brought his gaze upward, and there stood Gail. She stood poised for a moment; then, taking the stairs two at a time, she was in front of him before he could escape. "Hold on! Hold on! You'll have me over, you big horse."

As she reached up and kissed him, she cried, "It's snowing, it's snowing and it's going to lie."

"All right, all right. It's snowing and it's going to lie. Let me get my things off."

"What's that?" she was whispering. "Coo! It's a big parcel. Who's it for? Me?" She dug her finger between her small breasts, and he said, "You! Of course not." Then bending his head quickly down to her, he whispered, "Your mother."

"Oh, what is it?"

"I'm not telling you; you'll give the show away."

"Honest, I won't, I won't."

"It's a set of frying pans."

7

"Oh, Dad!" She pushed him, and he drew her to the side of the curtain that bordered the passage leading to the loggia and, his voice low, he said, "Do you think you could get it up into the attic without her seeing?"

"Leave it to me," she said. "You do an evasive tactic and leave it to me."

He left it to her to see that she hid her own Christmas box. He could imagine her reactions on Christmas morning when she saw the fitted dressing case that she had admired in Pomphreys months ago. Esther had been against him getting it. She considered it too sophisticated for a girl of fifteen, but he considered that Gail needed something sophisticated to help her over her present stage of plumpness. His daughter couldn't as yet see her plumpness as a prelude to beauty, but he could. He knew that in two or three years' time she'd be breathtaking. In a strange way she had inherited all the good points from Esther and himself; Esther's height, her pale complexion, his own brown eyes and his hair, but whereas his hair was a sandy nondescript color, hers, though of the same thick strong texture, was a tawny shade.

If he had been asked what made life worth living for him, he would have answered airily, "Oh, a number of things"; his wife, his home, his family. But deep in his being, where no question penetrated, the truth lay, and the truth was that it was his daughter and she alone that answered that question.

He had been proud when his first child was born and that a boy, but he had experienced no feeling of wonder until Gail had been put into his arms, and then it was as if a miracle had been performed for him alone. He had no longer believed in miracles. He had sung of miracles in choirs and concerts for years; miracles had been ten a penny. And then Gail happened to him.

Esther had, at first, been jealous of his feeling for the child; then the next year Terry had come, and things balanced themselves out. She had John and Terry, and he had Gail. Sometimes he had felt guilty about his almost utter lack of feeling for the boys and had tried to rectify this by being more friendly toward them. Yet with the insight of children they had gauged the parental balance of his affections. That was why, he had surmised, they had teased and tormented Gail until she was able to stand up for herself.

His wife came toward him now. "I thought it would hold you up," she said.

8

"Another hour and the way it's coming down and it might have."

When he shivered slightly, she said, "Go in the drawing room, the meal won't be more than fifteen minutes."

As he went into the room, John's voice came up through the floor again, bawling, "I can't find it, Mother." And he heard Esther exclaiming impatiently, "Leave it! Leave it! That'll be the day when you're able to find anything without it jumping up and hitting you."

There was a big fire roaring in the open grate. The room looked comfortable, colorful, and lived in. He sat down on the couch and stretched out his feet, and all of a sudden he had a longing for a drink. That was the only thing that was lacking in his home life . . . well, perhaps not the only thing, but something that became an irritation at a moment like this, a moment when he wanted to relax. But Esther was firm that no intoxicating drink of any kind should enter the house. This was one of the standards she had brought over from her mother.

He often wondered how his father-in-law had managed over the years to cover up the smell of liquor on his breath. He didn't do it with scented cachous or mints; he must have had some special formula because he had come into this very house, his eyes hazy with whiskey yet not a smell from him, and Esther had never suspected a thing. When her father was gay and he talked loudly and laughed a lot, she put it down to a business success. In a moment of weakness, once she had admitted that his manner embarrassed her at such times. He had, on this occasion, stared at her amazed, wondering how such an astute woman could be hoodwinked. But there were none so blind as those who did not wish to see. It would have been unthinkable to Esther that her father should take intoxicating liquor on a Saturday night, then on Sunday walk with stately step up the aisle to his pew, not paid for any longer but definitely reserved for himself and his family.

The sound of congenial commotion now came to him from the hall and he heard Esther say, "Why, Robbie, it's beautiful, but you shouldn't, you know you shouldn't," and a thick voice answer in airy tones, "Why shouldn't I, Mrs. Blenheim? Why shouldn't I?"

"Harry!" He hitched himself up straight on the couch and looked toward the door where Esther was entering the room carrying a square box. "Look what Robbie's brought me for a Christmas present. It's too much I'm telling him."

9

He got to his feet as she came toward him and looked down at the highly polished foot square box inlaid with mother-of-pearl. "What is it?" he said.

"A workbox. Look at it." She lifted the lid to disclose a tray of small compartments with inlaid tops and pearl knobs, holding strands of colored silks and boot buttons studded with colored glass. "It's got everything," she said. "Look!" She put it down on the couch and lifted out a tray to disclose beneath more compartments holding small bobbins of thread, needles, pins, and all the accouterments necessary for a Victorian lady's needlework.

Harry lifted his eyes to the young man standing by Esther's side. "It's an exquisite job, Robbie," he said. "Where did you pick it up?"

"Oh, you know . . . I get around." Robbie laughed and his thin parted lips showed a wide set of blunt-looking white teeth.

Harry laughed back into the face before him, the face that yelled out its inheritance.

Some Jewish faces were distinguished only by the shape of the nose, but every feature of Robbie Dunn's face proclaimed him to be a Jew. His skin was thick and of a slightly greasy texture; his eyes were round, keen-looking, and black; and his hair was thick, straight, and black. His face was long and, if it had followed its structural design, would have ended in a pointed chin, but here it leveled itself out, leaving the jaw square, which in a subtle way emphasized the whole.

Robbie Dunn, at nineteen, was only five foot six and a half, but he was thickset, and if when he spoke, he had hunched his shoulders and stretched out his hands, the onlooker wouldn't have been surprised; but when he did speak, his voice surprised most people because he spoke with the idiom of the working-class Tynesider.

Robbie Dunn, like most of his race, had a business head on his shoulders and was out to make money. He was both calculating and discerning. There were in him two strong and overpowering emotions: one was gratitude even for the smallest kindness, the other was hate for even the smallest insult. He had brought Esther Blenheim a present, but it was out of gratitude to her husband, because it was Harry Blenheim who had helped his mother when she had needed help most, at the time when she was left without a husband, mother, or father, all three being killed in an old car that should never have been on the road. And it was this man

10

who had given him ten pounds to get started. He hadn't loaned him ten pounds, he had given it to him.

Robbie now stood looking at Esther as she went into ecstasy over the box. Then his eyes came to rest again on Harry. He liked Harry Blenheim. He was a nice bloke, a good bloke was Harry Blenheim. If he told the truth he was the only one he liked out of the whole bunch, except perhaps Mrs. O'Toole, the grannie. He wondered why he didn't cotton on to Gail because she had always been nice to him, but he had the idea she was tarred with the same brush as her brothers.

"It's a beautiful thing, Robbie," said Harry now, "but as Mrs. Blenheim says"—he nodded toward Esther as he gave her her full title, which he always did when speaking of her to either Janet or Robbie because she had made this a stipulation of the association between them and the Dunns —"it would bring a good few pounds today. It's real Victoriana."

"Daresay," said Robbie nonchalantly; "but I only paid fifteen bob for it. Honest." He nodded. "Fifteen bob in a village yon side of the river, down by Washington way you know. But I've cleaned it up a bit since I got it. There was a bairn playing with it on the steps of a house, pulling all the buttons out. I went straight up and knocked on the door and said, 'That's too good for a bairn to play with, missus, I'll give you ten bob for it.' Quick as lightning she said, 'You'll not, you know.' 'All right,' I said, 'fifteen.' 'I'll take it,' she said, an' whipped it up out of the bairn's hands and set it screaming, and I didn't linger to do any comforting but made off with me box, and here it is."

They were all laughing now. Robbie could spin a yarn. He'd always had the power to make Harry laugh. His tales very seldom enhanced him; they were nearly always told against himself, which was clever Harry thought, as it tended to make people like him rather than otherwise.

Harry had not the slightest doubt that Robbie would one day get to where he wanted to go, and he would take pleasure in climbing the obstacles that were set up against him. And he was aware inwardly that Robbie hadn't to go any farther than this house to find barricades being erected against him. But as he had told himself before, it was as well to ignore them. Young men garnered wisdom as they garnered years, at least he hoped that this would happen to his sons, especially his eldest.

Gail came running into the room now, she rarely ever

11

walked anywhere. She was saying loudly, "Gran's starving, and she's not the only one." Then she broke off and exclaimed, "Oh, hello, Robbie. Coo! what's that? Who's that for?"

"It's for me, madam," her mother said, inclining her head slowly toward her daughter. "And remember that."

"Oh, isn't it sweet!" Gail was fingering the tiny bobbins of thread. "Did you bring it, Robbie?"

For reply he jerked his head, and again she said, "It's lovely." Then looking at her mother, she remarked bluntly, "You won't use it, Mother."

Esther Blenheim closed her eyes and pressed her lips together and assumed annoyance before she said, "Well, if I don't use it, miss, I can assure you you're not going to get the chance."

"Oh!" Gail flounced now. "It'll be mine someday." She grinned at her father, and as her mother exclaimed on a high note, "Really!" Harry Blenheim burst out laughing again.

It was at this moment that John came into the room. He stopped just within the door and surveyed the group; then said sullenly, "Gran's waiting."

John Blenheim was seventeen, as tall as his father, and as fair as his father was dark. All his features and coloring were those of his mother. His appearance in the room changed the whole attitude of the group, even Gail stopped her chattering.

As Esther now said, "We're coming, we're coming," Robbie Dunn walked down the room toward John Blenheim, and the nearer he approached him the shorter he felt, but he kept his eyes on him, and the tall fair boy returned his stare. It wasn't until Robbie was at the room door that he said in a casual way and over his shoulder, "I'll wait for me mother if you don't mind, Mrs. Blenheim. It's pretty rough out; I had to leave the car on the main road."

"You've got a car now?" Gail's voice was high as she pushed past him into the hall before confronting him squarely.

He looked at her for a moment in silence, then said, "Aye, I've got a car."

"You don't mean the van?"

"No, not the van. I've still got the van, but I've got a car an' all. And I'll tell you somethin' else." His glance now swept from Harry Blenheim to his wife, then to their son before it returned to Gail, and again he allowed a silence to

12

elapse before delivering his news: "I've taken a shop the day, in Pine Street off the market."

The silence was engendered now by amazement. It went on and on until Harry Blenheim said quietly, "You've taken a shop in Pine Street, Robbie?"

"Aye, Mr. Blenheim, a shop, I'm goin' in for antiques."

Harry shook his head slowly. At fifteen Robbie Dunn had started with a fruit barrow. He had given him the money to get going. He had only kept on fruit for six months, then had taken a stall in the market, a cheap-jack stall selling tawdy souvenirs and throw-outs from the warehouses, a stall at which John had once said only mentals or dimwits would leave their money. When he was sixteen he had gone in for secondhand clothes. But that didn't last very long; there were too many at that game, at least in the market. And then he had taken up the white-elephant trade. Going around the jumble sales, he had collected enough bric-a-brac to fill his stall, and when it went in almost a day, he said he knew that this was the line he had to follow, and he had done so assiduously for the last two years. He had made enough money on a Wednesday and a Saturday to provide him with a van and to pay three women on a Saturday to do the jumble sales. And now, here he was saying he had a car and he was taking a shop in Pine Street; rents in Pine Street were to be reckoned with. He had to hand it to him, he had push. He only hoped that John, in his way, would show as much initiative when the time came. He dismissed the doubts that rose to the surface of his mind and said, "Does your mother know of this?"

"No." Robbie grinned now at Harry. "I was keepin' it for a sort of Christmas box for her, but . . . but somehow it just came out."

It came out, Harry knew, because he wanted John to hear it. It was odd about the feeling between his son and Janet's son. They had never hit it off from the first moments they had come into contact when Robbie was seven and John was five. The feeling between these two boys had worried him at times. It was a feeling that was not the result of association; it had been from the beginning a feeling that stemmed from a deep elemental knowledge of an old hate, a hate that was beyond their consciousness, a hate that went far back down into the rock of time but which was held to the present by a gossamer thread of awareness—racial awareness.

Janet Dunn came into the hall now. She looked at Esther

13

Blenheim and said, "Mrs. O'Toole's getting restless," and Esther said, "All right, Janet. And look, don't you stay, you get off with Robbie here. I suppose you've seen this wonderful present he's brought me." Without waiting for Janet's comment she went on laughingly, "I'll enlist the battalion to see to the dishes. But anyway, you get yourself off now. And Robbie wants to talk to you, he's got something to tell you."

Janet Dunn looked toward her son. Her eyebrows were raised in inquiry, but her face held a blank look, giving nothing away. She said flatly, "That'll be the day when he hasn't got something to tell me." The remark too was flat, seemingly holding no meaning except to convey that this mother was used to her son's chatter; yet when they exchanged glances, there passed between them a language that only they could read, and Robbie gave a hick of a laugh and turned away and walked across the hall and through the door that led into the kitchen, and the Blenheim family went into the dining room, there to be met by Mary O'Toole, Harry Blenheim's grandmother.

"Is nobody hungry in this house except me?"

"It won't be a minute," said Esther Blenheim, going down the length of the room to the hatch at the bottom.

Taking her seat by her great-grandmother, Gail leaned toward her and said under her breath, "You've got a tapeworm, Gran."

"Watch it! Watch it!"

This remark sent Gail off into high peals of laughter and she leaned her head against the old woman's arm and hung on to it. She loved her great Grannie O'Toole; she was more with it than some of her own pals. She said, "Watch it! Watch it!" just like Tivvy on television said, "Watch it, pigeons! Watch it!" Oh, her grannie was wonderful.

"Sit up and don't be silly." Her mother's voice, coming at her from behind, brought her upward in her seat. "And make yourself useful; serve the potatoes."

As Gail went around the table with the vegetable dish Mary O'Toole looked at her grandson and said, "It's a terrible night; I hope you're not going out again."

"I'll have to, worse luck," Harry replied as he set about ladling the stew out of a casserole dish. "I've got to relieve Peter Thompson at eight o'clock."

"What! You're going to do Father Christmas?" It was Terry speaking now, his voice cracking on a laugh. Terry was short and promised to have the build of his father, but his coloring was that of his mother and his brother, John,

14

and what he liked above all else was to raise a laugh. His father, looking at him, said heavily, "Why can't you keep your tongue quiet!"

"You're not going to play Father Christmas on a night like this!" Mrs. O'Toole's thin body was erect in her chair. "Are you mad? Standing around for hours like Johnny-cum-canny; you want your head lookin'— Why don't you do something about it, Esther? He'll get his death, sitting in an office all day, then going and standing in the market till God knows what hour."

"Gran!" The word fell deep, admonishing, and Mary O'Toole closed her eyes against her daughter-in-law's voice and listened to her own inward one saying, "In the name of God will I ever get used to it." Five years she had been under this roof now and it had been pleasant enough, oh, she had to admit that. Esther tried her very best, her Christian best—aye, that was the word, her Christian best—but she only had to hear God, damn, or blast used and then she came all over starchy. She had the power to make you feel like a child who had wet its knickers, and her at seventy-five, it wasn't right. One of these days she'd let fly and she'd swear for ten minutes and not use the same word twice. Begod if she didn't!

Janet Dunn, putting the last dish on the table, said to Esther, "I'll be off then"; and Esther, smiling up at her, said "All right, Janet. And thanks. Elsie should be back in the morning. If I don't see you again before the holidays, a Merry Christmas, Janet."

"Yes, yes, a Merry Christmas, Janet." They were nodding all around the table, all seemingly oblivious that Janet did not keep Christmas, but she answered, "The same to you. The same to you," before going out.

"That was daft," said Terry.

"What was?" asked Gail from across the table.

"Wishing Janet a Merry Christmas."

"I can't see what's daft about it," said his mother; "we always do."

"That doesn't make it any the less daft." Terry had an impish grin on his face now and he turned it toward Gran O'Toole, saying, "Does it, Gran?"

"I suppose not," said Mrs. O'Toole. "But it's courtesy like, and she's a nice woman, is Janet Dunn, sensible. And have you noticed"—she swept her glance around the table—"she's got a presence about her, a dignity?"

"Some dignity!" They all looked at John now, and he

15

finished putting some food in his mouth before ending, "Working at an all-night café. Some dignity."

"There's never anything undignified about honest work, John." There was a strong reprimand in his father's voice.

"Honest! The Dunns? Huh!" John jerked his head backward. "That sharpshooting little squirt, honest."

"JOHN!"

"Well, he is. How's he come by a car so soon?"

"By hard work." His father was leaning toward him over the edge of the table. "He's turned his hands to all kinds to make a living and worked from early dawn until late at night. You don't know you're born, so I don't want to hear any more of it."

They were all looking at Harry now. It was rarely they heard him talk like this, rarely saw his face set as it was at the moment, and his manner aggressive.

"Oh, I should have known better than say a word against him." John's voice was a mumble now. "Better to keep your mouth shut altogether about the Dunns."

"You needn't keep your mouth shut about the Dunns. Talk as much as you like about them, only be fair. Robbie never had your chance but by the time he finishes . . ."

"Yes, yes, go on say it." John's head was up, his chin out. "He'll get farther than me, that's what you mean isn't it? . . . The dirty little Jew boy." His chair scraped back on the polished floor, and as he rose to his feet to leave the table, Esther said, "Sit down, John, and have your meal and no more of it."

Now also on his feet, Harry silenced her with a wave of his hand, and confronting his son, he said harshly, "You use that term ever again, my boy, and I don't care how old you are, I'll give you a hiding. You understand?"

John stared for a moment longer at his father, then swung around and dashed out of the room.

As Harry resumed his seat, a door banged overhead and they all started eating again, Harry and Esther, Gail and Terry slowly, but Gran O'Toole, munching rapidly, one mouthful hardly swallowed before she took on another, threw into the embarrassed quiet one of what Gail called "Gran's tactless bombs." "If he had half the brains of Robbie," she said, "and with the advantages he's had he wouldn't be going to the technical school next year, he'd be working for one of those big universities. . . ."

As Harry stopped eating and bowed his head deeply on to his chest, Esther's knife and fork clattered to her plate at

16

the same time as she exclaimed in hurt indignant tones, "There's one thing we can always rely on you for, Gran, and that's your loyalty to the family." And on this she, too, left the table.

"What have I said? What have I said?" Gran O'Toole looked from Harry to Terry, and then to Gail, and Gail, as truthful as her great-grandmother answered, "The wrong thing as usual, Gran, the wrong thing, and at the wrong time."

"I wish you a Merry Christmas, I wish you a Merry Christmas, I wish you a Merry Christmas and a Happy New Year."

"Shut up! Shut up, boy!" Harry now barked at his younger son. "There's a time and place for everything."

Terry applied himself again to his food. Gran was already applying herself, but Gail looked at her father, where he sat with his head resting on his hand staring down at his plate, and she thought, "He likes Robbie. He likes him better than he does John, I'm sure he does, and it isn't fair really."

It was quarter-past eleven that same evening when Harry returned to the house. He felt frozen to the marrow in spite of the double whiskey he'd had. He and Tom Vosey had paraded around the town center for two and a half hours and collected the almighty sum of one pound, eight and threepence. Was it worth it? He could have put the one pound eight and threepence into the fund and had the benefit of a night at home, and without the prospect of flu looming up before him.

On the kitchen table there was a tray set, and on the stove a pan with some milk in it. He didn't want to be bothered making coffee—he would have welcomed it if it had been ready—all he wanted was to climb into bed and get warm, but he reminded himself he'd had whiskey and it would be on his breath even though a half hour had elapsed since he had drunk it, so he'd better make the coffee.

The coffee made, he had just sat down by the side of the table when the kitchen door opened softly and Gail came tiptoeing in. "I heard the car," she whispered. "You're late. Did you get much?"

"One pound eight and threepence."

"Oh, the mean beasts. You took over five pounds last Christmas Eve."

17

"It was a fine night and people were out. Only mad dogs and fools would be out tonight."

"You're not a fool." She came close to him and rubbed her face against his cheek, and he put his arm around her and hugged her to his side, and when she sat on his knee, her shorty nightdress and dressing gown rode almost up to her thighs. But she didn't pull them down, her mother wasn't here to chastise her. Looking at her father's weary face, she said, "It's been a rotten night."

"I'm sorry; I'm to blame I suppose."

"Half and half," she said candidly.

"Thanks."

"Well, you said it. And, you know, you did go for John."

"He shouldn't have used that term about Robbie."

"But Robbie is a Jew, Dad."

"There's nobody disputing that fact, but would you like to be called the dirty little Englisher. And what's more, when people like John use terms like that, what can you expect from other boys? It's about time that kind of thing was squashed, good and proper. People don't seem to learn ever." He shook his head slowly, then went on, "Robbie's a good boy. What he does, he does for his mother. I think, his one aim is to make enough so that she won't have to work."

"But Janet likes work, she told me she does. I asked her only yesterday wasn't she tired after getting up at half-past five in the morning to get to the café, and she said no, she was used to it. I asked her wouldn't she like another job and she still said no; she said the hours had always been convenient, half-past six till half-past eleven. They were convenient when Robbie was at school so she could make his dinner. He would never stay for his dinner, she said. She said the job gave her a lot of time to herself and she doesn't mind coming and helping Mother when Elsie's off. So you see, she doesn't mind work."

"That isn't the point, at least how Robbie sees it. Anyway, it's a pity it happened. And at Christmas too. It's bound to mar the atmosphere. Did he go out?"

"Yes, he went to the club. But he was in before ten, and he wouldn't have any supper, not even a drink. Mother was worried, but Gran went in to him."

"Gran?" Harry raised his eyebrows and jerked his head quickly as he said under his breath, "Gran should stay out of this; she's caused enough trouble. Trust Gran."

"She didn't mean it; it just comes out. And you know, it's funny, she can manage John. He takes things from her that

18

he wouldn't from anybody else, and she tells him the truth to his face. If I was to say half the things to him that Gran does, he'd scalp me."

He said to her now, "How long has your mother been up?" and she answered, "Not long. She looked tired. Grandfather came in. He's not coming for Christmas after all; he's going to his friend in York. He said he's ill and wants to see him. It's the one he was in the army with, I think. Mother was disappointed about that and all. He brought a lot of parcels. They're up in the attic." She hunched her shoulders and smiled at him.

"Come on," he said, tapping her leg. "To bed."

She walked to the end of the table; then turning and looking at him where he was putting the tray on the draining board, she asked, "What are you going to do about John? If it isn't cleared up, he'll sulk all over the holidays and it'll be frightful. He can you know, I mean sulk for a long time."

"You leave John to me. Go on, get yourself up."

She made four tripping steps and came back to him, and flinging her arms around his neck, she hugged and kissed him. Then in a manner that was individually hers she drooped her head to one side and smiled gently into his face and whispered, "You're nice, Mr. Blenheim. As a certain Gran O'Toole would say, you're a nice bloke."

"Go on with you." He rapped her buttocks smartly once and she ran toward the door with her hands on her bottom. Then again hunching her shoulders, she adopted a stealthy attitude and crept out into the hall. . . .

Esther was sitting up in bed reading when he entered the bedroom. She didn't put down her book but looked over the top of it as she said, "You're late."

"Yes."

Dutifully she now asked, "How did it go?"

"One pound eight and threepence."

"One pound eight and threepence!" She clicked her tongue twice, then asked, "Did you have a hot drink?"

"Yes." He began to undress, and she said nothing more until he was in his pajamas and standing by the side of his bed. She laid down her book then and asked, almost in the same words as Gail had done, "What are you going to do about John?"

He had a sudden and unusual desire to turn on her and cry, "I'm going to let him get cold in the grease he got hot in," but that would mean that her face would tighten, then

19

her eyes would take on that hurt look, and when she spoke there'd be that slight tremor at the end of her words, which indicated the effort she was making to remain calm. Esther laid great stock on remaining calm. All the books she read, especially last thing at night, were to aid calmness. Waldo Trine's *In Tune with the Infinite* was her second Bible. Daily she imbibed its philosophy. He had once said to her, jokingly, "I bet you could repeat that book backwards," and she had taken his remark as censure. His thoughts darting off at a resentful tangent now, he said to himself, "She even took the damn book on her honeymoon, and the second night she sat up reading it." He shook his head at himself. He was tired, weary. That business with John had upset him, together with the lack of Christmas spirit emanating from the citizens of Fellburn. It was ludicrous, but if he hadn't stood outside each of the three pubs that lined Market Square, it would have been three and threepence he would have collected, not one pound eight and threepence. So much for Christian charity. God! he felt tired and irritable, all at cross-purposes with everything. It wasn't only the business of John, he had felt off color lately. Some of the joy had gone out of life; there was a sameness about it. Why? Oh, well, it was his age he supposed. They all said it happened to you as you neared forty. Looking at it squarely, he'd had a long run for his money. He'd known contentment for years, and that was taking into account the frustrations of the bedroom too. He glanced now at Esther. She was looking at him. Her fair hair was smooth and shining. She hadn't a wrinkle on her skin. She didn't look thirty-seven, she didn't look the mother of three children. She was wearing a pink brushed-nylon nightdress; on someone else, like Gail, it would have looked cosy, cuddly, but on Esther it only looked warm and sensible.

He sat on the edge of his bed. He wished Esther was cuddly. He wanted to go to her now and snuggle down beside her and feel her arms going about him. He imagined her pulling his head down, pressing it in between her breasts. He imagined himself pushing the cuddly nightie up to feel her flesh. He wanted comfort. Lord, how he needed comfort at this moment, wifely comfort, motherly comfort, mistressy comfort. The lot combined. His mouth was working and his hands moving against each other. He was sickening for something; the cold had got into his bones. He could see himself in bed with flu over the holidays. . . . "What?"

"I said are you going in to him . . . John?"

20

He stood up and looked at her. She was a good woman, Esther, a good mother, a good wife. But what made a good wife? There must be various opinions on that one. Some men had their wives every night—two and three times a night, so he understood. Huh! From once a week, Esther had regulated it to once a month. But that was only up till Terry was born. From then it was once every time she felt like it, and Esther very rarely felt like it. It must be four months now since he had lain with her. He was only thirty-eight; he felt no different from what he had felt at eighteen. He wasn't, he supposed, what you'd call a passionate man else there would have been hell to pay, but he was human, natural; and besides, he was considerate. He had always been considerate with her, too damned considerate.

"What are you standing there for, like that? You're shivering. Either get into bed or go along and see him and get it over with."

He turned from her and went to the wardrobe and took out his dressing gown. He was putting it on as he went out onto the landing.

Harry opened his son's bedroom door and went into the room. The light was on and the lower bunk was empty. Terry turned from his back onto his side and looked from the upper bunk at his father. He looked wide awake, as if he had been waiting for him coming. He said under his breath, "He's in his study." He motioned his head toward the wall and the boxroom that his mother had turned into a workroom for his elder brother and given it the title of study.

Harry put his hand out and ruffled Terry's already unruly head, saying, "It's time you were asleep, isn't it?"

Terry chuckled, then laughed softly before he asked, "Did you take much?"

"A mint, one pound eight and threepence."

"Coo! Could they spare it?"

"That's what I've been asking. It wasn't worth it, was it? I mean standing out there all night."

"No, I should say not. Are you cold?"

"I was, but it's wearing off." Again Harry touched his son's head. Terry was a nice boy. His character was akin to Gail's, kindly, thoughtful, just the opposite from John's. Who did John take after? Not himself, nor yet Esther. His grandfather? Perhaps, for Dave Rippon had his own particular form of sulks.

"Get to sleep now," he said as he went out.

21

He did not knock on the door next to the bedroom but opened it quietly and paused as he saw his son sitting at the small desk in the corner of the narrow room. The boy did not turn his head to look at him. He had likely heard his voice from the other room and was waiting for him. Perhaps he had been waiting for him all evening. This wasn't the first occasion when his son had remained stubbornly silent until he had gone to him and, if not actually apologized, made his peace. He stood by his side now, looking down on his hair, but he had no desire to put his hand out and touch it as he had done a moment ago with Terry.

"Time you were in bed, isn't it?" he said.

There was no reply from John, no movement whatever.

"I'm sorry about tonight; we were both a bit hasty."

Still no reply, no movement.

"I know you don't like Robbie. I know you're an entirely different type from him, but that's no reason to call him names." Harry now saw his son's jaw work, first to one side and then to the other, before his teeth came hard down on his lower lip.

"It's Christmas and this is no time to have quarrels or disagreements. Your mother's worried. Shall we forget it?" He put out his hand now and gently touched his son's shoulder; then, before the lack of response should make him angry, he turned about, saying, "Come on, get to bed. It's well past midnight." He paused at the door without turning around and added, "Good night."

He didn't even expect an answer to this, for this was John acting according to pattern, but tomorrow morning things would be as they had been before the incident at this evening's meal.

Esther was lying down when he returned to the room and she didn't speak until he had got into bed and put the light out, and then she said, "Good night," and he answered, "Good night."

He hadn't kissed her good night for more than five years now.

It was almost half an hour later when he heard her give a genteel little snort which meant she was asleep, and he turned on his side and put his hand under his cheek and lay staring wide-eyed into the darkness. And it came to him that he was lonely.

Two

"Good Morning, Mr. Blenheim."

"Good morning."

"Good morning, Mr. Blenheim."

"Good morning."

The female voices of the packing staff chorused through the outer office of the first floor of Peamarsh's.

When Harry passed a little cubicle where an elderly man was sitting at a desk on which there were three telephones, he paused for a moment and said, "Good morning, Mr. Hogg," and the man stood up quickly, saying, "Oh, good morning, Mr. Blenheim. And it is a morning, isn't it? How did you manage to get the car in? Mr. Waters has just phoned to say he can't get his out of his gate and if he could he wouldn't dare risk it down the hill."

"Oh, I carried mine," said Harry laughing, and Mr. Hogg laughed too.

He was the only man in Peamarsh's who gave the outer clerk, as the man was called, the title of mister. To the other members of the staff, according to their positions, he was Hogg, Charlie, or Dogsbody; the last, mostly from the men in the packing departments on the ground floor and in the basement.

Before he entered his office he had to pass a glass-partitioned room which housed four typists and was given the glorified term of pool. The members of the pool this morning weren't sitting industriously at their desks but gathered together in the middle of the room looking at something that one of them held in a small square box. A shadow passing their window brought their heads around apprehensively; then seeing who it was, they smiled and nodded and mouthed, "Good morning, Mr. Blenheim." And Harry nodded back to them.

An engagement ring in that box, he bet, likely belonging to the tall blonde, Miss Rice, wasn't it. Yes, Miss Rice. Well, he hoped she'd keep house better than she took down dictation. He'd had her once when Ada was off sick. Which reminded him; he hoped Ada was in this morning. Although there wouldn't be much work done on the premises today,

23

he had one or two things he wanted to get off, but if that cold of hers hadn't eased, she would have likely taken his advice and stayed in bed.

She had. His office was empty when he entered and the door to the little cubbyhole which was his private secretary's domain was closed. It was always open for the first half hour of the day while she bustled backward and forward from his desk to hers.

He had hardly got his coat off when the phone rang. He picked it up and heard his father-in-law's secretary, Miss Bateman, nicknamed The Paragon, say, "Mr. Blenheim?"

"Yes."

"This is Miss Bateman speaking."

"Yes?" he said again.

"Miss Cole has phoned to say that her cold has got worse and she won't be in this morning."

"Thank you, Miss Bateman."

"I'll send someone from the pool."

"Very well. Thank you." He almost added laughingly, "But don't let it be the blonde, she'll be very preoccupied today." But he was dealing with Miss Bateman, and so, instead, he said, "There's no hurry, I haven't much to go off."

"Very well, Mr. Blenheim."

He put the phone down and walked to the window. It was coming down harder than ever now; he couldn't see the clock on Howard's, the jewelers, across the street. If it wasn't for the party this afternoon, he would have those letters off and get home while the going was good, for if this kept up till dinnertime, all cars, those that had got in, would be bogged down.

He had just seated himself behind his desk when there came a tap on the door, and he said, "Come in." And when he saw Jim Whelan enter the room, he exclaimed on a surprised note, "Why, hello! What's brought you indoors without being dragged? Sit down, sit down." He pointed to a chair.

Jim Whelan was known as the outside man. His title was appropriate, for most of his work dealt with estimates and valuations. He was not quite a chartered accountant, not having stayed the course long enough to pass his exams; he was not quite an estate agent and valuer, having no private business of his own; but he was a bit of both, and a number of other things besides. He had been with Peamarsh's for thirty years and Harry had the idea that the longer he stayed the less he liked it. As he had once said to Harry, "It

24

was all right when they stuck to their own line, but now you don't know where you are." Recently he had been dangerously loud in his condemnation of the firm when they had spread out another tentacle and embraced the building trade. Acting as middlemen, they secured contracts, then passed them on, raking off a healthy percentage in the process.

"Something on your mind, Jim?"

"Yes, there is." Jim Whelan settled himself opposite Harry, then leaned forward and said, "You remember about two months ago I did an estimate on that job for Halliday, the man who took over Benson's garage down Cromwell Road?"

"Yes, yes, of course I remember; I dealt with it. It went through here."

"Do you remember what the price was, the one I quoted?"

"Let me see . . . well, I can't say offhand, but just a minute, I can get it for you in a tick." As he made to get up, Whelan said, "You needn't, only to confirm it. It was six thousand five hundred for having the garage extended, the car park made, ladies room put up, and so on."

Harry screwed up his eyes before saying, "That's right. But what about it?"

"Then why was it raised?"

"Raised?" Again Harry was screwing up his eyes. "To my knowledge it's never even been confirmed, I mean by Halliday. . . . Wait a minute." He got up quickly and went to a cabinet by the side of the window, and opening a drawer, he flicked through some files; then pulling out a folio, he said, "Here it is, a copy of the estimate, six thousand five hundred."

"Did you send that out?"

"No, I don't send them from here, not now; they go from the next floor, Rippon's office. It's a new arrangement, since they started on the buildings and contracts."

"Well, look at these figures, will you?" Jim Whelan now handed a sheet of paper across to Harry. "I've taken them letter for letter from the correspondence that was sent to Halliday. The typist there's my niece. We got talking and this is what came out of it."

Harry looked down at the paper in his hand and read, "Peamarsh's estimate to Halliday for work on garage, etc., seven thousand two hundred and fifty pounds. Lovell's estimate to Halliday for work on garage, eight thousand pounds."

Harry stared at Jim Whelan and said slowly, "Lovell's?

25

What's Lovell's got to do with this? We only took them over a month ago. We haven't started doing anything under their name yet, I mean nothing new; we're only finishing off the jobs that were already in hand, at least the contractors are. What does it mean?"

"It means that somebody sent an estimate from the firm of Peamarsh to Halliday quoting in the first place seven hundred and fifty pounds more than the reasonable price, and at the same time they've answered Halliday's letter to Lovell's firm asking for an estimate from them too. How was the poor bugger to know that Lovell's was Peamarsh's and some clever Jack was working off one against the other on him?"

"I can't believe it. And the risk!"

"Risk. What do they care about risk when there's lucre involved? They were out to show how much cheaper Peamarsh's could do the job and at seven hundred and fifty above what I put in at that. And my estimate of six thousand five hundred was leaving them a warm profit, I can tell you."

Harry looked grimly down on the figures on the paper; them drawing in a deep breath, he said, "Leave this to me, will you?"

"Yes, I'll leave it to you, Harry. But mind you, I want this straightened out; I don't like to see people taken for double suckers. Single suckers yes, it's happening every day, but this is a bit much."

"I'll see to it right away, Jim."

"Will you give me a ring?"

"I'll give you a ring."

"So long, Harry." Jim Whelan got up and made for the door. And he had reached it before Harry said, "So long, Jim."

When he was alone again, Harry sat staring down on the evidence of jiggery-pokery. He didn't need to ask himself whose work this was, he knew. He had a father-in-law with what was called a business head. But business head be damned, he wasn't going to get away with this. For his own peace of mind he must see that he didn't. Over the years he had closed his eyes to one piece of chicanery after another, but there was a limit.

He took the lift to the top floor and stepped straight on to a thick pile, cherry-colored carpet. This was Peamarsh's directors' sanctum. There was a wide oak-paneled corridor with two doors on either side. The name plates on the doors

26

said: Mr. Arthur McMullan; Mr. Tom Vosey; Mr. Frank Noland; the fourth door said Gentlemen. The corridor opened into a hallway studded with more doors. These were named: Mr. Graham Hall; Mr. Peter Walters; Mr. David Rippon. Another door had on it the simple statement Boardroom.

He thrust open the door marked Rippon. Miss Bateman was sitting behind her desk. She looked up and said, "Oh, Mr. Blenheim, I was just going to ring the pool."

"Oh, that's all right, Miss Bateman. As I said there's no hurry, I just want a word with Mr. Rippon."

"He was on the phone a moment ago. I'll see if he's free."

She pressed a button and listened, and said, "He's still on, but I don't suppose he'll be a minute. Take a seat, Mr. Blenheim."

It was all very formal; it was always formal with Miss Bateman. He could call his own secretary Ada, but he would never dream of calling Miss Bateman Marie.

Miss Bateman was a power in Peamarsh's. Before the building had been reconstructed and the top floor given over to the directors Miss Bateman had run the staff, and this included the men in the packing department, and now, not because she hadn't time, but solely because of the situation of her office, her domain of power reached only to the floor below, where she continued to wield it firmly; except over Ada Cole, who, having worked in Peamarsh's longer than Miss Bateman, would have none of it. Harry had always been vaguely surprised that his own able but timid secretary refused to be pushed around by The Paragon.

Marie Bateman was in her early forties. She was of medium height and thin, and from her fair hair to her long narrow feet she was perfectly groomed. Altogether she gave off a kind of restrained elegance, which deceived you into thinking she could at one time have been pretty.

Looking at her now, Harry understood why she intimidated most people. But no matter how off-putting her manner, she was a good businesswoman and secretary, or else his demanding father-in-law would never have kept her on.

"He's finished now."

"Thanks." He tapped on the communicating door and went into Dave Rippon's office.

"Hello there. I expected you."

Harry paused in the middle of the room and Dave Rippon added, "I knew Esther wouldn't be able to keep that."

27

"Keep what?"

"Keep what! The car, of course. I told her not to mention it until after the holidays, but that's women for you, same all over. Sit down, sit down. Well what do you think? Do you want it?"

"This is the first I've heard of it. You mean your car?"

"Oh, so she didn't tell you then." Dave Rippon leaned back in his high-backed, black swivel chair and laughed. It was a small sound coming from so large a man. Then he passed his hand over his forehead and on to his thick graying hair before he said, "Well, I'm ready for a change, it's over two years. Esther said you liked it."

"Yes . . . yes, I like it." His tone held no enthusiasm. "But you always put your old one in for exchange, don't you?"

"Usually. But that one of yours must be dropping to bits."

"It's a good car, it's only five years old."

"Only five!" The voice was scornful. "It might as well be fifty. Anyway there it is, it's up to you. As you know, it cost me nearly two thousand. They'll give me fourteen hundred for it or more, but I'll let you have it for twelve fifty. It's up to you."

Harry looked at his father-in-law, at his round fleshy face, at his round pale blue eyes, which you could have called a sailor's eyes, farseeing; and the description was certainly true in his father-in-law's case for Dave Rippon was farseeing where Dave Rippon was concerned. People said he was a handsome man, a fine figure of a man, a man you would never put fifty-five years to, fifty yes, even forty-five on some days. His body was big, thick, and hard. He had been an athlete in his time and the effect was still with him in spite of his sly drinking, although that was showing now in a thickening above his belt.

He had never liked his father-in-law, perhaps because he knew that everything Dave Rippon did for him was really for his daughter. He was where he was, he knew, because he had married Esther. This knowledge hadn't irked him during the first years of marriage, but latterly it had got under his skin, more so as he took his father-in-law's real measure. He knew, for instance, that his father-in-law couldn't make a straight deal if his life depended on it. Even about the car he had to be crooked. He wouldn't get fourteen hundred for it; it had only cost him eighteen hundred in the first place, not two thousand. If he got twelve hundred he'd be lucky, and that's what he wanted him to

28

pay. Moreover the car wasn't two years old; by his reckoning it was three, nearer four.

"I'm a fool for letting it go in any case." Harry blinked as his father-in-law leaned across the desk toward him, "I'm just going to get the same type—same color, in fact, I think—but you know after a couple of years things start going. Oh"—he leaned back again and flapped his hand toward Harry—"that's bad business, isn't it? I'll have to look out, I'm slipping. Well, you know how she's been taken care of, there's nothing wrong with her really."

Harry just stopped himself from saying, "No, you've only beaten the guts out of her."

Dave Rippon waited for Harry to make some comment, and when none was forthcoming, he blew his nose on a silk handkerchief before adopting his business attitude and saying, "Well, if it wasn't about the car, what brought you up on this the slackest morning of the year, for I don't expect there'll be two penn'orth of work done in the whole building today?"

Harry swallowed, wetted his lips, then said, "I've come up about the Halliday estimates."

There was a long pause before Dave Rippon spoke, and then he said one word, "Yes?"

"Whelan got the estimate out."

"I'm aware of that."

"It was for six thousand five hundred."

There was another pause before Dave Rippon said, "I'm aware of that also, so what?"

He held his father-in-law's eye as he said, "The estimate was sent out to them for seven thousand two hundred and fifty."

There was no reply from Dave Rippon now and Harry, wetting his lips again, said, "And there was another estimate sent to Halliday, apparently from Lovell's for eight thousand."

"Now look here, Harry." Dave Rippon was sitting very straight in his chair, his two hands flat on the desk. "This is not in your department and I'll thank you—"

"But I think it is, Dave. You see, the letter came to me from Halliday; I got Whelan to make the estimate and that came to me too."

"And then it came into this office. From then on it isn't your business."

Harry took a deep breath and dared to say, "I don't like it. To me it's bad business."

29

If he had thrust out his arm and punched his father-in-law right in the middle of his face, Dave Rippon couldn't have been more taken aback, so much so that he could only stare at his daughter's husband and think, once again, she let herself in for something there. But his agile mind told him at this moment that he would have to tread carefully with his son-in-law, because it would never do for this to get around, at least off this floor. He made himself lean back, take a deep, deep breath, and smile; then his voice calm-sounding, he said, "You know, Harry, right from the first I knew you weren't cut out for business, you're not ruthless enough. Now this is just a simple business deal; you've been long enough with the firm surely to realize that there are rules within rules, wheels within wheels."

"You sent an estimate supposedly from Lovell's for eight thousand for the same job."

Dave Rippon took a folded handkerchief now from his breast pocket and wiped something from the corner of his eye, stretching his mouth wide the while; then he said, "Well, that's easily explained. But it shouldn't need any explaining because you know yourself you send out an estimate and some of these beggars will beat you down to the last penny. They say A, B, and C have put in theirs at hundreds less; you know this quite well, you're getting them every day. Well now, the job was six thousand five hundred, right?" He paused, waiting for a reply, but when Harry continued to stare at him, he went on, "We put on another seven hundred and fifty. Why? Again because Halliday is a new customer, and if we can drop a few hundreds, say, down to six five, the original estimate, we've got him for good and all . . . see?"

"Yes, yes, I can see that." But even as he said it he knew that Halliday's estimate would never be dropped to six five, not while his father-in-law was dealing with it.

"Now about the Lovell's estimate; nobody outside those immediately concerned knows we've taken over Lovell's yet. Lovell's was a small private building company; their work was very high class and you've got to pay for high class work; so, therefore, when Halliday sent to Lovell's for an estimate I gave an estimate according to the work that Lovell's would likely have put in. . . ."

"But that's the point. You'll give this job to Bradley or Kershaw or one of the others; they're not of Lovell's standard."

Dave Rippon closed his eyes and leaned against the back

30

of his chair, and then he said, "If you were getting an estimate in from one firm for seven thousand two hundred and fifty and for the same kind of work you got an estimate for eight thousand from another firm which would you take? Go on, tell me which one would you take? You know damn well which one you would take." Again he was leaning forward, his forearms stretched across the desk now, his hands flat as before, "We sent Lovell's out just as a matter of business. It's BUSINESS. We're not thieves or gangsters, we're businessmen. This is a business house. Oh, Lord!" He now rose to his feet, thrusting his chair back against the wall. "At this stage of your career I shouldn't be giving you a lecture on business ethics."

"Perhaps you should."

"What!" Dave Rippon turned and looked down on Harry.

"What if Halliday, being a finicky kind of man, I don't know if he is, but just say he is, what if he plumps for Lovell's estimate?"

"Then he deserves to pay eight thousand, that's all I can say." Dave Rippon was bending down to Harry now, his face on a level with his, and below his breath he said, "Why these scruples all of a sudden?"

Harry looked away from his father-in-law's face before saying quietly, "I don't think they are sudden." Then he dared to add, "A decent profit, that's business, but . . . but this is jiggery-pokery. And have you thought what this man's going to say when he discovers that Peamarsh and Lovell are one and the same firm."

"I don't care what he thinks." Dave Rippon was standing straight now and his voice sounded calm and cold. "The point stands that Lovell's was a high-class firm and had highly skilled workmen, we've taken them over; nothing has changed."

Oh, my God! Harry groaned to himself. What could you say, how could you come back at this kind of twisted thinking? Half of Lovell's men were scattered among Bradley and Kershaw's. Whatever good work Lovell's men had done as a combined force was finished, but could you convince a man like Dave Rippon that this was so.

"Look." Dave Rippon's voice came in sharp and high. "What you want is a holiday, or"—he poked his face forward again—"a change of job."

"Perhaps you're right."

Harry got to his feet, and Dave Rippon, sensing the battle of words he'd have with his daughter should her husband

31

for any reason leave his protection, swallowed deeply and his tone, conciliatory now, said, "Come on, come on. Look, leave this to me. I'll straighten it out to fit your conscience. It's Christmas; come on, forget about it." He put his hand on Harry's shoulder and walked him toward the door, and as he opened it, he remarked casually, "I'm off to York this afternoon; I suppose Esther told you."

"Yes, she did say something about it."

"It's a blooming nuisance. This fellow—he was my colonel, I hadn't seen for years until we met at a reunion a little while ago—he's in a bad way, dicky heart, lives on his own . . . well he's got a housekeeper, sort of. Anyway, he phoned me yesterday begging me to come up. And what can you do at Christmas, somebody lonely, eh?" They were passing Miss Bateman's desk and he turned his head toward her now and asked, "Oh, by the way did you get me the reservation?" And when she answered, "Yes, it's here," he turned to Harry again and said, "There'll be thousands traveling today, and if this keeps on I can see us being stranded in some siding over the holiday." He laughed his other laugh, a deep belly laugh, then added, "But I must look in on the jollification for a little while, so see you again at three then."

"It's beginning at two-thirty today." They both looked at Miss Bateman, and she added, "I'm having word sent round, so that everyone can get away earlier."

"Half-past two it is then." Dave Rippon nodded at Harry and Harry returned the nod, then went out and down the passage and to the lift, and when he was inside, he leaned his head against the wooden partition. He had never felt so small and inconsequential in his life before. From the beginning to the end of the interview his father-in-law had treated him like a cross between a young clerk and a man depending on his livelihood from the perks of his wife's father.

When he opened his office door, a girl was standing at the corner of his desk. He said, "Oh, hello," and she said, "I'm Betty Ray. Miss Bateman sent me in."

"Oh, yes. Sit down, Miss Ray."

Seated behind the desk, he picked up some letters from the in-tray, saying, "There's only about half a dozen, they won't take long." He smiled at her now and said, "Nobody wants to work this morning." And she smiled back at him and replied, "Oh, I don't mind. I'd rather work, it passes the time away."

.32

"Yes." He inclined his head toward her. "There's something in that. Now then, this is to Farrow, Barrett, and Soames."

As he dictated the letter he looked at her and thought, "She's the one that sits farthest away from the window." The girls in the pool were mostly faces to him; they came in before he did in the morning and they went before he left at night. Sometimes he passed them on the stairs at lunchtime, but he had never managed to put a face to a body until now. Miss Ray looked a vivacious girl, medium height, black hair with a fine pair of eyes. Brown or black? He waited until she looked up again. Brown.

When she had finished typing the letters and she was about to go, he said, "If it wasn't for the party you could go home now I suppose," and she answered pertly, "But what would I do there? Well, I mean, I've got nothing to do at home; I'd rather stay for the party and risk being snowed in."

"You would?"

She nodded at him, "Yes," and they both laughed, he freely.

"How long have you been here?" he asked.

"Just over two months."

"Do you like it?"

She shrugged her shoulders. "It's a job."

Yes, they were all jobs, just jobs. He looked at her now as a whole. She was what they would call petite. She sounded lively, different from poor old Ada. But Ada was twice her age. He guessed this girl to be twenty. When he said, "Thanks, Miss Ray," she said, in a manner which would surely have caused Miss Bateman's back hair to stand on end, "Any time, any time, Mr. Blenheim," and went out.

He found himself still smiling as he straightened the papers on his desk. For the moment he had forgotten about Halliday, Lovell's, and his father-in-law.

Three

The basement storeroom was crowded with staff, ranging from the second director to the tea boy. A transistor was blaring forth dance music, but no one would have thought of dancing; they didn't dance at the office party, they just drank, talked, and laughed.

Harry, carrying a tray of filled sherry glasses, stopped in front of a group of men, and one of them said, "Well, there's no need for the old seasonable advice today, Mr. Blenheim, eh?"

"What's that, Barney?"

"Well, if you drive, don't drink, and if you drink, don't drive."

"Oh, yes, yes, that's true. Well, we're going to get something out of the snow after all, you could say."

An elderly-looking man said, "I've seen some snow in me time but never anything like this. I've never seen it so thick that you couldn't get the cars out of the yard."

"They say the buses are only running on the flat; they can't tackle Brampton Hill or the cemetery road."

"Well, the weather's not going to worry me," said another man. "I mean to get bottled and stay corked for the entire four days."

Harry moved on amid laughter and went to a corner where two girls were sitting on upturned boxes. As he neared them, one got to her feet, saying, "I'll go and bring Ada," and Harry, offering the tray to the remaining girl, said, "Well, Miss Ray, how are you doing?"

"Quite well, Mr. Blenheim, quite well; I've still got some." She raised her half-filled glass; then putting her hand out, she added, "But I'll take another, just to keep the kettle boiling."

"To keep the kettle boiling!" Harry laughed down on the girl. "It's a long time since I heard that one. Which part are you from?"

The pert face pushed up toward his and the voice, hushed a little, said, "I'd better whisper it, Bog's End."

"No! Well, the same here."

34

"You, Mr. Blenheim!" The brown eyes were stretched wide, the mouth agape.

"Yes, I was born there."

"Well, I never. Small world. Some go up, some go down, and some just stay put. The last's me. Although we don't live actually in Bog's End, but not a kick in the backs. . . . Oh, Lord!" She put her hand over her mouth and spluttered, "Aw, well, it's Christmas, I might as well say it."

Harry was laughing freely again. She was a card, this one. He wondered how she ever became a shorthand typist; her kind always ended up in a store or a factory. There was nothing of gentility, faked or otherwise, that he had come to expect from the typists in Peamarsh's. And she was a looker too, full of personality.

When her companion and another girl came scurrying back and sat one on each side of her, he offered them glasses of sherry, and they giggled as they said, "Oh, thanks, Mr. Blenheim."

He smiled widely at them, saying, "It's my pleasure, ladies." Then, again amid laughter, he moved on.

When he went to the trestled table to replenish his tray, his father-in-law was standing talking to Graham Hall. Hall was senior to Dave Rippon, but by how much was anybody's guess. He suffered from a stomach complaint, and it was rumored he was going to retire long before his time. Harry knew that his father-in-law could hardly wait for Hall's shoes, or for that matter Mr. Walters' whom everybody said should have retired years ago.

Dave Rippon, showing his consideration for the staff, called in a voice that he aimed to raise above the din, "You're seeing to everybody, Harry? How about Miss Bateman?" He pointed to where Miss Bateman was standing condescending to talk to Jim Whelan, it being the one day in the year when position and seniority were supposedly forgotten.

Harry looked toward Miss Bateman, but she was looking at her boss, and her boss was smiling at her and waving his hand. The atmosphere was very genial, very.

Mrs. Streatham, who saw to the tea each day, was now busily filling glasses. As she piled half a dozen onto Harry's tray, she said, "What about yourself, Mr. Blenheim? I haven't seen you take a drink yet."

"You must have had your eyes closed then"—he poked his head toward her—"I've downed three so far, and there's

35

still time to double it. They're saying back there we've no need to worry about drinking and driving today."

"That's true, Mr. Blenheim; we're going to get something out of it anyway."

"That's exactly what I said." They laughed together as if at a hilarious joke.

When he handed a glass of sherry to Miss Bateman, she smiled thinly at him and said, "Thank you, Mr. Blenheim," and he thought, "That's your fourth to my knowledge and not even a sparkle in your eye." She could certainly carry it.

As he was threading his way through the groups sitting and standing about the storeroom, he bumped into Tom Vosey. He, too, had a tray in his hand and he bowed to Harry, saying, "Can I press you to a drink, sir?"

Vosey was the youngest of the directors. He had risen to where he was because he was related to Graham Hall. Nevertheless, to Harry Tom was all right. There were buddies. And now, with a number of sherries down him, Tom was being skittish and playful; and Harry answered him in like vein. Assuming a pompous air, he said, "Thank you, my boy, thank you. Well, just one to keep out the chill, or let's say because there won't be any bill. Hah, hah, hah! Doesn't sherry make you witty? Drink it, my boy, drink it."

Tom Vosey put out his hand and pushed Harry in the shoulder, almost upsetting him and the tray. He was spluttering as he said, "You know, that's old Walters to the tee; I could even smell the boardroom." Then he added, "I say, how are we going to get home? . . . We'll have to shank it, won't we?"

"I'm afraid so."

"God, I've got a mile to go. But you've got two, or more. Harry, I say." He was whispering now confidentially, "Do these affairs bore you? Honest now, honest."

Harry considered a moment, then said thoughtfully, "Yes and no. At one time I used to look forward to them, but now . . . well."

"Me too. I know what you mean. We enjoyed them when we were young, boy, when we were young." Again he pushed Harry in the shoulder, then went on his way, laughing.

At a given signal someone called for order and Mr. Hall said his usual few words, apologizing for the absence of their esteemed head director and thanking the staff, one and all, for their faithful service to the firm of Peamarsh.

Immediately this ritual was over, Dave Rippon came up to

36

Harry and spoke as if the altercation in the office hadn't happened. "Well, I'm off, Harry," he said. "Give my love to them all at home. It's a damn nuisance having to go to York on a day like this, but there it is. We let ourselves in for these things and have to stand the consequences. Well, have a good time." He slapped Harry between the shoulders. "And by the way, if it thaws, come down and take the car to the garage, will you?" He hiccuped slightly, then laughed as he added, "It's going to be yours anyway, so you'd better look after it. . . . Happy Christmas." He slapped him again between the shoulders, then cried loudly to those about him, "Happy Christmas, everybody. Happy Christmas."

"Happy Christmas, sir. Happy Christmas, sir."

When he came opposite to Miss Bateman, he actually took her hand and shook it, saying, "A happy Christmas," and she, looking into his face, replied, "A happy Christmas, Mr. Rippon." Then waving his hand about him, he went out.

"That should have given her a thrill," said Jim Whelan nonchalantly as he passed Harry, "having your hand shaken by God. By the way, did you see him about that business?" and Harry replied, "Yes, I'll go into it after the holidays, Jim."

"Good. Well, now, I'm off an' all. Happy Christmas, Harry."

"Happy Christmas, Jim."

Ten minutes later he was back in his office. His head was buzzing. He did not know how many sherries he had got down him, at least half a dozen. He had never taken on that many before. He'd better get a cup of tea somewhere before he arrived home; it wouldn't do to greet Esther starry-eyed. He gave a little laugh to himself, then sat down at his desk and rested his head on his hand. He felt he could just drop nicely off to sleep; but he'd better not do that, he had a trek before him.

He rose and got slowly into his outer things, looked around the office, switched out the light, and went down the stairs to the main hall.

The hall was quite empty and he stood listening for a moment. There was no sound in the whole building. Funny, fifteen minutes ago the laughter and chatter had been rising to the top floor. He went out through the glass door and into the porch, and was met by a flurry of snow. It was still falling in thick, steady flakes, and although it was only a quarter to four, it was almost dark.

As he stood pulling his collar tightly up around his neck, a

37

small figure darted up the three steps in front of him, and as she brushed past him, she said, "Oh hello. Hello again. I've forgotten my bag. Fancy doing a daft thing like that. And it's got me pay in it!" She pushed out her lips and blew the snow away from her face, then laughed before disappearing through the glass door. He went slowly down the steps into the street, and he had just reached the corner when she caught up with him again.

"Dreadful, isn't it? It's getting worse."

"Yes. Have you far to go?"

"Pullman Street." As she finished, she slipped, and one leg disappeared into what had been a gutter but was now an eighteen-inch drift. As he steadied her, he said, "I know Pullman Street. I can go part of the way with you; we could cut across the market, they've likely cleared that a bit."

They had cleared the market earlier in the day, but the constant falling had beaten them for the square was knee-high in places. He said to her now, "They're going to find it difficult putting their stalls up tomorrow, and they generally do a roaring trade on Christmas Eve."

She turned her face toward him as she laughed and said, "We always wait until the last minute and get our turkey at a throw-out price. My mother can remember getting one one Christmas Eve for half a crown. But they hadn't the big freezers then. But who needs a freezer in this?"

When they had to step over a drift to get onto the pavement, he took her arm and said, "Come on, jump it. One, two, three!"

She squealed as she landed on the other side, then cried, "I've lost me shoe!"

When he dug out the high-heeled shoe, he said, "Why didn't you put on something sensible when you knew it was like this."

"Oh, who wants to be sensible? Here, can I hang on to you while I put it on."

He supported her with his arm around her shoulders and she held on to him as she bent her leg back and put on her shoe. And she squealed again, saying, "Coo! it's freezing. Me other one is wet and warm but this is like ice now."

The farther they got away from the center of the town, the deeper the snow. In the side roads nobody had bothered to clear it away as yet, and when they came to Taunton Square, from where his road lay in the opposite direction from hers, he said, "You're never going to make this on your own, I'd better see you to your door."

38

"Thanks." She peered up at him through the falling snow. "It's only about another five minutes' walk. At least it used to be; I don't know how long it will take us now."

"Come on, let's see then." And he laughed as he took her arm.

After they had gone a little way she pulled him to a stop and said, "Listen! Isn't everything quiet, hushed like?"

He listened, then answered, "Yes, nice and quiet, hushed like." He was smiling down at her.

"Do you like things quiet?" They were trudging on again now.

"Yes, moderately so."

"Oh, I don't; I like bustle, plenty of people, talk, noise, laughter . . . life. That's what I like, life."

Although he couldn't see her face, he said, "Yes, I can see you do."

Her comment to this was cut off when they both slipped together and overbalanced in the snow. When they righted themselves, they had their arms around each other, but only for a second, for, taking her arm again, he made the incident casual by saying, "It's treacherous; you could break your neck."

"We're nearly there; two more streets and up the cutting."

In the cutting they had to walk in single file, lifting their feet high to make progress, and when they came to the end of it, she pointed to the first house at the end of a short street and said, "Well, we're here."

He raised his hat now and said formally, "Well, I'm glad you've made it. I think I'll make my way back into the market and keep to the main roads; they must have made some attempt to keep them open."

"But you're not going straightaway"—she was peering up at him again as she searched in her bag for her key—"you're wringing and frozen as much as me. Come in and have a cup of something hot."

"It's very kind of you but . . ."

"Kind, me foot! Come on in."

He smiled to himself as he followed her into the house. She certainly was an uninhibited little miss, and she certainly had no respect for rank or class distinction.

"Take your coat and things off, I'll switch the fire on. The house is warm, the boiler's always on, but we'll need something more than the boiler to thaw us out." She had flung her coat and head scarf aside, and now, balancing on one

39

leg, she undid her stockings from her suspenders and dragged them from her wet legs.

"Here, give me your coat, I'll put it on the boiler."

"Oh, no, no. It's perfectly all right, it's waterproof."

"Waterproof or not, it's soaking wet across the bottom. Here, give it to me." She almost dragged it from him. "There now, sit down an' make yourself comfortable."

As she went to go through a door, she paused and, looking over her shoulder, laughed back at him, saying, "Make yourself at home; it's Christmas . . . remember."

He found himself sitting on a very comfortable couch before an electric fire which flickered over artificial logs and smiling widely to himself. Make yourself at home. Make yourself at home, because it's Christmas. She was a little star turn.

"Tea?" Her voice was calling from the other room, the kitchen presumably.

"Yes, please." He listened to a kettle being filled and the plop of the gas being lit, and when she came back into the to the room, she said, "It won't be a tick."

He looked at her standing in her bare feet, her dress coming just above her knees—Miss Bateman wouldn't allow mini skirts—she looked like a child, no older than Gail. For something to say he said, "It's a very comfortable room this." He spread out his hand.

"Yes, I like it." She came and sat on the sofa, not in the corner but not close to him. "My mother did it up; she's a dab hand with paper and paint."

"Your mother does the decorations, not your father?"

"I haven't got a father."

"I'm sorry."

"Oh, don't be. I don't remember him; he died when I was young."

"Have you any brothers or sisters?"

"No, just me and me mother, two lone women." She laughed, and he laughed and said, "Woman indeed!"

"What do you mean? Woman indeed! What do you take me for? A girl?"

"Well, yes, I would. I'd take you for a girl, a young girl."

"Coo! That's nice."

The kettle began to whistle and she jumped up and went into the kitchen, and from there she called, "How old do you think I am?"

He thought for a moment and said, "Nineteen."

"Thanks very much; I'm twenty-four."

"You're not!"

"I am." She came in with the tray, and putting it down on a pouffe to the side of the fireplace, she said, "I'm shivering, I want something to lace this. How about you?"

"Oh, not for me, thank you."

"Oh, go on." She went to a sideboard behind them and bought out a bottle of whiskey. "It's Christmas. Have you forgotten? It's Christmas, and we've just trekked through the Yukon, and you've saved me life and we've come to the log cabin and we're going to be marooned here for three weeks."

He was laughing loudly now; he couldn't help but laugh at her.

"There, get that down you."

He'd never had whiskey in tea before, and he clicked his tongue against the roof of his mouth and said, "Hmm! Very nice."

"I'll say it's nice; it's me lifesaver."

"Yes?"

"Yes." She drew in a deep breath and lifted her legs and put the soles of her feet toward the fire. Then leaning back, she said, "Everything's nice at Christmas; everybody's nice to everybody at Christmas. Have you noticed it? For a couple days everybody's nice to everybody, and for the rest of the year they're bitchy."

"Is that how you've found life?"

"Mm! Well no." She shook her head. "There are nice people. You're nice."

"Thank you."

"But you are, seriously." She now sat straight up on the couch and turned her body toward him until her knees were within an inch of his. "That's what they said the first day I came to Peamarsh's. You'll like Mr. Blenheim, they said; he's nice."

"They didn't. You're teasing me."

"Honest, they did, all the girls in the pool. They said there were one or two not bad, Mr. Vosey and Mr. Whelan, and one or two on the bottom floor, but for the rest they were stinkers. Oh, you should hear what they say. And they know some things about a lot of them an' all, all the darling goodie-goodies. Make your hair stand up on end, it would. But never about you." She took another long drink from her cup, her eyes fixed on him all the while. "A nice bloke, that's what they said you were, a quiet, nice bloke. And you know what else they say?"

His mouth was tightly closed, he was trying to stop him-

41

self from laughing. He shook his head. "That you're above-board."

He stared at her, his face bright. He felt warm inside, the whiskey was seeing to that. Yet it wasn't the whiskey alone, it was a good feeling to know that people thought you a nice fellow, a nice bloke. Gail had said that too. It was worth being aboveboard after all.

"They think Rippon, your father-in-law's, a stinker."

"Oh, do they now?"

"Yes. He's rotten rich, isn't he? They say he's got more than Mr. Walters, or Mr. Hall or any of the others put together. They say he's loaded down with shares in everything from oil to ointment."

He drooped his head onto his chest and bit on his lip. He should stop her talking, but he couldn't; nor did he want to. It was all so good to hear that they thought Mr. Dave Rippon a stinker. It was good to know that some people could see through his church facade.

"Have another sup?"

"Oh, no, thanks."

"Come on." She pulled the cup from him. "You can only get really drunk once."

He was leaning against the back of the couch laughing loudly. He had never laughed like this in years. Suddenly he put his hand over his mouth and said, "Dear! dear! Have you got near neighbors?"

"Only Ma Tarrant next door and she's stone deaf. We're lucky."

Half an hour later he had got through three cups of tea and almost the equivalent of three double whiskeys; he had his shoes off and they were set at a safe distance from the electric fire drying. Betty was now in a knee-length, padded dressing gown because she had found that her dress was damp. She sat on the couch with her legs curled under her, her head and hands moving as she talked; and he lay back in bemused contentment and laughed at her. He had never met anyone like her. She was gay, happy, full of the joy of living, and strangely, she didn't make him feel old. He felt younger now than he could remember feeling in his twenties.

"Loosen your collar and tie."

"No, no. What do I want to loosen my collar and tie for?"

"Go on, make yourself comfortable, there's nobody'll come in. Me mother won't be back until nearly eight. Here." She had her hands at his neck, and they were struggling now; then she was lying across his knee looking up into his

42

face, her hands still at his neck but quiet for a moment under his grip. He looked down at her in silence, and then he said thickly, "You know, you're a naughty girl."

"My! You've been quick finding that out. You're sharp." Her tone, the deriding manner in which she said it, her candidness, set him off laughing again. And now she had her head snuggled under his chin and his tie was off and the buttons of his shirt were open.

"Have you any hairs on your chest?"

"What!"

"Let's see if you have any hairs on your chest."

They were struggling again.

"Here, here, you little devil. Give over."

She gave over and lay back on his arm, her head on the end of the couch, looking up at him. Then, her hand coming out, she traced her red-nailed finger gently around his mouth, saying softly, "You're nice, nicer than nice, sort of innocent nice."

"What!" He tried to pull himself up in mock indignation and she emphasized now, "But you are. Do you know what? If you weren't, you'd have had me clothes off afore now."

"Oh, Betty. Really!"

"Oh, Betty, really!" she mimicked his voice, then tweaked his nose.

As she lay gazing up at him, her big brown eyes mere slits now, his sanity, rising on a strong wave, told him to get out of here and quick, and he muttered thickly, "I'll have to be making my way; it's getting on and it's going to take me some time to . . . to get back."

"Why go when you don't want to?"

"What do you mean, I don't want to?"

"You know what I mean. You don't want to go."

They were staring at each other again, and he said softly, "You seem to know everything, don't you?"

"Pretty near everything." She was her skittish self again, her chin bobbing and her hand waving in the air. "Anyway, I know enough that you don't want to go."

"What if I prove you wrong?"

Her body became still for a moment. Then raising her head from the couch, she brought her face close to his. Her eyes, wide now, stared into his, and of a sudden she was kissing him, holding him and kissing him with such a ferocity that it was like an attack. And it was seconds before he responded to her.

When she pulled him up from the couch and led him

43

across the room and into a bedroom, he made no resistance. When she switched on the light, one thing his bemused mind did notice was that the curtains were already drawn; it was as if she had prepared for it.

He sat on the edge of the bed, as much from weakness at the knees as pressure from her hands, and when, slowly unbuttoning the dressing gown, she slid it from her and stood before him stark naked, he closed his eyes against the sight of her. He hadn't seen Esther naked more than half-a-dozen times in his life, and then only when he had barged into the bathroom, when she had been quick to cover herself up. Yet here was this girl standing before him without a stitch on. It was unbelievable. For a moment he thought that he must be dreaming, until her hands came on him again and she pulled off his jacket.

All his life afterward he was to remember the next half hour. Even when he hated the thought of it, every incident and happening in it was to remain clear before his eyes. At night when they turned the key on him and he was alone within those four cold, soul-crushing walls, he was to remember. Later, through ostracism and shame, the memory was still clear. Even when his life flowed through a channel that brought him a peace he had never known before, the memory remained vivid, bringing him out of sleep, pushing the sweat from his pores, bringing groans and remembered moans of ecstasy from him.

He had been married for eighteen years and he knew now that, compared with her, he was as inexperienced as a virgin boy. He felt ravished, raped. She was wild, savage, almost demented at times. Such intensity and passion coming from such a small frame was unbelievable, and more unbelievable still when he thought of her as a young girl. But once it was over he never thought of her as a young girl again.

He lay still on the top of the bed, nothing moving but his bare chest. He wasn't at peace as was the case after he had been with Esther; every nerve end in his body seemed frayed, yet he had a strange sense of exhilaration and achievement. But he had achieved nothing; the achieving was hers. He wasn't aware how long he lay unmoving, but when he turned his head and looked at her, he expected to find, like Esther, she would have her eyes closed as she dropped into relaxed sleep. But instead, her eyes were wide, laughing, waiting. She said softly to him, "Do you believe me now?" He did not answer but made a questioning move-

44

ment with his head, and she replied, "That I know everything." He still did not answer her, but as he looked at her, he thought, "Yes, she certainly does." And where had she learned it? She looked nineteen, she said she was twenty-four, and she had the knowledge of an old whore mistress. The last thought brought him up on his elbow to stare down at her, and it was as if he was reading the words written on her naked body: She was a tart. A little prostitute, that's what she was.

He got off the bed and dressed with his back to her, pulling on his clothes with jerky movements. When he made for the door, she said to him, "Some people are never satisfied." He turned and looked at her but could find nothing to say. As he went to close the door behind him, she said, "I'll be seeing you." It sounded like a threat.

He pulled on his shoes, got into his coat, wound his scarf around his neck, took up his hat, and let himself out into the street. It was still snowing heavily, and he stood for a moment bemused. He must have been stark, staring mad.

He entered the long Cut, lifting his feet high with each step, and when he reached the end of it, where the wind had drifted the snow to the side and left a small clear space, he stood for a minute leaning his back against the wall. What had he let himself in for? This is what happened when men went abroad. Peter Thompson had told him why Arthur Rice went off on his lone tour at least once a year. It could happen abroad and no consequences. But this had happened in Fellburn, in the town where he was known by practically everyone, where he was known as a churchman, for the simple reason that he sang in the choir, and as it happened, with a young girl in his firm, a girl he'd see every day in the week, even if it was only her head through the glass partition of the pool. God! What had he done? He must have been raving, balmy. He hadn't been all that drunk, he had known what he was doing. Or had he? He'd never had so much whiskey at one go before. And on top of all that sherry. He rubbed his hand over his snow-covered face. It was no use making excuses for himself, it was done, and he, Harry Blenheim, had done it. Or had he? He was feeling again her bouncing, struggling bare body. But it didn't tie up with the everyday picture of her, small, neat, and soft. Yet he'd heard of women like her; he had heard body-hungry men easing themselves with stories of loving amazons. But she hadn't been just one amazon, she had been half a dozen. How long was he there altogether? He pushed

45

his coat sleeve up to peer at his watch, then realized with deep dismay that he had left it in the bedroom. The strap had caught at her skin and he had dragged it off his wrist and thrown it on the side table. It was a gold watch with a gold-link strap and had been Esther's present to him on their seventeenth wedding anniversary and had an inscription inside to that effect. God! What was he going to do now? He'd have to go back. He turned, but didn't go immediately down the Cut; he had to will his body to move.

He had just reached the end of the Cut when he saw a woman standing by the door he was making for. She was banging on it as she kicked the snow from her feet. When the door opened, he caught a blurred glimpse of the girl. Within a second the door was closed.

That settled that. He wasn't going in there and have to face the mother; no, not if he never got the watch.

When he again reached the end of the Cut, he stopped once more, his thoughts racing now. How was he going to face them at home, Esther and Gail? Gail? It would be harder to face Gail.

"You all right, mister?" The man coming out of the Cut was looking into his face, and he pulled himself from the wall and said, "Yes, thank you. Just a little exhausted. It's heavy going."

"You're telling me. Far to go?"

"Holt Avenue." They were plodding along side by side now.

"Oh, that's yon side, isn't it?"

"Yes, it's some way. But I'll cut across the market and keep to the main road. That should ease things."

"That's going out of your way," said the man. "Why don't you cut up Barrack Road. Look, we're coming to it. You cut up there; that'll take off the market and bring you out in Champlion Place."

"Oh, as near as that?"

"Yes," said the man; "it'll cut a good third off."

"That's very helpful." Harry nodded at him. "Thanks, I'll try it."

They parted at the corner of the next street, and the going here wasn't so bad as the people had attempted to clear the snow from the pathways. But when he came out into Champlion Place, it was almost knee-high again. As he crossed the square, his knees almost buckled under him. From the square he cut up side street after side street; then of a sudden he realized he was walking down Baker Street.

46

This was where Janet lived. In the ordinary way he would have approached his home from the other direction. So deep was the snow here that he had to support himself with one hand against the wall, and when he found his hand flat against a door, he made out the number 17. Janet lived at 23, three doors away. He would knock and go in and rest for a while. It would appear quite natural. He could say he had taken a short cut that had turned out to be the long way around. He was frozen right to the bone. When he had left the other house, he felt that he would never be cold again, but now he was shivering and he knew that it wasn't only with the cold but with the thought of entering his own home. He was aware that he was still slightly drunk, and if he went in like this, Esther would be sure to smell it from him; there were no secret Rippon breath formulas for him.

Within a few seconds of his knocking on the door of No. 23 it was opened, and Robbie stood there, silent for a moment, until recognizing the figure. Then he exclaimed loudly, "Good Lord! Mr. Blenheim. Come in, come in." He put out his hand and almost dragged him over the threshold, exclaiming loudly, "Lor! You are in a state. Mam! Mam!" he called over his shoulder, then went on, "Let me get your coat off; it's sodden. You're all sodden."

Some whimsical part of Harry endorsed this. Yes, he was sodden both inside and out.

"Why, Harry!" Janet Dunn was standing at the end of the passage. The name Harry sounded natural on her lips, yet she never used it in his house. She came forward holding out her hands, saying, "How did you come down this way? Is anything wrong?"

"Let him thaw out and then he'll tell you," said Robbie bluntly. "Let's get him near the fire." He spoke as if Harry was unconscious, and he could have been, for he felt powerless to open his mouth. They went into the living room, one each side of him, and lowered him into a chair before the open fire.

Harry now looked up at Janet. He wanted to explain to her but still found it impossible. But when she put her hand on his brow and said, "You are hot, but you're shivering. You've got a chill. Bring a drop of whiskey, Robbie," he made an effort and protested in a croaking voice, "No, no! A cup of tea, please. That's all, a cup of tea, or . . . or if you have c-coffee."

"Yes, yes, certainly. You'll have it in a second." When she

47

left the room, Robbie, dropping on his hunkers before Harry, asked quietly, "You been out in this long?"

"An hour, I think. No, longer. What time is it?"

"A quarter to seven."

"No!" He sat up in the chair. "As late as that? I . . . I should be home, they'll be worrying."

"You haven't been home?"

"No. No. There was a party at the office." He leaned back in the chair again. "Some of the staff had a job getting back, I . . . I helped them." And how, he thought.

Straightening himself up, Robbie said, "Well, another half hour isn't going to make much difference; you're not fit to go out again yet." He stood looking down at him. An office party. That's why he stank of whiskey. He had been under the impression that he didn't drink. Perhaps that was only when in the house, Madam Blenheim being a strict teetotaler. "What you want," he said now, "is something to eat; it'll steady you."

"Oh, no, no!" Harry shook his head, but Robbie insisted, saying, "Never mind no, no; it's packing you want inside you, I'd say. We were just about to have something, anyway."

As his mother came through the doorway with a cup of coffee in her hand, he said, "It's something to eat he wants, what do you say?"

"Yes, indeed," said Janet. "That's the thing. So drink this, then sit up; it's all ready."

Harry took a long drink of the scalding liquid, then muttered, "No, Janet; I'm not going to trouble you any further."

"Trouble!" Her voice was high. "We're only too pleased to have company. And what better day than on the queen of the Sabbath."

He looked up at her inquiringly for a moment. Then lowering his head he said softly, "Oh, dear me, I forgot it was Friday, Janet."

"All the better," she said. "We couldn't have wished for better company, so come on, drink that coffee up and we'll get started."

She returned to the kitchen and brought in a large covered dish which she placed in the middle of the table set to the side of the room. The table was covered with a white cloth and at each end was a candle in a tall holder.

He watched her lighting the candles and heard her mutter something as she did so. Then she turned to him, smiling, and said, "They should have been lit at sunset but that would

48

have been at half-past three. Do you remember looking through the window when you were a lad and Dad going to the door to bring you in and you flying down the backyard as if the devil was after you?"

He shook his head and she laughed, "Well, you did." Then she motioned him to the table, and he rose slowly and took his seat.

Robbie was already standing at one end of the table. He had a bottle of wine in his hand and began to pour some in a glass while unselfconsciously saying, "Blessed art thou, O Lord, our God King of the Universe, who created the fruit of the wine." Then he sipped it and poured out another two glasses. Next he lifted the white napkin that was covering a large object to reveal a loaf of plaited bread. Again he repeated the words he had said before, but adding now, "Who bringeth forth bread from the earth." Then nodding impishly at Harry, he added, "All in English for your benefit. Geordie English. Funny that, but me Yiddish isn't in Geordie, at least I don't think it is." Janet and he now laughed together. Then he broke the bread, dipped it into wine, and handed it to Harry, saying, "It's very good."

"Thank you." Harry put the bread on his plate, then looked at the wineglass in his hand. From the smell of the contents it was port and just the thought of it intensified the sickness that was already in his stomach.

When Janet lifted the lid from the dish in the center of the table to disclose what looked like a stew and which gave off a strong aroma of herbs, she said, "You do like fish, Harry, don't you? So you should like this."

"It's got everything in but the pan scrub," said Robbie, laughing, "and it's guaranteed to stick to your ribs."

Harry smiled but said nothing; he was doing his utmost to quell the rising swell of sickness, but when Janet placed the plate of steaming chopped fish and vegetables before him, it was more than he could stand. His head down, his hand to his mouth, he stumbled to his feet, muttering, "Sorry, sorry, bathroom."

"This way." Robbie had him by the arm, and when they got into the small kitchen, Harry, still pressing on his mouth, groaned, "Lavatory."

"That's outside, man," said Robbie brusquely. "Get it up in the sink here. Come on."

Harry was now past protest, and leaning over the sink, he vomited. A strong smell of whiskey and dead sherry and the

49

stodgy meat pudding he'd had for his lunch in a restaurant in town erupted.

A few minutes later, when Robbie handed him a towel, he wiped his mouth; then putting his forearms on the draining board, he rested his head on them.

"Here," Robbie pushed a plain kitchen chair toward him and said quietly, "Sit down."

He sat down; then looking up at the young man, he stared at him for a moment in silence before saying, "I'm so sorry, Robbie."

"What's to be sorry for? You've been sick, and no wonder, the way you came in. I'll tell you something." He put his head down to Harry and whispered, "Gin does the same for me. Two glasses and I'm flat. She doesn't know." He nodded toward the kitchen. "She always thinks it's something she's cooked." He was grinning now, but Harry couldn't grin back. Getting to his feet, he said, "If you don't mind, Robbie, I'll make my way home."

"Yes, yes, of course. And I'll come along of you."

"No, no, you won't."

"Well, you might as well stop talking because I'm comin.' I won't go in, don't worry, but I'm going to see you there. I don't want them to find you lying in the gutter stiff the morrow mornin'."

At this moment Harry thought he wouldn't mind being found in the gutter stiff tomorrow morning.

Janet helped him into his coat, and she pushed his fumbling fingers aside and tucked his scarf over his chest, then buttoned the coat. He said to her too, "I'm sorry, Janet." And her voice brusque now, she replied sharply, "Don't be silly, Harry. What have you got to apologize to me for? I'll remind you that I've had to hold your head before the day when you were sick. Do you remember the night we went to the fair and you went on the shoggies."

He had a faint recollection of the event and he smiled at her weakly. And she went on. "And that wasn't the only time. There were school treats when you stuffed yourself and got it up in the bus coming back."

He could remember one such occasion. "I must have a weak stomach," he said.

"There." She handed him his hat. "Now when you get in, go straight to bed and have a rest over the holidays. It isn't only today that has caused this stomach upset, it's doing that Father Christmas stunt. That marketplace is a

50

death trap any day in the winter, even without snow. I don't know how Robbie escaped."

As he looked down at her, part of his mind registered the fact that Janet Dunn in 23 Baker Street was a different creature from Janet Dunn when she came to help out in Hollytree House, Holt Avenue. This was the Janet he remembered from years back, and he had never seen her for a long time because their meetings were always in his own home, with Esther in either the foreground or the background. He said, "Perhaps you'll invite me to dinner some other time, Janet?" and she answered, "Any time. You know you're welcome in this house anytime, Harry. And you don't need an invitation. Dear, dear! You should know that."

He looked at her face. It was plain, homely, and good. Her hair was black and straight; her eyes were round and dark; her skin had an olive tint; her nose was not large but it was the nose of a Jewess. Yet somehow he had the impression she had just missed being a beautiful woman. She had a good figure, and as his grannie had said, she had a presence, a sort of dignity. She was a good woman altogether, was Janet. He took her hand and nodded at her but said nothing, then they went into the passage, where Robbie was waiting. She opened the door and let them out, saying, "Go careful, the both of you mind. Go careful." She spoke as if they were of one family.

As he went down the street with Robbie supporting him by the arm, he thought, "It's been the strangest day of my life."

Robbie left him at the bottom of the steps, saying, "Now you do what Mam said and go straight to bed. And if I were you, I'd stay there over the holidays; you're right down low if I'm any judge."

"I'll see to it, Robbie." He tried to smile. "And thanks for your help, for everything."

"You're welcome. There's nobody I'd rather give me shoes to, you know that."

They peered at each other through the snow, then Robbie turned away and he went into the house.

When he reached the hall, they all gathered around him, all talking at once, until Esther, her voice raised unusually high, cried, "Stop it! Be quiet, I can't hear myself think. Now"—she looked at Harry—"you might tell me where on earth you've been. They said you left the office before four, your car's still there. We couldn't find out anything from anyone with Father gone to York."

51

Before he could answer, Gail said, "Let me get your coat off, Father. Oh, it's wet. And your shoes and trousers, look."

"Well, don't stand there," said Esther; "the carpet will be filthy. Go in to the cloakroom and take them off. Get your father's slippers, Terry. And stop dancing about, Gail. John, put the kettle on."

As she gave her orders, she pushed Harry toward the cloakroom, and there he sat down and pulled his shoes and socks off and turned the bottom of his trousers up. When she bent down and felt them, she said, "They're absolutely wringing," and at this he was forced to retort sharply, "Well, perhaps you haven't noticed, Esther, it's snowing outside."

She answered this with a stiff silence for a moment; then she asked in her usual controlled tone, "Where have you been?"

He bowed his head and rubbed his brow with his hand as he said, "After the party some of the staff couldn't get home, I . . . I helped one or two on their way, then I got sort of lost and found myself round by Janet's, and I was so exhausted I went in."

"You mean to say you've been at Janet's all this time!" Her voice was indignant now.

"Not all the time; I don't know how long." He couldn't say not more than twenty minutes. "But I just had to call in, I was dead beat. You've got no idea what it's like outside."

"She could have sent Robbie to say you were there. That's the least she could have done."

"I wouldn't let her," he lied. "She wanted to but I wouldn't let her. Now if you don't mind, Esther, I want to get near the fire." He got to his feet and pushed past her in the narrow space and went out into the hall, there to see John standing with his slippers in his hand. He took them from him, saying, "Thanks"; then still in his bare feet, he went into the sitting room, and as he dropped onto the couch, Gail took the slippers from him and slipped them on to his feet, then said, "You should go upstairs, Dad, and change your trousers, they're very wet."

"I will in a minute, dear." He nodded at her.

"Do you want anything, a hot drink or anything?" Esther was standing before the couch, and without looking at her, he shook his head and said, "All I want is to get to bed."

"I'll go and put your electric blanket on." Gail ran out of the room and he pulled himself to his feet again, saying,

"I'll be all right tomorrow, I just want to sleep." He had not looked Esther straight in the face yet.

When he entered the room, Gail was turning down his bed, and when she came at him and flung her arms around his waist, saying, "Oh, Dad, I was worried; I thought you had dropped into a drift or something," he felt his whole body stiffen. She was the same size, the same height as Betty Ray. Her body felt like Betty Ray's. When she put her hands up on to his lapels to help him off with his coat, he thrust her from him, and his voice rough, almost a growl, he said, "Don't. Don't do that."

It was the first time in his life he had repulsed her. Always he had opened his arms wide to her; always he had hugged her close. She stepped back from him, her hand up to her cheek, her eyes wide and slowly filling with tears, and then she was running from the room.

He followed her swiftly toward the door, but when he reached it, he stopped abruptly and closed it and leaned his back against it. This was only the beginning.

Four

It was three weeks before Harry returned to the office, and if he was grateful for anything during that time, it was for the respite.

When, on Christmas Eve, his temperature having risen with alarming rapidity, Esther sent for the doctor—who pronounced a severe dose of influenza—the one clear thought in Harry's mind was "Thank God I won't have to go in on Wednesday."

Looking back, he didn't remember much about Christmas Day or Boxing Day, only that he had made his peace with Gail. She had come into the room several times and stood at the foot of the bed and asked politely, "How do you feel now, Dad?" until he had made the effort to put out his clammy hands to her and croak, "Come here." And when she had stood at the bedside, he had said, "I'm sorry, pet. I'm sorry," and she had answered without her usual gusto, "It's all right, Dad." He had moved his throbbing head slowly and said, "No, I was rough with you but . . . but I felt ill, more so than I do now; I'd . . . I'd had a trying day, and the snow."

"It's all right, Dad," she had answered, and again he had moved his head. Then pulling her down to the side of the bed, he had whispered, "Listen, pet. If ever again I'm bad-tempered and beastly, take no notice, just tell yourself that I love you better than anyone else in the whole wide world, will you?"

On this she returned to the daughter he knew, and she threw herself on his neck, crying, "Oh, Dad! Dad!"

"There now. There now. Look, you'll catch this cold. But remember what I said."

She had lifted her head and looked at him and dropped it to one side, saying, "You never could be bad-tempered or beastly, not you."

"I was last night."

"It wasn't you, it was the flu."

"Get up out of that, child! Do you want it too?" Esther's command had brought Gail to her feet, but she had smiled lovingly at him before leaving the room.

54

After this little incident he let himself dissolve into the sweating depths created by a hundred and four temperature.

But now the time of the respite was over and Esther was at the door to see him off, driving in her father's cast-off Jaguar. Under other circumstances he would have got a thrill out of driving the Jaguar. Who wouldn't? But passed over as it had been, almost in the nature of a gift, the joy of possession was tainted somewhat. He knew that his father-in-law wouldn't have let him have a smell of the car if it hadn't been that he wanted to please Esther. That was the only good point in his father-in-law's favor: his constant aim to please his daughter.

But the business of the car was not really bothering him at this moment. What was tensing the muscles of his stomach and bringing his jaw rigid was the uncertainty of what attitude Miss Betty Ray would take toward him. Remembering her brashness, he shivered with apprehension.

But he needn't have worried. After Mr. Hogg had greeted him warmly, there came the chorus of "Good morning. Nice to see you back, Mr. Blenheim. You feeling better?" To all of which he had said, "Yes, yes, thank you very much." And then he was passing the window of the typing pool, and the girls inside, having heard the chatter in the hallway, all had their faces turned toward him, and they smiled at him. And among the smiling faces was Betty Ray's. He did not let his eyes linger on her but nodded through the glass to them as a whole. Then he was in his office and Ada Cole was taking his coat and saying, "Oh, I am glad to see you back, Mr. Blenheim."

"Thanks, Ada."

"Sure you're feeling fit now?"

"Fit as a fiddle, Ada. Well"—he paused—"not quite. Let us say, I don't feel like dying any longer."

Her round face smiling, she looked at him kindly, saying, "It's an awful thing, flu. It gets you down. It's left its mark on you; you've lost weight, and your tan's gone."

"Tan? I never knew I had a tan, Ada."

"Oh, well, you know what I mean, you were a bit browny."

"Well, I suppose the snow bleached me."

"Eeh! It did that. Wasn't it dreadful? A number of old people in the town died, and no wonder. We've never had anything like it for years; and we don't want it again, do we?"

55

"No, Ada." He took his seat behind the desk, drew in a deep breath, then asked, "Anything new?"

"One or two small jobs have been completed. Bradley's doing the alterations in Temple Street and Kershaw has finished the council job. There have been some inquiries in, estimations. And Halliday, you remember, he accepted the quotation."

"Halliday?" He lifted his chin upward. "Oh, yes, I was dealing with that just before we broke up, at least I went to see Mr. Rippon about it. There was a muddle about prices."

"Well, they accepted the stated price."

"And what was that?"

"Oh." She screwed up her face. "I can't think offhand. I'll get it." On her way to the filing cabinet, she turned around and said, "I've just remembered, we haven't got it. I had orders to pass on all that correspondence to the upper office." She jerked her head toward the ceiling.

"Was it six thousand five hundred?"

"Oh, no, more than that, I'm sure. Now I remember. That was the estimate Mr. Whelen put in, but Miss Bateman told me they'd worked it out upstairs and that wouldn't cover it. It was over seven thousand. Yes, it was over seven thousand." She was nodding her head now.

He looked down at his desk for a moment, then bit on his lip and asked, "Who's to do the work?"

"Bradley's, as far as I can make out. They're starting this week. Their estimate is likely in. It's bound to be, but I haven't seen it. Everything's been mixed up lately, hasn't it, Mr. Blenheim? I mean not just lately, for months now. You don't know where you are, do you?"

"No," he said slowly, "you don't know where you are."

She looked at him for a moment longer. He was vexed. She could always tell when Mr. Blenheim was vexed. She turned and gathered up some papers from a side desk and went into her cubbyhole.

Harry sat staring at the phone. He had a desire to pick it up and say what was on his mind, but he knew that he daren't, not if he wanted to remain in Peamarsh's. But it was damnable, damnable. Bradley's estimate would be in the region of five thousand five hundred, give or take a pound or two. When Jim Whelan had put the job down at six thousand five hundred, he was giving Peamarsh's a good percentage for the small amount of negotiating work they were doing, but that didn't suit Mr. Rippon. He had to put it up another seven hundred and fifty. And who would get

56

a cut of that? Would it be plowed back? Not if Dave Rippon had anything to do with it, it wouldn't; it would be fiddled into the directors' pockets. But how? Yes, how? There was Miss Bateman to get over. She must know a lot, Miss Bateman.

As bad as old Walters was, this kind of robbery hadn't been so blatant when he was active. Their percentage had never been moderate, but they had usually stuck to Jim Whelan's figures.

What would happen when his father-in-law became head of the firm, which was very much on the cards? Would he be able to work directly under him? When Dave Rippon moved into Peter Walters' office, Frank Nolan, Arthur McMullan, and Tom Vosey would all move up a step and there would be a vacancy on the directors' board, and that vacancy would come to him, not because his father-in-law would want it like that but because Esther would want it like that. But what did he himself want? Well, it didn't matter what he wanted, did it? He was fast stuck under Dave Rippon's thumb. Everything that came his way would come via Rippon, that is, as long as he remained in this firm. And being Esther's husband, he couldn't see himself leaving it ever. He took his handkerchief from his pocket and wiped his face, he was sweating.

It was as he returned from lunch that he came face to face with Betty Ray. She stopped on the bend of the stairs. Standing above him and her eyes wide and bright, she looked into his face and said, "I'm so glad you're better, Mr. Blenheim."

His answer to this should have been "Thank you," but all he could do was to swallow and stare at her.

"It was the snow; it was dreadful wasn't it?" Her eyes were swelling over with laughter; he could almost hear her gurgling inside. He couldn't believe that she was the same girl who had acted like that. His mind interpreted, in a flashing picture, the words "like that," and he saw her naked, savage and writhing, totally uninhibited.

"Did you get my card?"

He heard himself repeating dully, "Card?" at the same time seeing Esther holding out a card to him, saying, "This one's got no name on. Gaudy-looking thing; it must be from one of the choirboys. Very nice, though, to think of you. That makes thirty-one altogether. You're doing well."

"Yes, I sent you a get-well card. I didn't sign it." Her voice was a mere whisper now. "I thought I'd better not.

57

By the way, I have your watch. . . ." She stopped abruptly. She was looking over her shoulder at someone coming up the stairs and she finished in a clear voice, "I'm so glad you're better, Mr. Blenheim."

As Miss Bateman came abreast of them, he said, "Thank you, thank you," then followed the stiff trim figure up to the landing. When they reached the hallway, Miss Bateman turned to him and, smiling quite genially for her, said, "I endorse that, Mr. Blenheim, it's very nice to see you back again."

"Thank you, Miss Bateman. It's good to be back; you get very bored at home."

Then they went their separate ways.

Standing at the window of his room he looked down on the street and breathed deeply. The pattern was set; she wasn't going to blab. She had taken the incident like a night out at the theater, say. He looked unseeing now across the street and wondered how many men she had practiced on to become so proficient at her hobby, for likely that was what it was with her. During the days around Christmas, when he was at his lowest, he had thought the whole thing was a nightmare and had been relieved at the idea, but his temperature, returning to normal, had brought with it the unpleasant fact that it was no nightmare. Well, it was over, and there'd be no repetition, not if he knew it. Although it was a pretty uncomfortable feeling to have the awareness of this thing between them, he imagined that he wasn't the only man that shared such a secret with her. He supposed he really should be getting a kick out of the incident. Many men would, but it held no kick for him, only revulsion; and this was mainly created by the thought that one so young could be so damnably knowledgeable and, moreover, had used him and made him feel like a schoolboy fumbling at his first affair.

She had mentioned his watch. He was relieved about that. Now he was back, she'd likely send it to him here at the office. Esther, fortunately, hadn't missed it. That was something.

But Betty Ray didn't return his watch; instead, she sent him a letter. Ada usually left his mail, the envelopes slit open, in a pile to the right of his blotting pad. But next morning, on top of the pile, lay an envelope with the words "Private and Personal" printed in bold letters above the address. As he picked it up, he looked at Ada Cole standing in front of the desk, then said aloud, "Private and Personal,

58

huh!" He was smiling as he slit the envelope open. There was a single piece of paper inside and on it he read simply, "I have something belonging to you, don't you want it?" He had no power to stop the blood rushing to his face. He folded the letter in four again, crumpled up the envelope, and dropped it into the wastepaper basket; then looking up at Ada Cole, he remarked with as much casualness as he could muster, "Something silly; I'll deal with this."

"Yes, Mr. Blenheim." And on this she turned and went into her room, and being a woman, she thought, "Now what could be in that letter that would make him look like that, absolutely startled, and red to the ears?"

Harry did a lot of thinking during the day. Should he ignore the letter and wait until he met her, perhaps by chance on the stairs again, and ask her point-blank if she would kindly return the watch. But remembering her volatile personality, he could see her marching into his office, a wide grin on her face, and slapping it down on his desk . . . and in front of Ada Cole or anyone else who might be there. One thing he decided he wasn't going to do, and that was write to her and ask her to return it by post, for if she was nettled in any way she was just as likely to send it to his home address. And then how would he explain it away? Finally, he knew that the only thing was to do what the letter suggested and go to the house for it.

Having made up his mind on what course to take, he knew he mustn't put it off; that would just be piling up the agony; he must settle this business tonight. So he phoned Esther and told her not to hold up the meal as he had some outdoor business to attend to and would be a little late.

The staff left the office at five o'clock, but he didn't leave until a quarter to six, gauging that this would give her ample time to get home. One other thing he was careful not to do, and that was to drive up to her door. He left the car at the bottom end of Carey Street, then went through the Cut, no longer knee-deep in snow but brittle underfoot now with ash.

When, following his knock, he heard one female voice call out and another answer, he hesitated whether to turn and run into the darkness. But too late; the door opened and a woman said, "Yes?"

He was standing in the shadow and she in the light. He took her to be about forty, and she was as fair as her daughter was dark, and instantly he summed her up.

"Mrs. Ray?"

59

"Yes." Her tone was intended to appear refined but resulted in being mincing.

"I would like to have a word with your daughter if I may."

"Oh. Oh, come in. Come in. You're Mr.—?"

"Blenheim."

"Oh, yes, yes. Betty's told me about you, lots. Come in, Mr. Blenheim. Oh, come in. Betty! Betty dear, here's Mr. Blenheim."

After closing the door, she went before him along the passage, her arm extended, ushering him into the room like a stage servant before a personage.

Betty was standing at the bedroom door. She had a comb in her hand, and after looking at him for a moment, she began combing her hair, then said casually, "Be with you in a tick. Sit down."

"I . . . I can't stay."

As he spoke, the bedroom door closed, and Mrs. Ray, smiling with every feature of her over-made-up face, said, "Oh, do sit down for a minute, Mr. Blenheim. She always likes to tidy up after she's been in the office. You get sticky, don't you? So do sit down; you might as well get off your feet." She was wagging her head at him. "You're quite better now? Betty told me you had been ill. It was the day in the snow. You had a time of it, hadn't you? It was very good of you to bring her home. She told me all about it."

"Did she?" he thought. "I wonder." And yet he wouldn't put it past her. He could see them sitting on this couch here roaring their heads off. He stared at the woman. He knew the label Esther would put on her after just with one glance. Common. And if Elsie saw her, she would go further. "Common as muck, Mr. Blenheim," she would say. "Common as muck. An old tart." Like mother, like daughter. They were a couple of tarts. Yet Betty had a better camouflage . . . as yet. Anyway, she had deceived him. But perhaps in a way he was easily deceived.

Mrs. Ray was now adjusting an earring the size of a walnut; she was looking into the mirror above the mantelpiece and talking to him through it. "We don't see much of each other, Betty and me; it's lonely for her. I'm so happy when she gets a nice friend." She paused here and let her eyes rest on his before going on, "You see, I'm on twelve till seven one week and six-thirty till midnight, or sometimes later, another. I'm at the Three Dolls, you know, on the main road. It's a restaurant like, and does a night show.

60

Very popular. Very popular with motorists. I don't mind the twelve-o'clock shift, but I always feel a bit worried about the late shift, leaving Betty, you know. But when she has a friend, I don't worry. It's a comfort."

There was a solo he sang with the phrase repeated throughout, "Holy, holy, holy, Lord God of Hosts," now he found himself saying just that "Holy, holy, holy, Lord God of Hosts. . . ." It was strange. Although he went to church every Sunday, he had never prayed very much, and of latter years not at all. When the prayers were being said, he was thinking of the next hymn and hoping yet once again that Robbins would not drag the end out; or he was going over his solo, singing it in his mind. But now he was praying, actually praying, "Holy, holy, holy, Lord God of Hosts, get me out of this."

"Oh, there you are, dear. Oh, that's nice. I always say you suit red."

Out of habit, Harry had risen to his feet when Betty entered the room, and now he stared at her in the tight-fitting red woolen dress and red mules as she came toward him. She didn't speak as she sat herself on the couch, but her mother said, "Well, I'll have to be away; time's flying, as the man said as he threw the clock at his wife." This quip was followed by a high kick of a laugh; then hurrying across the room, she added, "It'll never do if I miss that bus." She was going into the bedroom when she swung around. "Wait till we get that car, eh, Betty? And we will, won't we, girl?"

"We will, Mam." Betty jerked her head toward her mother and smiled; then she turned and stared at Harry. She stared at him for a full minute, during which he could find nothing to say. Her scrutiny unnerved him; and when at last she spoke, she said softly, "It's nice seeing you again," he was more unnerved still.

Mrs. Ray came hurrying back into the room. She was wearing a short green coat with a fuzzy fur collar turned up high, and over her bouffant hair was lightly dragged a chiffon scarf. "Well, I'm off, so I must say good-bye, Mr. Blenheim. It's been very nice meeting you."

He was on his feet once more, watching her pulling on a pair of fur-lined gloves, and when she smiled widely at him and said, "Now, don't you be a stranger, just pop in when you feel like it. I know our house must appear homely and not what you're used to, but you're very welcome to what we have," he groaned to himself. And following on

61

"Glory, glory, glory," he added, "Oh Christ!" and the exclamation now had no connection with prayer.

"Bye-bye, ducks."

"'Bye-bye, Mam. Be good."

"Well, you know your mam." Mrs. Ray went out laughing. And when the front door closed, Betty looked up to where Harry was standing some distance away on the hearth rug, and her face unsmiling and tight now, she said, "You didn't think much of her, did you?"

"What do you mean?"

"Just what I say. You almost turned your nose up at her."

"You've got a vivid imagination. How do you know what I think?"

"I happen to know men, that's how I know. And you dubbed her straightaway as a cheap piece, didn't you?"

"I did nothing of the sort," he lied firmly.

"Well, you could have fooled me." She uncrossed her legs, then recrossed them, then said almost vehemently, "She's been good to me, has Mam. She's worked for me all me life until I could do it for meself. She could have let me go into a factory as soon as I left school and that would have made things easier for her, but no, she wanted something different for me, so she sent me to the typing college and I passed out top. Do y'know that? Top! And if it wasn't for all the old frozen-faced nits in this town, especially in Peamarsh's, holding down the good jobs, I'd have an office of me own instead of being in the blasted pool. But once the Miss Coles and Batemans get in, they're there for life, old maids' last hope."

He didn't see what all this had to do with his visit, but one thing was evident, she was bitter about her position. He said, "You could always move; there are always vacancies of the kind you're after in Newcastle."

"Yes, I know I could, but I don't want to leave me mam; this is her home, she's made it."

"It's very commendable of you."

"Oh, come off it." She swung around, turning her head fully away from him and looking across the room, leaving him feeling bewildered. She was talking from such a personal plane that one would have imagined that they had known each other for years. She turned her face toward him again, and now she was smiling, and her whole attitude underwent a lightning change as she said softly, "Come and sit down, I'm being naggy."

"I . . . I can't stay."

62

"You can for ten minutes." She patted the couch. "Just ten minutes. Come on, sit down."

It was impossible to refuse her request, and when he took a seat once again on the couch, she curled her legs up under her as she had done on the first occasion they had sat together, but she didn't snuggle up to him or tease him; her tactics were different tonight. She kept her distance as she said, still softly, "It's nice seeing you again."

"Now, Betty." Her name had a strange sound on his lips, and as he paused, she put in, "Now, now, don't get panicky, relax. I'm not going to eat you, you know." She gave a little giggle. "You're scared stiff of me, and it's funny."

"I'm not scared stiff of you." He jerked his head to the side. "Only there's no point in going on with this."

"Why?" The question was quiet.

"Because"—he brought his head round to her again—"I'm a married man with three children, the eldest one not much younger than you."

"Are you happily married?"

"Yes, I'm happily married."

"I don't believe you. You've got a son seventeen, so you've been married eighteen years or more. It doesn't last that long, not eighteen months in some cases. You prove to me one middle-aged man in this town who's happily married and I'll enter a convent. And look, I'm tellin' you I'm not talkin' from hearsay, I'm talkin' from knowsay. I know a lot of men in this town, and I could spill some beans if I liked. But there's one thing about me, I'm not spiteful, I never have been. I don't want to cause trouble for anybody, but what I do want"—she paused, and her hands gripping her forearms across her chest, she repeated—"but what I do want, Harry"—she drew out his name, paused again, then ended—"is a bit of happiness. That's all I'm asking, just a bit of happiness."

What could he say to this? For a moment he felt sorry for her, in sympathy with her, and he wished, he wished deeply that it was in him to make her happy, but he knew that if he was going to have an affair it wouldn't be with someone like her.

She was compelling him to look into her eyes as she went on talking. "I liked you from the first time I clapped eyes on you, but mind, mind, I never planned anything. I just thought it was heaven sent that snow and you bringing me back, like an answer to a prayer that you didn't know you had prayed. You know . . . sort of. After you had gone

63

that night I knew I'd frightened you. You had never been with a woman, had you, except, well, your wife? You knew nothing about it. To all intents and purposes you could have come straight out of a monastery. I know I'm a bit wild when I get going, but that's me. I'm warm inside, hot, boiling, in fact, like them volcanoes, just like them, burstin' out every now and again." She shrugged her shoulders now and grinned slyly at him. "But I don't need to tell you, do I? Anyway, there it is." She leaned back from him and now stated flatly, "I like you; I want to be friends with you."

He turned from her and, leaning his elbow on his knees, cupped his forehead; and from this position he muttered, "It's impossible, quite impossible."

"Are you afraid your wife might get to know?"

When he didn't answer, she went on, "Nobody would ever see you come here; we're very fortunately placed in this house. You just need nip through the Cut and you're in. There's only six houses in the row, and from the time they come in at half-past five until they start to go out to the clubs or some place at half-past six, the street's empty. And in front there's only a warehouse. It's a hundred-to-one chance you'd ever be seen, so what are you frightened of? And look, look, don't think me mam would say anything; me mam's the soul of discretion, as they say."

He almost sprang to his feet now and, looking down at her, said, "It's impossible. You must take this for final. Apart from being a married man, we work in the same office. Then besides being a member of the church I'm in different societies in the town. What you're offering is most generous, I realize that, but I just cannot accept, I cannot be a hypocrite. You know for a fact that if I hadn't drunk so much on Christmas Eve the . . . the incident would never have happened. Now"—he undid the top button of his waistcoat, then did it up again, before adding—"if you'll be good enough to return my watch, I'll be grateful, and . . . and we can . . ."

"And we can forget it ever happened." She was on her feet confronting him now, her eyes almost black, her mouth tight. "You know what you are, you're a weak-bellied, pious bastard. That's what you are. Now you listen to me, Mr. Blenheim. What if I have a baby?"

He had heard about people blanching, but now he was experiencing it. He felt the blood draining from his face down through his stomach. Even his words seemed white as he whispered, "You're not?"

64

"I don't know yet. It could happen quite easily; I wasn't prepared. I'm over me time, so I don't know."

Holy, holy, holy, Lord God of Hosts . . .

"As things stand, I think I'll just hang on to your watch, sort of mind it for you for a little while longer."

"I want my watch, and I want it now."

"Oh, Mr. Blenheim, stop shouting; somebody might hear you next door. I know she's deaf, but she has friends come in."

He was no longer feeling blanched; the blood was pounding in his head. This was the kind of situation that other men got themselves into too. From his own experience he had known of a number in his time; one had been a close friend, a churchgoing man and a visitor to the house. Esther had liked him; she always thought Bill Caldwell such a genuine man. That was until he had got himself mixed up with a young married woman and the affair had ended in divorce. After that his name had never been mentioned again. Esther didn't hold with divorce; what God had joined together was a holy law with her. He had the wild idea of thrusting this blackmailing little tart aside and dashing into the bedroom and searching for his watch, and he might have done just that except that he knew that to prevent him she would come to grips with him, physically, and he wanted no more of that.

He picked up his hat and, without looking at her again, made for the door; and when he reached it, she called, "I'll write to you when I want to see you again."

As once before he had stood at the end of the Cut and wiped the sweat from his face, so now he stopped at the same spot again and stood gasping as if he had sprinted from the house. What was he to do? He should get advice, tell someone . . . and make himself out to be as she said, a weak-bellied pious bastard. And what if she should be— He couldn't even think the word "pregnant." He saw his whole ordered world in fragments about him. He saw the chaos after exposure. He saw the reactions of the individual members of his family. First Esther: the ground cut from beneath her, her ideals and lofty thinking sullied by the sordid affair. But the reaction he knew he dreaded most was that of his father-in-law. What would it be? Wrath, yes, indignation, and of course the demand that the whole affair be hushed up for his daughter's sake; and for the remainder of his life he'd be under his thumb. And all this because he took a girl home in the snow. It didn't seem possible. If

65

someone had put the situation to him as a hypothetical case, he would have said the whole thing was highly improbable.

He got into his car and drove home.

The house was quiet when he entered the hall, and after he had hung up his things in the cloakroom, he went into the sitting room, where Esther was sitting reading. She laid down her book and stared into his face, saying, "You're looking peaky again. Why did you work so late when you're not feeling too fit?"

"Oh, I'm all right." He went to the fire and held out his hands to the flames and asked, "Where's everybody?"

"Terry's gone to his piano lesson, John's doing his homework, and Gail's having tea with Anna Birkett. By the way, are you going to choir practice?"

"Yes, yes, I suppose so. I'd forgotten about it for the moment."

"I told Gail you might pick her up and bring her home before you went, but then I didn't know you were going to be so late."

"I'll go straight off and fetch her after I've had a bite," he said flatly.

"Good, I hate her to be out alone in the dark. I'll get your meal now, I've kept it hot."

As she brought his meal into the dining room, she said, "Father rang a short while ago. Colonel Callow's housekeeper had just been on the phone to him. The colonel wants him to go through again for the weekend, so he won't be coming into the office tomorrow and will likely stay in York until Monday night. He said he thinks the old fellow's lonely."

"Hasn't he any relations of his own?" Harry asked, and she answered, "No, I understand not. He's lived with the old housekeeper and a manservant for years."

"Is he wealthy?" Harry asked this question thinking it might give the reason for his father-in-law putting himself out for an old man.

"I don't really know. But he must have some money, although he doesn't appear to spend more than is absolutely necessary. He's a bit of an eccentric, I think, won't have the phone in, no television. The housekeeper's got to use a call box. Father said this was the third time she had phoned in the last three weeks, so he felt he was obliged to go. He's silly like that, about wartime loyalties. He seems to forget that the war's been over more than twenty years."

When you enjoyed the war as much as Dave Rippon did

66

on his own saying, you didn't forget it easily. He could hear his father-in-law leading forth, his back to the fire, swaying on his toes as he regaled him with his wartime activities. "Best years of my life, grand days, great days. Such comradeship'll never come again. Oh, boy! Did we have fun." And all this from a training camp in a corner of the country where the nearest bomb had been dropped twenty miles away.

"What's on your mind?"

"What?"

"I said, what's on your mind? You've been staring at your plate for the last five minutes."

"Oh. Oh, I was just thinking."

"Can't you scrap the choir practice tonight?"

"No, Gregory's got the idea that the TV might do a service from the church. As far as I know, he's written away asking someone to come down and hear us."

"I . . . I knew nothing about this." She looked slightly affronted, and he said, "Well, it's the choir business."

"Well, the choir business is also the church committee business and nothing was said at the last meeting."

"Oh, I think what he's done he's done since then."

"I should hope so."

She certainly was affronted. As he watched her taking some empty dishes out of the room, her back very straight and expressive, he thought, "I wish to God that was all I had on my mind at the moment, whether or not Gregory had taken too much upon himself.

Fifteen minutes later, when he was on the point of leaving her to pick up Gail, she said to him, apropos of nothing that had been mentioned since she showed her displeasure of the choirmaster's initiative, "Does Father know of this?"

He had almost forgotten the matter and he turned a blank face to her and asked, "Know what?"

"What's the matter with you tonight, Harry? You're miles away. What were we talking about just a short while ago? Gregory writing off to the BBC on his own?"

He stared her full in the face, then said loudly, "I don't know, Esther, if your father knows about it or not, but if someone has omitted to inform him, is that going to be looked upon as a crime?"

"Harry!" She spoke his name in a tone that was weighed with censure; then she waited. But on this occasion he didn't, as was usual when he had raised his voice to her, apologize immediately by saying, "Oh, I'm sorry, dear," and so preserve the tranquil atmosphere of the home. On this occasion he just walked out.

Ten minutes later, when he reached the Birketts' house, he got the impression that Gail, for once, wasn't overjoyed to see him, and the reason was presented to him when Paul Birkett came out of the garage, where he had obviously been tinkering with a motorbike, and joined his sister, Anna, who was seeing her friend off at the gate.

When he started the car up and the waving had stopped, Gail said to him, "That was Paul, Dad."

"Yes." He raised his eyebrows and nodded at the windscreen. "Yes, I think I saw him."

When she took her elbow and dug him in the side, he cried, "Careful, careful! That's a police car just passed us; they'll have me up for drunken driving."

"Do you like him, Dad?"

"Do I like Paul? Well, I hardly know him. I don't come across him much, him not being in the choir."

"Well, he sits in the third pew on the left . . . no, on your right, and in the end seat; you can't help but see him."

He was forced to chuckle. So this was it. He was glad. She was nearly sixteen and she hadn't had a boyfriend yet. Some of them at the church were going strong at fourteen. He wondered if young Paul, like himself, could detect the butterfly emerging from the chrysalis. He doubted it. He said teasingly now, "Oh, yes, I remember seeing him. He's lanky, isn't he?"

"Oh, Dad, he's not, not lanky, tall."

"Oh, perhaps I haven't got the right one. Has he got red hair?"

He could hear her swallowing. "It isn't red, it's auburn, and it's lovely hair."

They stopped at the traffic lights and he cast a glance at her as he asked softly, "You like Paul?"

She dropped her head just the slightest as she answered, "Uh-huh!"

"Does he like you?"

"Yes, Dad." She was looking at him squarely now, but he kept his eyes on the road as they moved over the crossing; then he asked casually, "He's told you so?"

"Well . . . well, not exactly. He wrote me a letter."

"Oh, he did, did he?"

"He . . . he didn't give it to me himself; he gave it to Anna to give to me. He wondered if I would go out with him."

68

"And what did you say?"

"Well, I haven't said anything yet. I'll write the answer tonight and give it to Anna tomorrow."

He bit on his lip. For all the talk of being with it, of being groovy, of LSD and free love, for some youngsters love still started like this. He could understand young Birkett writing; he was a shy lad in spite of his red hair, or perhaps just because of it. The Birketts were a nice family. A bit starchy, he thought, at least the parents were, but nevertheless nice.

Out of curiosity now he said, "Have you just got to know him—I mean, well? Doesn't he go to the Youth Club?"

"Not very often, and then he plays chess most of the time."

They were about three minutes' ride from home when, after a thoughtful silence, she suddenly asked, "What's it like, Dad—I mean marriage?"

He actually grazed the curb, and when he straightened out again, he didn't know whether to laugh outright at her question or to treat it seriously. It was natural, he supposed, she should be thinking of marriage, even at fifteen, well near sixteen, but this was jumping the gun a bit. And what a question to tackle, and coming from her. Had it come from either of the boys he would have dealt with it in a straightforward manner; but even with them he knew he would have evaded the truth, because the young should not be disillusioned. If that was to come, it should come only after they had tasted wonder. Had he ever tasted wonder? The answer was a little while in coming, and then it was "No." Happiness, a kind of happiness, but never wonder, because he thought that when you tasted wonder it would leave a mark on you. He had only once seen the result of wonder and he had been very young then. He had seen it on the faces of Mr. and Mrs. Fielding. They would sit in the front row of the church, and often he would find himself singing his solo to them alone. They walked in the street hand in hand, and some of the choirboys said they were potty. They were of no account, the Fieldings. He had worked in an ironmonger's shop all his life, never even rising to manager, and she had done daily work until she fell and broke her leg. She died at seventy-three, and the following day he put his head in the gas oven.

"Dad! Did you hear what I said?"

"Yes, I heard you, dear; I was just thinking. But . . . but I

69

think it's a question you should ask your mother; she'd be able to tell you better than me."

"Why?"

"Why? Well, because she's a woman; she'd see it from her side."

"If I asked Mother, I know exactly what she'd say?"

"You do?"

"Yes. 'Don't probe; you'll know in God's good time.' "

He gulped in his throat. Again he didn't know whether to laugh or to treat this seriously. That his young daughter could have got the measure of her mother utterly nonplussed him. That Gail, who was always obedient and loving toward her mother, should yet see her through a mirror of cool reasoning amazed him, for in that simple sentence was embodied Esther's character and, stemming from that, her way of life.

Thinking it advisable to ignore her statement, he said hesitantly, "Well, marriage is a very wonderful thing if two people love each other, really love each other."

"But how will I know—I mean, really know. You see, I feel I really love Paul, I've been gone on him for ages. I've dreamed about us being married and all that, but I want to know if I'll still feel like this . . . well, I mean, when I'm married and have a family."

"Oh, my dear! you mustn't trouble your head about such things yet. Look." He swung the car around into the avenue. "You'll have other boys, dozens of other boys. Well, if not dozens, you'll know and like a lot of boys before you marry. What you want to do now is to enjoy yourself. Go to parties and dances. The summer will soon be here, you'll be playing tennis, and you'll meet other boys and . . ."

"I don't want to meet other boys, Dad. I've just told you." Her voice was earnest now. "I like Paul, I always have."

"Well then, go on liking him, there's nobody stopping you. And there's one good thing about it, your mother likes the Birketts." He felt he shouldn't have said that.

"Do you love Mother, Dad?"

He was startled again by this question and he wanted to evade it by saying, "What's got into you tonight?" but he knew what had got into his daughter. She was awakening to life; the puppy fat was slipping from her mind as well as from her body. She wanted to talk about this thing which was persistently with her and which took on the shape at present of Paul Birkett.

70

As he turned into the drive, he said, "Of course I love your mother." When he stopped the car, he found she was looking at him, and he wouldn't have been at all surprised if she had come out with "Then why do you have single beds? Because if you love somebody, I would have thought you would always want to be close to them." Or she could have said, "Well, why have you stopped kissing Mother when you go out in the morning and when you come in at night? You used to do it when I was small." But what she said was, "It's funny, Dad, but I can talk to you better than anybody else, even Anna, and we talk about some things, I can tell you."

He laughed gently and touched her cheek with his hand as he said, "I bet you do. But I'm glad you can talk to me, I hope you always will."

She said now, "Aren't you coming in?" and he answered, "No, I haven't time; I'm late for the squawking session as it is. It's an absolute nuisance having to pick up modern misses from parties."

She put her arm through the window, her fist doubled, and aimed a punch at him; then said, in what she imagined to be a haughty grown-up voice, "Will you look me up, Mr. Blenheim, on your return?" And he answered in the same vein, "It'll be a pleasure, ma'am. A pleasure."

As he drove the car around the circular flower bed and out of the drive again, he thought, "She could be married in two or three years' time. And the boys, too, for that matter." When they were gone there'd be only he and Esther. What would it be like, just he and Esther alone? But the thought brought no mental picture to the screen of his mind.

71

Five

It was a fortnight later when he saw the second letter marked "Private and Personal" lying on top of his mail. Ada was in her office, her door open, but before he had finished reading the letter, she was standing at the other side of the desk and once again she saw his face giving him away.

The letter said simply. "You can have your watch. I'll be in about the same time."

He had given up all hope of getting his watch back and had decided to go into Newcastle, buy a similar one, and have it engraved. In fact, he would rather have done this than visit her house again. But then there was the damning inscription. With a thing like that she had a hold over him.

Ada was still looking at him as he folded up the letter and casually opened a side drawer and thrust it in. When she laid an order sheet on the desk and turned away without speaking, went into her room, and closed the door, he quietly opened the drawer again, took out the letter, and put it in his pocket.

Behind her closed door Ada Cole stood looking into space. It was a woman. He had got himself mixed up with a woman. That was the only reason he would look like that. She bent down and opened the bottom drawer of her desk, and from beneath some papers she took out a crumpled envelope and studied it yet again. There was something vaguely familiar about the writing. She had a good memory for people's handwriting. Well, so she should, she told herself; she had dealt with handwriting all her working life, and whoever had written the address on this envelope had got her claws into Mr. Blenheim. Yet she couldn't imagine him going off the rails, him happily married and with such a nice family. And besides which, he was such a nice fellow. But he'd had that scared look on his face again when he had read that letter. Now where had she seen that writing before? Something about the P. "Private and Personal." If she had seen it recently then, she deduced, it must be somebody in the office. Mentally she now went over all the female staff from the ground floor up. She went through the

72

directors' secretaries, but the improbability of it being one of them was too high, two of them being over fifty and the others, Miss Bateman excluded, were of an appearance, she decided, that wouldn't attract any man, not a man like Mr. Blenheim anyway. That left only the pool. Now who was there in the pool? Rose Weybridge, Betty Ray, Olive Standford, and Mary Cheeseman. Mary Cheeseman was getting married next week. That left three, and he could count Olive Standford out; a man would be hard put to take on a girl like Olive, poor soul. There were plain girls and plain girls, but Olive was in a category of her own. That only left Rose Weybridge and Betty Ray. Now she wouldn't put it past Rose Weybridge to try it on with any man. She was a young madam, was Rose Weybridge. And what about the other one? She was a cheeky piece, Betty Ray, always with an answer ready and brazen sort of eyes. But when would either of them have come in contact with Mr. Blenheim? Christmas! The word hit her like a blow. When she returned after the holidays she found a note signed by Betty Ray stating briefly what work she had done and adding that she had filed the copies of the letters she had typed. Ada Cole remembered that she had commented to herself at the time about the handwriting, thinking, "They get worse." She hadn't the note now, but she could easily get a sample of that girl's handwriting, and she would do so without further delay.

On their third meeting she said to him, "You know I could love you or hate your guts," and he replied, "I'd rather you didn't do either."

"What're you frightened of, anyway? Oh, I know." She flapped her hand at him. "There's your wife, and the church and the Choral Society and the Rotarians, and the Save the Children Fund Committee, and, oh, God knows what. I know everything you're in, I've done my homework; but when all that's said, I say, 'What are you frightened of?' I'm not a blabber, I've told you. Have I let on in any way over these past weeks that I know you other than as one of the bosses?"

"No, I can't say you have. But you've written to me twice and your letters, to say the least, stand out. 'Private and Personal.' You know yourself that when a letter like that comes into an office it means just that, 'Private and Personal.' But there's very little of private business that one can keep from one's secretary."

73

"Oh, if that's all you're worrying about. Old Ada wouldn't smell a dead pig if it was hung under her nose."

"You'd be surprised."

"Yes, I'd say I would be if I found out different. But anyway"—she turned her head to one side—"you don't want anything to do with me, do you? I'm not your type. That's it, isn't it?"

"No." He had to be kind. "It isn't a case of you not being my type, it's a case of not wanting to be involved in anything underhand or—" He almost said unseemly, but that would have made her laugh. "Oh!" He moved impatiently on the couch. "We've been through all this before. You said you'd return my watch and that's why I'm here."

She stared at him. She wasn't sitting on the couch tonight but on a chair to the side of the fireplace, and after a moment she said, "If I give it you back, will you do something for me?"

He groaned inwardly. Another catch, another hitch. Not the bedroom again. "It all depends what it is," he said, "and if I'm in a position to grant it."

"Oh, you're in a position all right. I want to go up."

"Up?" He bent his head toward her, not understanding.

"Yes, up on to the top floor. Mr. Nolan's secretary is going to America; I'd like her job."

He took his eyes from hers and looked into the fire. He was thinking rapidly. If he told her the truth, that he had no power to help her here, it was just a possibility she might hang on to the watch. He listened to her saying, "Mary Cheeseman's getting married and Rosie Weybridge hasn't got the sense she was born with. That only leaves Olive Standford and me. Now Olive has been there for over a year and her work isn't bad, but if you've seen her, you'll know that she isn't what every man wants about the office." Her mouth curved upward now, then her face broke into a smile as she ended, "So that only leaves me. A little word from the right direction, a little push, and I'll be upstairs. The last word, I know, is with Miss Bateman, but you could tell her that I've done work for you and it was all right. It was all right, wasn't it?"

"Yes. Oh, yes."

"Well then, will you? You could say sort of offhand like to her when you're going through the office to see his nibs, 'I hear Mr. Noland is losing his secretary. Who were you thinking of putting in her place?' And if she doesn't say me

74

you could say, 'Well, there's that Miss Ray, she did some very good work for me.' "

He was staring at her again. She really believed that this was how things could be done. She didn't think that Miss Bateman would be asking herself why he should want Miss Ray promoted, why his interest. He couldn't understand how she, being what she was, could be so naïve. He said, "I'll do what I can."

"You will?" She was laughing now. "Good. You won't regret it. I'm a good secretary, I know me own worth, and if I've got somebody to take an interest in, and an office of me own . . . well, I'll go ahead like wildfire. I know I will."

Not in Peamarsh's, he thought, not if I can help it. He would, he knew now, never know a moment's peace as long as she was in the building.

He watched her get up and go into the bedroom, and when she came back, his watch was dangling from her finger. She came and stood in front of him and swung it before his face like a pendulum. Her own face had an impish look as she said, "The evidence."

He put out his hand and took hold of the end of the strap, but she still held on to it, and as she looked down at him, she said, "I hate to let it go; it was me only hold over you."

Thank God for that, he thought, remembering the threatened pregnancy. He wanted to pull it from her hand, but restrained himself in case this should be a prelude to a tussle. He felt she was just waiting for that. He took a slow deep breath as the watch dropped onto his hand, and putting it in his pocket, he said, "Thank you."

As he got to his feet, she said, "You won't forget about what I asked you, will you?"

"No, I won't forget." He picked up his hat and walked out of the room and into the passage, and there, slipping before him, she put her hand on the sneck of the door and turned her face up to him as she said, "Well, I suppose this is the last tête-à-tête."

He made no answer to this and she said softly, "You're a fool, you know; you could have had fun. I'm not a gold digger. There's something I put much more value on than money, and I'll give you three guesses at it." She put her head back now against the door and laughed a high cracking laugh, saying, "You blush easily. I've never know a man blush like you; you're like a lad in some ways that's never

75

been tried out. All right, all right." The slow movement of her hand before his face indicated he keep calm.

When the door was pulled open, he stepped into the dark street and moved swiftly away toward the Cut, and he was some way along it before he heard the door bang. It didn't close, it banged.

For the third time he stood at the end of the Cut and got his breath. It was over. Thank God, it was over. It had been a lesson, a nerve-racking lesson. But he was out of it, clear. Never again would he let himself in for anything like that, NEVER, NEVER.

The third letter marked "Private and Personal" arrived the day after Olive Standford was told to take over in Mr. Noland's office. The letter said briefly, "You're a dirty stinker! You didn't even mention my name to Miss Bateman, I asked her. Well, the last laugh might be on me."

As the morning wore on, the sick feeling in his stomach increased. She had said she wasn't a blabber, but that was when she imagined she had something to gain. Thwarted, God knew what she would do, or say! He even dreaded going out to lunch in case he would run into her on the stairs. The only thing to do was to get out early and return early. And he got the opportunity to do this when, at about ten to twelve, Jim Whelan phoned to say he would like a word with him and would he join him for lunch at The Oak? Yes, Harry said, he'd be very pleased to. Was it something connected with the business? No, Jim replied, nothing connected with the business, but nevertheless it was of some importance. But more over lunch. How soon could he make it? Right now, Harry said.

Jim Whelan was waiting for him in one of the wooden-framed cubicles which distinguished The Oak, and after asking him if he would like anything to drink and Harry saying, "No, thanks all the same," they got down to ordering lunch. This over, Harry sat back and looked across at Jim and said, "Well now, what's this you've got to tell me?"

"Ah, yes." Jim tapped his fingertips gently together then asked, "Am I right in thinking that you don't actually love your father-in-law?"

It was a moment before Harry answered very quietly, "You're right; but why do you ask?"

"Well, for the simple reason I wanted to make sure, although I was pretty certain how you felt."

"What you've got to say concerns him?"

76

"Yes."

"Regarding the business?"

"Oh, no. No, nothing to do with the business. . . . By the way, do you know if he goes to York very often?"

"York? Yes. At least he's been a few weekends this year."

"Do you know why he goes?"

"To see this old colonel, I understand. He's still war crazy, good old days, and all that."

"His old colonel? Oh, that's a good one! Now let me start at the beginning and put you in the picture from my side. It's like this, Harry. My in-laws live in York and they were celebrating their golden wedding at the weekend, and the wife and I went through on Friday night and for a treat we had arranged to take them to the new hotel that's been opened recently. The Splendide. In the ordinary way we would never go to a place like that, but this was once in a lifetime. Well, it was when we were in the foyer, they were waiting for me, Marge and her mam and dad, and I was just coming out of the gents when I see a man and a very smartly dressed young woman being led to the dining room by the headwaiter. And the man was . . . guess who?"

"No!"

"Yes, Rippon. And the woman was Alice Howell."

"Alice Howell and him, in . . . in York!"

"Alice Howell and your father-in-law in York, yes. You remember Alice Howell, don't you? She was in the storeroom. She married, and her husband had a nervous breakdown—two, in fact. He's in the asylum now."

"Yes, yes, I know." There was an utterly bewildered note in Harry's voice. "She was a member of the church. They were both members. She moved to York to stay with a cousin or someone last back end, in November some time."

"Does that coincide with the colonel?"

Harry sat back and tried to digest this news. It was unbelievable. He said as much. "It's unbelievable, Jim. Now are you sure?"

"Look, Harry; I know the old man, I knew him even before you did—I started in this business when it was a pup—and I also know Alice Howell."

"He couldn't have just met her."

"Just met her be damned!" Jim tossed his head. "The headwaiter was taking them in like old friends and headwaiters are not given to charity; the only thing that causes them to stoop their backs is the thought of picking up crinkly paper."

77

The stinking hypocrite, the psalm-singing stinking hypocrite! And all that business about his old colonel. God, he could be sick!

"Well, now, has that given you an appetite for your dinner?"

"Appetite? It's taken it away. I'm floored, Jim."

"I'm not; I wasn't surprised in the least. I've had my own opinion about Mr. Dave Rippon for many years; an' I've got a suspicion this isn't the first little offshoot he's indulged in. In fact, I've more than a suspicion. Dave Rippon never does anything for nothing, and if I've ever heard of him doing a good turn for somebody, a woman in particular, I've always wondered what she'd had to give him in return." He paused and looked hard at Harry and asked, "Aren't you tickled about it?"

"No, Jim, I'm not, I'm anything but. At this moment I'm flaming-well boiling, I'm bloody-well boiling."

And that was putting the state of his feelings mildly, for he was hearing Esther down the years extolling her father's virtues.

"I'm sorry I told you, Harry."

"Oh, no, don't you be sorry, Jim. Thank you very much, and I mean that. You see, I've had that sanctimonious old roué pushed down my throat for years; that was, when he wasn't being held up before me as a paragon."

"Oh, I guessed that much, Harry. That was why I thought I'd like telling you. What you going to do about it?"

"I don't know, Jim, not yet. I just don't know, I'll see how things work out. But there's one thing I do know. I feel in a stronger position than I've ever felt in my life before."

"Good. Good. Then my spilling the beans has done something."

"By the way," said Harry now. "Did he see you?"

"No. As it happened he didn't, and that was because he was escorted to the Rose Room. It's a smaller dining room, kept for select patrons or small parties, I understand. But would his face have been red if we had bumped into each other! Yet being Dave Rippon, I bet he'd have talked himself out of it."

"Yes," thought Harry, "being Dave Rippon he'd have talked himself out of it all right."

Harry ran up the office stairs, marched across the first floor, thrust open his office door, pulled off his hat and coat, and sat down behind his desk. He was still angry, but now

78

his anger was being attacked by a form of reasoning that seemed to be defending his father-in-law. It said, "He's a widower; if he wants to have a woman on the side that's up to him isn't it?" Yes, he came back, that was up to him. He could have had as many women on the side as he liked if he wasn't such a preaching prig, and if his moral code wasn't held up as a yardstick to himself. . . . And what would Esther make of her dear papa when she heard of this? But there was the rub; he wouldn't be able to tell Esther, for the knowledge would break her. And there was another point. Would he be able even to tell his father-in-law he was aware of his double life? . . . He didn't know. Yet there was one thing certain, he wouldn't be capable of listening to him doing the Colonel-Callow-and-the-honor-of-the-regiment monologue without retaliating in some way.

He sat now with both hands on the desk rolling a pencil back and forward between his fingers. Then, the action stopping abruptly, he put his hand into his inner pocket and brought out Betty Ray's letter again. When he reread it, it didn't appear so obviously threatening now. The knowledge he had acquired over the last two hours had in an odd way rid him of some of his fears, not all, but some. His thinking pointed out that even if she did open her mouth he wouldn't have his father-in-law wagging his finger at him. Then his reasoning, turning on him, again, said, "You're not in such a good position that you can wag your finger yourself. They would say you're worse than he is; a married man with three children!" It wouldn't be much use protesting it just happened that once, for who'd believe you? Certainly not Esther.

When the phone rang he lifted it abruptly and said, "Yes."

"Harry!" The name was rapped out, it was the great man himself.

"Yes?"

"Where've you been? I tried to get you at twelve o'clock."

"I've been to lunch."

"Going early, aren't you? Anyway, listen. I want you up here at four-thirty prompt. I'll likely be out of the board-room then, but if I'm not, wait."

He held the mouthpiece away from him and looked at it. The man on the other end of the line could have been a schoolmaster chastising an errant pupil. He was about to speak when he heard the phone click down.

Well! Talking about having the wind taken out of your sails. That demand augured no pleasant interview. There was

79

something amiss and he himself was involved, that was evident.

It was about ten minutes later when the phone rang again and he heard the voice of Miss Bateman on the other end. "Mr. Blenheim?"

"Yes." He was bristling now.

"Miss Bateman here."

"Yes, Miss Bateman?"

"Would it be possible for you to come up to the office now?"

He screwed up his eyes as he replied, "But Mr. Rippon's just been on the phone and told me he wants to see me at half-past four."

"I know, Mr. Blenheim; but I would like to see you now, if it's convenient to you."

Where his father-in-law's tone had been, to say the least, demanding, Miss Bateman's was persuasive, and this he knew wasn't like Miss Bateman.

"Are you still there, Mr. Blenheim?"

"Yes, I'm still here, Miss Bateman."

"Can you come up now?"

"Yes, I can." His voice remained stiff.

"Thank you."

When he put the phone down, he stared at it; then rising and passing Ada Cole's door, he called, "If anyone should ring, I'll be up in Mr. Rippon's office, Ada."

She opened the door and nodded at him, saying, "Very well, Mr. Blenheim." Her expression caught his attention, and stepping back, he looked at her and said, "Are you all right, Ada?"

"Yes, yes, Mr. Blenheim." For a moment he thought she looked frightened, but that, he supposed, was a ridiculous idea; she was just tired. "Not another cold brewing up, I hope?" he said.

"No, Mr. Blenheim."

He nodded at her now and went out across the hall and into the lift and up to the second floor. When he entered his father-in-law's outer office, Miss Bateman was seated behind her desk, apparently waiting for him. He judged this because her hands were on top of the blotter, joined together as if she had been sitting thinking. This, too, was an unusual pose in which to find Miss Bateman.

"Sit down, Mr. Blenheim."

He sat down and looked across the desk and noted that her expression, too, was different; she didn't look cool any longer, she looked sort of furious, yet in an odd way controlled. For something to say, he said, "Can I help you, Miss Bateman?"

Before answering she made a small motion of her head slightly to the side and her arched eyebrows moved upward. Then, her voice even, she said, "No, I don't think you can, Mr. Blenheim; but I can help you."

He found himself pursing his lips and bobbing his head and saying politely, "That's very nice of you, Miss Bateman."

"We won't waste time on being polite to each other, Mr. Blenheim. I have twenty minutes"—she glanced at her watch —"before I am due in the boardroom." She sat up stiffly in her chair now, her hands still joined together on the blotter, then went on, "Mr. Rippon wishes to see you at half-past four. You will have gauged from his tone that he didn't sound pleased. You might be wondering what he wants to see you about. Well, I'm going to tell you so you'll be prepared. It's about Betty Ray."

His stomach muscles jerked as if a bullet had hit them. The saliva left his mouth and his tongue seemed to swell making it impossible for him to comment in any way.

"The knowledge of your association with Miss Ray came to me through"—she paused—"Miss Cole, but believe me, Ada . . . Miss Cole told me of this only because she was worried about you. She felt you were being blackmailed by this girl because of the letters you were receiving. She told me in confidence about it. Perhaps that was foolish of her, but she wanted advice. You must believe that she sincerely wanted to help you. Well, Mr. Blenheim, I am secretary to Mr. Rippon; I've worked for the firm for a year longer than you and my loyalties have always been with it, especially to Mr. Rippon, and so I informed Mr. Rippon of what Miss Cole had told me."

The hell you did! Loyalty to the firm. He felt hot anger rising in him again, but it was checked when she said, as if she meant it, "I'm sorry now that I did so, very sorry. I want you to believe that, Mr. Blenheim."

That was some comfort. He opened his mouth to speak but found himself still unable to do so. Instead, he drooped his head and swung it slowly from side to side; but he brought it up sharply as she said, "But you needn't be concerned as to what he will do to you because you've got a comeback at him, haven't you?"

81

"Comeback?" The word seemed to struggle over the thickness of his tongue.

"Yes, his visits to York."

His eyes widened, his mouth dropped into a slight gape. "You know about them?"

"I didn't until about an hour ago. I happened to be sitting in the cubicle in The Oak and heard you and Mr. Whelan talking. I'm afraid I became interested and made a point of listening. It's odd that I should have gone into The Oak today, fate, you might say. I haven't eaten there more than half-a-dozen times before. Perhaps because it's a favorite with the men. Anyway, there I was alone in my cubicle and I had nothing to do but lean back against the partition and listen to two known voices talking."

"You know it all then, Miss Bateman, don't you?" he said now with a slight touch of sarcasm, and she nodded at him and said, "Yes. Yes, Mr. Blenheim, I know it all. I also know that your father-in-law was looking forward to the ribbing he would be able to give you because of your relationship with Miss Ray, although he didn't know exactly what it was. Nor do I or Miss Cole for that matter. But being, as he terms himself, a man of the world, he put two and two together."

"He would."

"Yes, he would, Mr. Blenheim. I can also tell you that he had decided that he wasn't going to inform your wife, he didn't want her to be upset, but"—she paused—"to use his own words he was going to take it out of your hide. Subtly, of course. The means he was going to use was the business concerning the outside building contracts. He was going to give you carte blanche except"—again she paused—"for the final word on estimates. He would make these himself, but they'd all be done through your office and you personally, and whatever trouble ensued he would see that you bore full responsibility. You have known your father-in-law a long time, but even so it might seem impossible to you, even at this stage, that he could, under those circumstances, make trouble for you, but I can assure you, Mr. Blenheim, that he could. His methods are legal and quite within the law, but dirty."

Miss Bateman sneered as she said the word "dirty," and there was such bitterness in her tone that for the moment he forgot his own predicament and wondered what had happened to turn her against the man she'd worked for for so long. Surely not just because she'd heard of his affair in

82

York. Yet women were strange creatures. Didn't he know! He asked her quietly now, "Why are you telling me all this, Miss Bateman?"

She didn't answer for a moment, but bringing her hands from the desk, where she had kept them during all this time, she joined them tightly together and pressed them against her thin neck as she said, "Because I'm leaving next week and I thought it might be a good idea that when you were called into the sanctum you should have in your possession some bullets to fire, not only for yourself but on my behalf, so to speak." She began now to gather some papers up quickly from her desk, and when she rose, he rose also and said, "I don't quite follow you, Miss Bateman. I can't see how letting him know I'm aware of the real reason for his visits to York can affect you in any way."

"That alone couldn't, Mr. Blenheim, but when you tell him that you are aware that I have been his mistress for fifteen years, and that I have a child by him—adopted, she is now thirteen years old—and that I expected him to marry me when his wife died, you'll understand that you are firing for me. Also, that right up to this very week he has visited me as usual. My home is very discreetly placed on the outskirts of the town; he arranged it so." She moved toward the door and his stunned gaze followed her, and there she turned and looked at him, her face, he thought, on the point of crumpling into tears. But her voice held a slightly cracked sound like laughter as she said, "I believed in Colonel Callow. Mr. Rippon kindly phoned me from a call box during his visits. The colonel, I understand, didn't like the phone. What is more, he actually made me feel sorry for the poor, lonely colonel. I was a fool, wasn't I, to be taken in? But I . . . I really can't blame myself for my stupidity because Mr. Rippon is a very clever man."

"Oh, Miss Bateman, I'm very sorry."

She turned her face toward the door for a moment, but she didn't go out, and he spoke softly to her back, "I won't say anything about this, Miss Bateman; you wouldn't really want me—"

"Oh, yes, yes, please." She was looking at him now. Her eyes were full of tears, but they weren't spilling over. "I ask you to do this for me. I want you to do it. I want him to know that you know. It may not give you any power over him because you're not the kind of man who would use that kind of power, but it will prevent him from using you as a battering ram because of his dislike of you. And he

83

dislikes you heartily, he cannot stand you. All crooks hate honest men."

As they stared at each other in silence, he had the strong urge to take her in his arms and comfort her. Then she said, "I'm acting in strict accordance with the saying, 'There's no fury like that of a woman scorned,' don't you think, Mr. Blenheim? But I've kept my fury quiet because I'm averse to brawls, but it will nevertheless have results." She blinked a number of times; then, straightening her shoulders and wetting her lips, she went out of the room. She didn't even deem it necessary to go to the cloakroom but marched straight to the boardroom, knocked once, then opened the door and went in.

He stood where he was, staring into the empty hallway. Amazing, unbelievable, fantastic. The words were of the superlative degree, of which his mind was capable at the moment. The whole affair was past description, at least that part of it in which Miss Bateman was concerned. Poor Miss Bateman. He felt utterly, utterly sorry for her. All these years he had judged her to be an unfeeling, prim, less-than-human being, a sort of highly powered machine. How wrong one could be. Yet, no one could be blamed for thinking her otherwise, for her attitude had created that impression. But he had just glimpsed the real Miss Bateman, an exceptional woman.

He forgot to close the door after him before he walked across the landing, and he was still in a state of bewilderment when he entered his office again, there to see Ada Cole standing in her doorway, her hand to her cheek. She went to say something as he passed her, but instead she broke down, and he turned quickly to her as if he had just recollected she was there and said, "Why, Ada, don't. Don't distress yourself like that."

"Oh! Mr. Blenheim, I don't know what to say; I don't, I don't really."

"Then say nothing."

"But it was me."

"Well, you did what you thought best."

"I did, I did, Mr. Blenheim. I was so worried. That girl's no good, I know she's not, I've found out things about her. I . . . I didn't know what to do. Miss Bateman was the only one, but . . . but believe me—" She now blew her nose loudly, then went on, "Oh, believe me, Mr. Blenheim, I never thought for a moment she'd pass it on to Mr. Rippon, I didn't. I would have died rather than open my mouth if I'd thought— And this morning when she phoned and told me, well, I nearly ran out of the place. Honest I did."

"Sit down. Sit down." He pressed her into a chair. Then sitting down himself, for he felt he needed support, he said, "Now you mightn't believe me when I say that what you did was the best thing that could have happened."

"Oh, Mr. Blenheim!" Her head moved in wide unbelieving sweeps.

"It's true. It's true, Ada. You've done me a great service."

"Oh, Mr. Blenheim, if only I could believe you, but I can't; it's just because you're kind."

"Kindness nothing, Ada. Look, I'm telling you." He reached out and took her hand. "You won't understand this, but I want you to believe me. Because of your concern and what you did, you've given me a kind of strength, power you could say." He didn't use the word his mind suggested, "handle." "Yes, that's the right word, 'power,' that I didn't have yesterday. And this was true, for if Miss Bateman hadn't heard of his connection with Betty Ray it was more than unlikely he'd ever have heard of her connection with Rippon.

She dried one eye after the other, then stared at him, her whole face showing her perplexity now.

"I can't explain anything more to you, Ada, but I just want you to believe that you've done me a service. That's what you wanted to do in the first place, wasn't it?"

"Oh, yes, Mr. Blenheim. And as I've said, I was so worried about you because I could see by your face when you got those letters that you were upset, and when I found out who they were from . . ."

"How did you find out, Ada?"

"Well"—her head drooped—"by the writing on the envelope, comparing it."

"You're very astute, Ada."

"No, not really, Mr. Blenheim, but . . . but when you're worried about someone. . . ." Her voice trailed away; then she blew her nose and went on, "I knew enough about you to know that you would never get mixed up with a person like her, not off your own bat; there must have been something."

"There was, Ada, but . . . it's difficult to explain."

"Oh, Mr. Blenheim"—her lids were blinking rapidly—

85

"you've no need to explain. But she's no good, Mr. Blenheim. But perhaps you know that already."

"Well, I know very little about her really; I've only seen her three times." He pursed his lips. "The last twice following the 'Private and Personal' letters."

"Oh." She seemed surprised. "Then you won't know that her mother's done time for soliciting . . . and shoplifting?"

His face stretched a little as he said, "No, I didn't, Ada."

"How that one ever became a typist at all passes my comprehension; commonness is sticking out all over her. Oh!" She put her hand to her cheek again. "I shouldn't say all this, but I feel I can, knowing your feelings are not concerned. They're not, are they, Mr. Blenheim?"

She was agitated and on the point of tears again, and he took her hand and patted it, saying, "No, of course not, Ada. There now, no more tears, let's forget about it. But before the subject is closed, I'll say again that I'm grateful for your concern."

"Thank you, Mr. Blenheim. But there's just one more thing I'd like to know. Will . . . will there be any repercussions for you because of your father-in-law knowing?"

"I shouldn't think so, Ada." His voice was firm as he got to his feet. "In fact, I'm sure there won't be. Now"—he bent over her—"do you think you could get us a strong cup of tea on the side?"

She fluttered to her feet, saying, "Oh yes, Mr. Blenheim. Yes, I'll see to it at once."

"For both of us," he added, and she hurried away, still sniffing but apparently reassured, and he thought, "Poor Ada, she's a small cog in the wheel of my life, but her concern for me has gummed up the works."

Six

He was standing in Dave Rippon's outer office at twenty-eight minutes past four. There was no one there. At twenty minutes to five, as he was pacing up and down before Miss Bateman's desk, the door opened and she came in, alone. Going straight to her desk, she put down a pad and some papers, and without looking up, she said, "He'll keep you waiting another twenty minutes or so. I'm leaving at five, a very unusual procedure for me following a board meeting. It's what you might call working to rule." She glanced up at him, her eyes cold and hard now.

He asked her quietly, "What will you do?"

"Do?" Her chin came up high. "I'll become secretary in another firm. That'll be no problem. I don't know whether you've realized it or not, Mr. Blenheim, but I've practically run this business over the past ten years." Her voice was steely.

"I have realized it, Miss Bateman."

He noticed now that in spite of her tone her whole body was quivering, her hands, her shoulders, her head, it was like an ague. Her hands began fumbling at the papers on the desk; she opened and closed drawers; she rose from her seat three times in succession and went to the filing cabinet, flicked over folios but did not take anything out. He felt he couldn't bear to watch her any longer. Her calmness had entirely deserted her and she looked possessed of a growing fury. He went to the window and stood looking out.

About three minutes to five she bounced up from the chair and, going to a cupboard, took out her hat and coat and handbag. She pulled on her hat without looking in a mirror and the result was slightly askew. As she got into her coat, she said, "If he wants to know where you got your information, and he's sure to, tell . . . tell him, I told you, just that." She emphasized the last three words with accompanying dips of her head.

He stared pityingly at her as she fumbled with her bag. There wasn't a shred of her usual composure left. He said softly, "What can I say, Miss Bateman?" and she turned to him and said, "What? What do you mean?"

87

"I'm . . . I'm so sorry."

Her lips worked soundlessly before she said, "You shouldn't be sorry for me, Mr. Blenheim, you shouldn't waste your pity on fools. But then you've been a bit of one yourself, haven't you?" When she made an effort to smile, even grimly, it was as if her skin had become stiff and was cracking in the process. As she went toward the door, it was suddenly opened and Dave Rippon marched into the room; at least he took three steps inside then stopped and stared at Miss Bateman and said on a surprised note, "You . . . you off?"

"Y-yes, Mr. Rippon, I'm off."

He glanced quickly at Harry, then looked back at his secretary, questioning now. "You not feeling well . . . Miss Bateman?"

"I never felt better, Mr. Rippon, and never more sane."

Again he glanced at Harry, furtively now, but his gaze was jerked back to her when she said, "I'm leaving early because I'm going away for the weekend. It's a long time since I went away for a weekend, Mr. Rippon, but now I feel I need a change. Good night, Mr. Rippon." Her voice and manner were touched with hysteria now. She moved toward the door; then, her head jerking around, she said, "Good night, Mr. Blenheim."

Harry did not answer; he merely acknowledged her words with a small movement of his head, then he watched his father-in-law stare at the closed door that she had almost scraped past his face.

But now Dave Rippon was recovering himself. Definitely his mistress' attitude had astounded him, but he was covering it up well. He passed Harry without looking at him, and going into his own office, he called over his shoulder, "Well, come on; let's get this over."

In the inner office Harry didn't wait to be asked to sit down. Pulling forward a straight-backed leather chair, he placed it dead opposite his father-in-law and sat down.

"Now—" Dave Rippon rubbed the palms of his hands together as if about to relish a meal; then he moved from one buttock to another before he said, "What I've got to say to you isn't going to be pleasant hearing." He waited, staring across the desk into his son-in-law's straight face. "You've been up to something, haven't you?"

Harry made no movement. He did not even blink his eyes. He kept them fixed on the pale blue ones glaring into his.

"Well! What's the matter with you, man? You've heard what I said. You've been up to something. Keeping your

88

tongue glued down isn't going to help. I'm going to start by telling you, you should be damned well ashamed of yourself."

"Oh, Esther wouldn't like to hear you using that kind of language, Father."

Harry had no intention of being facetious, but he just couldn't let the opportunity slip past. He felt for a moment like laughing; he felt drunk with power. He had it in him to break this man, this pompous, bigheaded, conniving, sly, lecherous man. He knew also in this moment that the feeling he'd had for his father-in-law, had always had for him, had been hate. Not a Christian feeling; that being so, he hadn't put a name to it before.

"Are you drunk?"

"I could be."

Dave Rippon brought himself forward in his chair and, leaning across the table, peered at his son-in-law. He didn't look drunk, he didn't sound drunk, but there was something different about him. After a moment of dead silence he leaned against the back of his chair again, and nodding his head slowly, he said, "You're going to brazen it out, eh?"

"Brazen what out?"

"Now look here. You know as well as I do what we're talking about. You've been having an affair, haven't you, with the girl, Ray, in the pool?"

"Having an affair? Me? What on earth gave you that idea?"

Dave Rippon again sat in silence; there was no indignation in his son-in-law's voice. His denial was smooth, calm. He tried again. "You've been getting letters from her, she's got something on you. She's been blackmailing you, hasn't she?"

"Blackmailing me?" Harry now dug his finger into his chest.

"Now look here, I don't know what your game is, but don't play it with me. Now stop acting the goat. I know you've been receiving letters from that girl, and a girl like that doesn't keep writing letters to no purpose. Now you either come clean or I'm going to go further into it. Take your choice."

"What do you mean, go further into it?"

"What do I mean?" Dave Rippon's bushy eyebrows were moving up to his receding hair line. "I mean just that, I'm going to get to the bottom of it. You happen to be my daughter's husband. You have a standard to keep up and I won't stand for any jiggery-pokery toward—"

"Shut up!" The spittle spurted from Harry's lips on the words, and if there had been bullets aimed straight at him,

89

Dave Rippon couldn't have been more startled. His face, in fact his whole attitude when he rose to his feet, looked comical. When at last he brought out, "What did I hear you say?" Harry said in the same tone, "Do you want me to repeat it? And I wouldn't bother standing up if I were you, it's going to be a longish session."

"Have you gone mad?"

"Yes, slightly, because hearing you putting on a sanctimonious act is enough to drive anyone mad. And I'm going to tell you something. I've listened to it for the last time. Sit down!" He now stabbed his index finger toward the chair, but Dave Rippon didn't sit down, not immediately anyway; he didn't resume his seat until Harry said, "I've told you, it's going to be a long session. Where would you like me to start? With Alice Howell, alias Colonel Callow, or nearer home . . . with Miss Bateman?"

He thought for a moment that his father-in-law was going to have a seizure. He watched his heavy face flush slightly, then turn a ghastly gray, a pasty doughy gray. He watched the blue eyes darken and swell out of their sockets; he watched the prominent Adam's apple jerk between the collar and the thickening chin. He saw one white hand, with its well-tended fingernails, paw at the end of the desk, and for a moment he thought the man was actually going to collapse; then he was sitting in front of him again, staring at him as if he was watching horns growing out of his head. He let him get his breath before he said, "Well now, take your choice."

Dave Rippon didn't speak but continued to stare at Harry. He was recovering himself, but not sufficiently to make any retort when Harry said, "Of all the two-faced, mealy-mouthed, dirty old swines on God's earth, you beat them all."

"Don't you dare speak to me like that." Dave Rippon's voice seemed to be dragged up from some great depths.

"I'll speak to you how I like. You've lauded it over everybody for years, held yourself up as a moral example—my home's been built on . . . Father's standards." He gave an impression of Esther's voice. "God, it's unbelievable. And all the time you've not only had one woman on the side but two."

Dave Rippon made no rejoinder to this; he just continued to stare at the new edition of his son-in-law, and Harry went on, "You'd like to know how I found out about your little games, wouldn't you? Well, I'll tell you this much be-

90

cause she asked me to tell you: Miss Bateman, she told me she's been your mistress for fifteen years and that she'd had a child by you and that you've visited her twice a week, never failing. She must have felt pretty grim to tell me that, don't you think, a decorous, self-contained woman like Miss Bateman? She must have gone through something and been pretty cut up to give you away in one fell swoop like that. You'll have to ask her on Monday why she did it, for as she said, she'll be away for the weekend. I'd like to be here when you explain about Mrs. Howell and the colonel. And you'd better be careful what you say, you'd better not make a bigger liar out of yourself than you already are, because she knows a great deal, does Miss Bateman."

"Get out!" The words were thin, hardly moving the lips at all.

Harry didn't move. He knew he had said enough, more than enough. Whichever way things went, this would likely be the end of him in Peamarsh's, but at this moment he didn't give a damn, except perhaps that it would all come as a shock to Esther. In a way he was sorry for her because she was so damned fond of her father, too fond. That kind of feeling should be cut out, or at least filed down, when a woman took a husband. Looking back now, he could see that Esther had never looked upon him as master in his own house; mentally she was still living under her father's roof. Well, there were lots of people going to get lots of jolts before this affair was over, but there was one thing he'd make plain to Esther from now on: he was running his own life, and hers, and the children's as long as the latter needed him. He thought quizzically that he might even have to do it on the dole, but however he had to do it, he would do it.

Now, in his own time, he rose to his feet. But he had to drag his eyes from those of his father-in-law before he turned about and went out of the room.

The clock in the outer office said twenty-past five. In his own office he found Ada still there, her face full of apprehension. He said calmly, "Everything's all right; there's nothing to worry about. Get yourself off home."

There'd be plenty of time for her to worry when the lid blew right off; at present it was only eased up slightly. How quick and how high the lid went depended on his father-in-law's reactions and these in their turn depended on the outcome of his meeting with Miss Bateman. He saw how things would work. His father-in-law would go straight along to her place now and try and patch things up. But with his new

91

knowledge of Miss Bateman he couldn't see her allowing the rift to close; she had cut too deeply. Yet at the same time he couldn't visualize her opening her mouth wide; if she wanted to get another responsible post, she wouldn't get it by blackening her last employer.

The weekend he saw as a time of waiting. Should he, he asked himself, use it to put his own case before Esther? Tell her everything that had happened since the office party? Then tell her why he was coming clean? He didn't know; he'd have to see how things turned out because bringing low in her estimation, at one go, the two men in her life would be too much altogether. It was strange, but if he had the choice of whom to expose, he would have chosen to tell his own story because he knew it would have hurt her less. The knowledge wasn't pleasant to face up to, but it was nevertheless true.

When he reached home, Gail greeted him in her usual boisterous way, and as she tugged off his coat, he said, "Hold on, hold on, leave me my shirt. What's all the rush, anyway?"

In answer she said, "I thought you'd never come." Then taking him by the arm, she led him toward the sitting room, and inside she pointed and said, "There! Isn't that nice?"

He looked at the low table set before the fire, and when he stood over it and saw only two cups and saucers and two plates arranged, he said, "Where's everybody?"

"Mother was at the Young Wives' Group meeting. She phoned to say she'd be held up, a committee or something, she'll be back about half-past six. And John is staying on for a lecture. Terry is down at Tony Barnham's and Elsie had to go to the dentist's, and so I thought, tea for two before the fire. Isn't it lovely? And look"—she pointed—"I've done a plate of toast, all dripping with butter, soggy." She wrinkled up her nose. "Sit down. There's your slippers. I'll just make the tea."

As she dashed out of the room, he looked after her and shook his head slowly; then he sat down on the couch and put on his slippers. From the hate-filled meeting of an hour ago to this. And would he ever have this again, tea before the fire, just him and Gail? As he turned toward the door and watched her coming in, her face bright, the teapot held out like a sacrifice, he thought, "Oh my God! What'll it do to her when she knows?" and of a sudden it became imperative that she shouldn't know, that all this messy business concerning himself and his father-in-law should be hushed up; no price should be too high to pay for his daughter to continue seeing him in the light of "a nice bloke." Esther didn't matter, not really; she could take care of her emotions, they were already set. Her reactions would be decided between her and God and she would receive comfort from righteousness. But not so his daughter; God would hold no comfort for Gail. If her father ceased to be "a nice bloke," it would affect her whole life. For one wild moment he thought of getting on the phone to his father-in-law and asking him if he could talk the matter over again. When he gave an audible "Huh!" Gail said, "What did you say?" and in reply he smiled at her and answered, "I've got the kindest and most beautiful daughter in the world."

When she fell across his knees, he actually groaned—she was lying in the same position as Betty Ray had lain, and it brought back the incident as plainly as if it had happened yesterday. But, contrary to when Gail had put her arms around him that night up in the bedroom and he had repulsed her violently, he now took her hand gently in his and said softly, "Don't ever stop loving me, Gail, will you?" and she, after a moment of surprise that brought her eyes wide and her mouth agape, said, "As if ever I could, Dad. Fancy even thinking a thing like that."

They were at their evening meal when Dave Rippon came into the room. Harry had his back to the door, and he did not turn around when Esther, from the far end of the table, said, "Oh, hello, Father. This is a surprise; I thought you were going away for the weekend."

"I've changed my mind, I'm getting too old for jaunts. Have you a bite for a hungry man?"

Harry had been about to carry some food to his mouth, but when Esther had spoken, the fork had become stationary in midair; now he returned the food to his plate and waited for Dave Rippon to come into view. He knew that Esther's attitude would have told her father immediately that as yet she knew nothing.

"Move up and let your grandfather sit down." Esther was speaking to Terry when Gail said, "Come and sit beside me, Grandfather."

"Thank you. Thank you, my dear."

Now Dave Rippon turned to his daughter and asked, "Sure I won't be robbing anybody?"

"Don't be silly, Father." Esther closed her eyes at such a question.

93

"Where's Mrs. O'Toole?" He always gave his son-in-law's grandmother her full title.

"She's got a slight chill," said Esther; "I'm keeping her in bed."

"Good idea, good idea." Dave Rippon nodded in agreement.

That he had not addressed himself in any way to Harry was not really unusual; they worked in the office and this made formal greetings unnecessary.

As Esther helped her father to food, she said, "I thought you were going to York to see the colonel." This was followed by a moment of complete silence; then Dave Rippon, looking down at his plate, said, "Oh, I think the old boy was having me on. I'm not going to rush off at his beck and call. I'm getting a bit tired these days, feeling my age, I suppose."

"Nonsense," said Esther soothingly. "But anyway, I've always told you, you work too hard."

"It's a modern complaint, my dear, and it's not going to get any better. And these two will find it out shortly." He nodded from John to Terry, then asked, "How's work going with you, John?"

"Oh, not too bad, Grandfather."

"You really have got your mind set on this engineering?"

"Well, yes, I suppose so." John smiled across the table, and the smile altered his face completely and made him appear strikingly good-looking.

"What about you, Terry? Still going to be an architect, eh?"

"No, Grandfather." Terry shook his head solemnly. "I've decided that my mission in life is to lead a pop group."

John spluttered part of the food from his mouth; Gail let out a loud crack of a laugh; Esther, too, laughed; her father smiled; only Harry's face remained straight.

"You know what?" Dave Rippon wagged his fork, first at one boy, then at the other, as he said, "You could both do worse than come into Peamarsh's. The firm's going places, getting bigger and bigger every year. You should think about it. And think about it very seriously from now on, with your father to be a director soon, and not exactly junior either."

Harry lowered his knife and fork to his plate but held on to the handles. So this was it. In some way or other he had silenced Miss Bateman; now he was making sure of him. For a moment a gust of fierce hot anger rose in him and he thought, "Be damned if he will!" Then Gail's hand came

94

across the end of the table and touched his arm, and Esther was saying, "Oh, Father! When did this happen?"

"Oh, it's been on the books for some time, but . . . but I like to be sure of things, know my ground so to speak."

"Who's leaving?" said Esther now, excitedly.

"Well, we knew today for certain that Walters is resigning —it's his age with him—but Graham Hall is also giving up. Poor chap, he's in a bad way. So I thought of my son-in-law." Slowly he lifted his head and looked at Harry. His blue eyes looked cold, almost opaque, and he said directly to him now, "Of course, it all depends whether your husband will take one of the vacant chairs on the first floor."

"Don't be silly. Don't be silly." Esther was laughing, her voice high, her attitude almost girlish.

"Well, it's up to him." Dave Rippon's glance was boring into Harry, and as Harry looked back at his father-in-law, the expression on his face brought a sudden quietness to the table. They were all staring at him now. What he might have said if Gail hadn't at that moment got up and, coming to his side, exclaimed excitedly, "Haven't you anything to say, Mr. Director?"

He turned and looked at her for a matter of seconds, then muttered thickly, "It's come as a sort of surprise, I wasn't expecting it."

"He who expecteth nothing." Terry's voice was mimicking their minister. Then speaking as his perky self once again, he added, "But I'll tell you what I expect, Pop. I expect a car the minute I'm seventeen, but I'll settle for a scooter to be going on with."

Amid laughter, in which she joined, Esther said, "You'll have nothing of the sort to be going on with! And don't call your father Pop. I've told you about that before."

"All right, Ma."

Whether Terry realized it or not, he was creating a diversion for which Harry was grateful; but shortly there came a lull in their laughter and chatter and they were all looking at him again, all, that is, except Dave Rippon. He was eating his meal with apparent enjoyment, and into the waiting silence he said, "This is an excellent casserole; I can never get Mrs. Hunter to do steak like this."

"Excuse me." His voice mumbling, Harry got to his feet.

"What's the matter?" Esther looked concerned for a moment, and he patted his stomach and said, "Overeating, I suppose, but carry on."

When he reached his room, he dropped heavily into a

95

chair. So this was how it was going to be; promotion, as a gob stopper. Working on the same floor and hating each other's guts. Miss Bateman had said that his father-in-law disliked him. Now that feeling had turned to black hate; it had poured out of his eyes as he had stared at him back there at the table. And on his part, the feeling was returned in full. And so how could they work together? He couldn't do it. He just couldn't do it. But the alternative was to bring everything into the open.

It must have been twenty minutes later when Esther came into the room. She stood looking at him for a full minute before she said, "What's the matter with you, Harry?"

"Me? Nothing, just tummy." He punched his middle.

"Aren't you coming down?"

"No; if you don't mind I'll turn in."

"You're going to BED!" Her voice was high in disbelief. "And after Father bringing you this news."

He could only stare at her until she said, "Talk about gratitude; you didn't even say thank you. What's come over you lately?"

He got to his feet and went to the dressing table and took off his collar and tie, and he said to her through the mirror, "What have I got to thank him for? If he hadn't done it off his own bat, you would have seen he did it off yours; so it was cut and dried anyway, wasn't it?"

"Aha!" She moved her head from one side to the other on the exclamation. "Now I have it. Well, let me tell you, Harry, you should be thankful and glad that there are people who have your welfare at heart, because, left to yourself—"

He swung around, saying sharply, "Don't say it, Esther, don't say it. I've heard it for years and once more would be just too much." He watched the color flush her pale face. Then she swung around and went out. But she didn't bang the door behind her; that wasn't Esther's way.

He returned to the mirror and looked at his reflection. She had explained his reactions to her own satisfaction; he would leave it like that and let things ride. For how long? He didn't know.

It was a nine days' wonder in the office, Miss Bateman was leaving. Why, nobody seemed to know; there were various rumors. She was going to be married to a man abroad with whom she had been corresponding for years; and this could have been so because nobody knew Miss Bateman's business. She'd had money left her; perhaps she'd won the pools, with

96

an X for secrecy, who was to know? Some more astute guessers said, perhaps she'd had a row with old man Rippon, for he had been acting like a white-skinned devil during the last few days.

But Ada Cole thought that she was the sole reason for Miss Bateman leaving and she said so to Harry. "It all stems from Friday, Mr. Blenheim, and what I told her. And then you going up there."

He assured her again and again that his own affair had nothing whatever to do with Miss Bateman leaving, until he finally convinced her, and then she said, "What will they do without her?"

"Everybody can be done without, Ada."

"But she's got everything at her fingertips, she's a wonderful organizer, you know she is, Mr. Blenheim."

"Yes, I know, Ada. But someone else will take her place and will soon get into the way."

"They'll never suit Mr. Rippon, he's very particular."

"Yes." He endorsed her statement. "He's very particular."

"They have had nine replies to the advertisement in the evening paper," she said.

"Well, that's hopeful." He nodded at her. "Now let's forget about the business of the upper floor and get on with this one."

Ada Cole looked slightly hurt. Never before had Mr. Blenheim told her in so many words to get on with her work.

By Thursday it was all over the office that Mr. Rippon had picked his new secretary. She was a woman in her forties with good references and she was to start on Monday.

Miss Bateman left on the Friday evening without any fuss, not going around, as some of the other staff would have done, to say good-bye to her colleagues. And there was no presentation made to her. She had asked Ada Cole to see definitely that there was no collection taken on her behalf.

On the Monday morning Olive Standford told the other girls in the pool that she had seen Miss Bateman waiting for a bus on the Friday night and she was sure she was crying, and on this she was howled down. Mary Cheeseman said, "That would have been quite impossible, as The Paragon hadn't any tear ducts."

On the Monday afternoon when Harry came back from lunch, Ada informed him that Mr. Rippon said she had to take over the management of the pool until the new secretary got into her stride.

The new secretary gave her notice in at the end of the

week; but this was no nine days' wonder, everybody expected it.

The next secretary stayed a month. It was when the news went around the office that she had given her notice in, too, that Betty Ray spoke to Ada Cole. She waylaid her in the main hall.

"Miss Cole, can I have a word with you?" Her tone was deferential, but the look Ada bestowed on her was cold and her tone prim, as she said, "Yes, Miss Ray. What is it?"

"Well, I'll come to the point. It's no use beating about the bush. Mr. Rippon . . . above"—she jerked her head—"nobody's staying with him; I want the chance to try."

"You!"

"Yes, me. Why not?" The deference had gone out of the tone. "I've been here nearly six months; I've got the hang of the work. Me shorthand's better than anybody else's. It's a hundred and twenty a minute and me typing's sixty. And what's more, I can pick things up quick. I want a chance to try."

"Well, you're not getting it, Miss Ray. And take that as final."

Ada was utterly indignant. That girl daring to ask to be sent upstairs. She felt like telling her all she knew about her. If she had her way, she'd dismiss her on the spot, cheap little blackmailing guttersnipe!

There was only one answer to a further advertisement for a secretary in the evening paper, and this applicant's inexperience disqualified her immediately. There was nothing for it but Ada should send someone up from the pool. But it certainly wouldn't be that Ray piece; on that she would remain firm if Mr. Rippon never got a secretary. So she sent up Rose Weybridge; and on the second day Rose came downstairs, crying, and stuttered, "He t-told me to g-get out."

When Ada went to the pool with the intention of sending the newest recruit upstairs, she found the typewriters quiet and the girls waiting for her. They all wanted to be the first to tell her that Betty Ray had taken her pad and things and gone upstairs to Mr. Rippon's office. They thought that Miss Cole was about to choke and they waited for her to grab the phone. Instead, they watched her march out and across the hall to the lift.

Ada Cole was incensed. That's how she would have termed her feelings, but flaming mad would have been a more accurate description. When she reached Dave Rippon's office, the outer room was empty. Knocking on the private

98

door and being told to enter, she saw Betty Ray seated at one side of the desk and looking as if she had been there forever. For a moment she was unable to speak; then almost spluttering, she said, "Mr. Rippon . . . Mr. Rippon, I didn't send this girl up here. She came on her own accord. She's—"

"Yes, she's just told me. Well, she can't be any worse than I've had lately. If she is, she'll go. In the meantime, you can leave things as they are, Miss Cole."

She stared at Mr. Rippon; then she looked down on the girl, and she had the most disturbing desire. She wanted to slap her face, not just once, but twice, three times, go on slapping it. She hurried from the room, and in the lift she said to herself, "And he knows about her and Mr. Blenheim. There's going to be trouble. Oh, dear, there's going to be trouble. And what will poor Mr. Blenheim say?"

Seven

"Do you like it?"

"I think it's smashing."

"Truly?"

He looked at her proudly. In the last three months she had put on inches; her puppy fat had almost disappeared, her legs were long and beautiful, she carried herself well, holding her head up as if, like the song, she was attempting to walk tall. Yet she had no need to try; two months past her sixteenth birthday she was already five-foot-five. Her face looked warm and kind and beautiful and so, so young.

She said, "It isn't mini-mini, it's only three inches above."

He smiled as he looked at the cream wool lacy thing she was wearing. Not mini-mini, as she said, but showing a surprising length of leg. He dropped his chin down and pushed his eyebrows up as he asked, "Has your mother seen it?"

"Yes." She pulled a long face.

"What did she say?"

"She said definitely no, until she saw Anna's. Coo! Hers is mini-mini-minus. But she said it was as well she wasn't with me when I went to buy it." She hunched her shoulders. "It was lucky I hung on to my birthday money, wasn't it?"

"I'll say it was."

She came slowly across the room and sat on the edge of the bed and looked at him as he stooped to tie his shoe laces. Then, her head on one side, she asked, "Could I have come with you to the dance if I hadn't been going to Paul's party?"

"Yes. Why not?"

"You would have taken me?"

"Of course. Why do you ask?"

"Well, Mother says I couldn't have gone in any case, it being a staff do; but you're taking John, so I said I didn't see why I shouldn't have gone, that is, if I hadn't been going to Paul's. And she got ratty with me."

"But you are going to Paul's, so why bother arguing?"

"Oh!" She wagged her head. "It's just a matter of getting things straight. Sort of standing up for me rights, as Elsie says."

100

As he got into his dinner jacket, he said, "But you'd rather go to Paul's party, wouldn't you?"

"Huh! Yes, I think so. Dad?"

"Yes?"

"Do you really think I'm pretty?"

He came slowly to the side of the bed and put his finger under her chin and looked down at her. "No, I don't think you're pretty." He moved his head from side to side. "Pretty is such a weak word. I think you're beautiful."

"Oh, Dad!" Impulsively she leaned her head against his waist and put her arms around his hips. "Do you know, you're the only one who's ever said I'm beautiful; Paul says I'm not."

"What!" He jerked her head up. "You mean to say he's told you you're not?"

"Yes. We were talking one night and he said I wasn't beautiful. I wasn't even pretty, I had the wrong features. But he said I had something. And when I asked him what it was, he couldn't tell me, he just said I had something that . . ." She stopped and chuckled, and he prompted, "That what?" and she blinked her eyes and bit on her lip before she ended, "That got him."

He laughed deep in his throat and walked to the wardrobe, saying, "Well, I'm glad you've got that something an' all, but he's wrong."

"I don't think so, Dad." It was her quiet tone that made him look over his shoulder at her. Her face was straight, almost solemn as she said, "You're the only one who sees me as beautiful. There's not another soul in the world thinks I'm even pretty. If Paul doesn't . . . well!"

He turned his head away, opened the wardrobe door, and took out his overcoat, and he didn't speak until he was ready to leave the room. Then, standing in front of her, he said, "People will come to my way of thinking before long, you'll see."

She stood up and put her hands on the lapels of his coat and drew them together, and buttoning the top button, she stared at it as she said, "I'm worried, Dad."

"What about?"

"You. You haven't been well for weeks."

"Nonsense. It's just the pressure of work. Fitting into a new job. Responsibilities and all that. But I'm all right."

She still played with the button as she said, "Mother's worried about you; we all are."

When he didn't answer, she raised her head and looked at

101

him, and then he said softly, "Well, you can stop worrying for there's nothing to worry about. Now you go out and enjoy yourself."

She smiled at him, then said, "It won't be much fun for you without Mother. Of all the luck, to go and sprain her ankle the day before the one night in the year she looks forward to."

"Did she say that?"

"Yes. She said she loves the staff dance. Didn't you know?" Her voice was high with surprise.

"Not really; I always thought she looked upon it as a bit of a bore, a sort of duty."

She seemed surprised by his answer, as if it appeared odd that her father didn't actually know what her mother thought. She picked her coat up from a chair and they went out together, down the stairs and into the sitting room, where John was waiting.

John at eighteen was an attractive boy, being above average height and startlingly blond. When he was happy he looked handsome, and he looked happy tonight.

From her position on the couch Esther surveyed her son with pride. She loved her first-born with a deep secret love that even outdid the feeling she had for her father. The affection she felt for her husband had never, even before she gave birth to her son, been given entry into the private chamber of her being. It could be truthfully said that only she and God were aware of such a place and the secrets it held.

She looked from one to the other now and said, "Well, that's it; you're all ready then." She didn't comment on her daughter's appearance but addressed her with "Don't keep your father waiting when he comes to pick you up. And mind what I told you."

"Yes, Mother."

"Well then, don't stand about, get yourselves away."

This remark could have had a dampening effect, but Terry, sitting on the head of the couch, said, "I don't see why I couldn't go to the dance. I've kicked more ankles than most at the club; I can do everything from the Charleston upwards, so why?"

"Because you're still in short trousers!" John pushed Terry's head with his hand, and Terry, jumping off the couch and taking up a battling stance, said, "Watch it, watch it, said Mary O'Toole."

At this moment Mary O'Toole came into the room and she

102

exclaimed loudly, "Who's taking me name in vain?" Then she paused before adding, "Oh, now! Don't you look grand, each and every one of you. My! It's a family to be proud of." She bent and kissed Gail, and Gail hugged her; then she said, "Let me have a look at your new dress."

When Gail opened her coat, Mrs. O'Toole covered her eyes and exclaimed, "What's the world coming to? It'll be nappies you'll be getting back to next."

"Gran!" After the note of censure, Esther exclaimed, "Let them get away, they'll be late." And Mrs. O'Toole said tartly, "Well, there's nobody stopping them."

With an exchange of bye-byes Harry, John, and Gail left the room somewhat self-consciously, but when they reached the front door, Gran O'Toole was behind them, and she patted their backs one after the other as if they were all small children, Harry included, and said, "Have a good time. Have the time of your lives. Forget about everything and enjoy yourselves." She gave Harry an extra pat and he turned and smiled at her; then bending, he put his mouth to her ear and whispered, "I'm going to get blind drunk," and she cried in a smothered laugh, "Now that's the best idea you've voiced in years. Just do that. Do that, me lad." And she pushed him out of the door.

The staff dance was always held at the old Coach and Horses. The word "old" was a misnomer, because although the hotel was half-timbered and could date its beginnings back to the eighteenth century, its interior was modern, yet complementing the old beams rather than at variance with them. The cuisine was of the highest standard; and what was more, the hotel was situated on the outskirts of the town in a setting of woodland and pastureland; and lastly it provided parking facilities for over a hundred cars.

The staff at Peamarsh's numbered fifty-two. Add to these wives or sweethearts and a couple of friends per head of staff—the inviting of friends was always encouraged—and you had a company of two hundred or over. This number always provided for the dance floor to be well covered even while the bar and cocktail lounge were crowded. Everyone's enjoyment was provided for at Peamarsh's staff dance.

Harry was standing at the bar in company with Tom Vosey; Ossie Ferndale, who owned the timber yard; Jack Lucas, a dentist; and Peter Jones, an accountant. The two latter were there as guests. Their wives were at present dancing and in the respite the men were drinking hard. The company were all well-known to Harry, all his friends you might say, being members of the Round Table.

This time last year, even this time six months ago, Harry would have been laughing at their risqué jokes, telling himself he must try and remember this one and that one; he never did, as he couldn't tell jokes, but that didn't stop him from enjoying them. But tonight he didn't laugh, he only drank. He had started on sherry; then, as on another memorable night, he went on to whiskey, not doubles this time, just singles, but they came regularly, and as their number increased so did the anger inside him. Every now and again his thoughts would be punctuated by the term "The dirty old swine!" Once he thought, and her playing up to him openly, brazenly. Well, she'd get all she was asking for. But this trite term, he knew, didn't really apply to the situation because Betty Ray would be very disappointed if she didn't get what she was asking for. Four times, to his knowledge, the old sot had danced with her; that would never have happened if Esther had been here—oh, no. Like the good impartial employer he was, his dances would have been doled out if his daughter had been present. And what was more, if Esther had been here her father would never have come near the bar. As it was, he'd been in and out all evening throwing them back.

A few minutes ago he had stood in the doorway watching the dancers, trying to keep his eyes on John wriggling in front of his young partner, trying not to let his fuddled gaze rest on his father-in-law whirling the dirty little piece around the floor. He seemed to have lost all sense of propriety and didn't care a damn what anybody thought, yet he must know that tomorrow all the staff would be talking.

Harry didn't have to be told that there was a reason behind his father-in-law's flouting; he was doing it because he imagined it would upset him. Doubtless the little bitch had put him well in the picture. And now Mr. Dave Rippon was thinking that he had him on a hook; he was showing him that he was in a position to enjoy something denied to himself. If it had been possible to explain the truth to him, he would still have remained unconvinced. In his own eyes he was a dashing fellow, swiping his son-in-law's mistress from under his nose. God! It was all so sickening.

And Betty Ray? She, too, in her own way, was showing him. He could almost hear her saying, "All I wanted was to be secretary to somebody on the top floor, anybody, but you put a spoke in me wheel, and see what happened. In

104

one jump I'm at the top. Now what do you think of that, Mr. Blenheim?"

"What's up with you tonight, Harry? You look about as happy as a whore at a rectory tea." Ossie Ferndale pushed his big red face close to Harry's. "Come on, what is it? Worrying about your missus not being here? Look, boy, count your blessings; go and have a dance. I've never seen you on the floor the night. You used to trip a pretty measure. Didn't he, Peter?"

Peter Jones, a thin dapper man, nodded and giggled. "A pretty measure. That's funny. Makes you sound like a ballet boy. A pretty measure." He giggled again into his glass; then almost aggressively he said, "You know somethin'? Those ballet boys on telly, they make me sick. How a fellow can push himself into those tights. I tell you, they work me up."

This brought a splutter from the group, and Tom Vosey, his arm around Harry's shoulder, his mouth wide with laughter, said, "Listen, it reminds me. Talking of ballet, there was this fellow. He was doing a film and he had to do the splits . . ." At this point Tom Vosey lowered his head and his body shook with the outcome of his story, and just as he was about to go on, the band stopped and Ossie Ferndale put in, 'Come on, Tom man, get on with it. They'll be here in a minute.'

"Oh, they'll enjoy this one." Tom Vosey flapped his hand. "I'll wait for them." He took his arm from Harry's shoulder and turned toward the door, where some of the dancers were now entering; then he turned back again and asked, "What you say, Pete?" And Peter Jones muttered quickly, "Not before mine, Tom; she's funny that way."

"Break her in, break her in. And where you goin', Harry?" Tom Vosey reached out and grabbed Harry's arm; and Harry said thickly, "I've just remembered, it's time I picked up Gail."

"There's another hour to go yet, man, and they've got an extension to the end." He nodded toward the bar.

"Sorry." Harry's face muscles were working as he mumbled, "The child'll be waiting."

"Child! Go on with you." Tom Vosey pushed him roughly in the chest. "Sixteen. Gail's no child. They don't thank you for butting in, not at sixteen they don't these days. She'll be glad of a little necking time." He now left the crowd and walked unsteadily with Harry across the room, saying, "What's up with you these days, anyway, Harry? You're not yourself. You want to take a pattern from your old man.

105

Now he's had a real randy night. Never been off the floor, and at his age. As for knocking 'em back . . . whew!"

Harry's teeth ground together. But he forced himself to speak calmly as he said, "I've left Esther at home; she'll be worrying. Oh, not about me." For a moment he adopted Tom Vosey's manner. "But she doesn't like them being out late."

"You know something?" Tom Vosey leaned toward him now, swaying slightly. "There's something I've wanted to say to you for a long time as a close friend . . . privileged friend, an' it's just this. You never brought her up right, Esther. You should have put your foot down from the start. She's still Daddy's girl. You should assert yourself, man. Here, Harry, just a minute, just a minute. Don't go off like that, man."

But Harry was away, hurrying erratically across the hall to the cloakroom.

When, a few minutes later, he returned from the cloakroom, he saw John standing talking with two girls, and he beckoned him over, and even in his fuddled state he noticed that his son looked different tonight because his expression held no trace of surliness. He tried to space his words as he said to him, "I'm going to pick Gail up; I'll be about half an hour; I don't want to have to wait for you when I come back, mind."

John stared at his father closely before he answered briefly, "O.K." then turned and walked back to the girls. And Harry thought, "There'll be no need for you to tell your mother that your father's been drinking; it'll be self-evident tonight. But will you tell her about your grandfather?" Ah! That was a point. John wasn't blind, nor was he stupid; he knew what his mother thought of her father; he was also aware of the handsome presents in the form of cash she received from him and which rubbed off on to himself. No! John would doubtless consider the matter carefully, for he was cunning was John. Oh, yes he had to own that, among other things, his son was cunning.

The party was still going strong at the Birketts when he collected Gail. But her reluctance to leave was compensated by the fact that Paul came out to the car with her.

Harry had just stared the car up when she leaned toward him and said in a confidential whisper, "Dad! You've been drinking."

He gave a short laugh and said, "How p-perspicacious of you, Miss Blenheim." When he stammered on the word she

106

burst out laughing. "And I was forbidden even to take sherry!"

"What! Who forbade you?"

"Mother, of course. That's what she said before I left, you remember? No, you don't. Well, she said, 'And mind what I told you.' She had warned me upstairs that I hadn't to touch drink of any kind. And here's you bottled!"

He put his head back and laughed a great rollicking laugh, and the car swerved as he cried, "You sound like Gran, and that's good, that's good." Then he asked, "Did you have a good time?"

"Smashing! Oh, really smashing. I jived till all my bones rattled. Mrs. Birkett had cleared one room right out. I danced with Paul nearly half the night. Roma Allsopp was mad, she's after Paul, you know."

"Is she indeed!"

"Yes, but Paul couldn't care less. He told me so."

"That was very chi-chivalrous of him, I must say."

"Did you have a good time, Dad?"

"Well, you've just said I'm drunk, so I'm bound to have had a good time, eh?"

She leaned her head against him as she said softly, "I didn't mean it nasty. Did you dance much?"

"I didn't dance at all."

"Not once!" She straightened herself up away from him, her voice high.

"Not once; there were no beautiful girls about. Now if you had been there, my shoes would have been worn out."

"Oh, Dad, you're sweet." When she dragged on his arm and snuggled up to him, he said, "Here, here; be careful. Look, I'm having my work cut out to drive this thing as it is, I'm seeing double."

She laughed and sat back in her seat and, sighing deeply, said, "Oh! Am I tired! And it's school tomorrow. Oh Lord! Oh, Lord!"

"Well, get in the back and lie down. John will want to sit in front in any case."

"That's an idea. I'll climb over." As she made to clamber over the seat, he said, "Wait, hold on, we're nearly there."

When he drew up in front of the hotel and got out of the car, an attendant came up to him and said, "Would you mind going to that side, sir?"

"But I won't be a minute. I'm just going to collect my son."

"Well, you see, sir, if anyone wants to come out"—he pointed to the left of the building—"they're going to have a

107

tight squeeze getting past you with the other cars parked alongside. You see, you've stopped at the narrowest point, sir."

"Oh, all right." He got into the car again; then putting his head out of the window, he asked, "Where do you want me to go?"

"Just along here, sir. Look, there's a space just around the corner." He walked by the side of the car. "There, sir. I'm sorry to trouble you, sir, but we've had a job tonight. We've moved those we could from the drive—the careless ones who leave their doors open." He grinned, then walked ahead and beckoned Harry on.

There were a number of cars parked around the side of the building and the attendant, coming up to Harry again, said, "We don't usually stack here, but there was an overflow from the main park, very unusual. Most times it can cope, but the whole town seems to have come out the night. Will you be long, sir?"

"Not more than five minutes," said Harry. Then taking off his overcoat, he leaned into the back of the car, where Gail was now curled up on the seat, and put it over her before asking, "Will I put the light on."

"No. No, thanks; I'll be clean off in two minutes flat. And don't wake me when we get home, just carry me in. Do you hear?"

"I hear, ma'am. Certainly, ma'am." He sounded jocular, and when he closed the door and turned about, the attendant said, "You could come in the side door here, sir; it leads straight to the lounge."

"Thanks," said Harry, "but my son'll likely be waiting in the hall for me and I don't want to be waylaid at the bar, if you see what I mean." And they both laughed.

The hall of the hotel was a large room with an open fire-place fronting the door and lounge chairs dotted about on the thick pile carpet. The reception desk was at the far corner on the right-hand side, and on the left-hand side were two passages, one leading to the gents cloakroom, the other leading to the ladies. The door leading to the ball-room gave off from this side of the hall, and as Harry made his way toward it, there emerged from the second passage the blue mini-dressed figure of Betty Ray.

"Well, well! Hello!"

Harry had paused for a moment, long enough to give her a cold wavering stare, but when he made to move on, she stepped quickly in front of him, saying, "I've never had a

108

chance to have a word with you tonight, or any other time for that matter. You're very elusive, aren't you?"

He didn't answer her; he just continued to stare at her. For weeks now he had ignored her; even when her voice came over the phone, saying politely, "Mr. Blenheim, Mr. Rippon would like a word with you," and adding, "at your convenience," he never gave her an answer. And when he passed through Rippon's outer office, he kept his eyes averted from her, although highly conscious all the time that she had hers fixed tightly on him and that they were laughing at him, as they were doing now.

"Have you enjoyed yourself the night?"

When he still didn't answer, she gave a little hick of a laugh and, her voice low, she said, "You're in a misery, aren't you? All the time you're in a misery. You're frightened of your own shadow, frightened to enjoy yourself. Look, hang on a minute, don't dash off"—she put her fingertips lightly on his sleeve—"or I might raise me voice, I've had a few drinks; an' I'm never dependable when I've had a few drinks, not to be counted on, you know what I mean?"

He knew what she meant. They were staring at each other now and her eyes were no longer laughter-filled as she said, "You wanted me out of Peamarsh's, didn't you? You were terrified of me; you wouldn't believe that I would play square. All I asked was to get on to the other floor and make something of meself, but instead of giving me a helpin' hand, what did you do? You kept mum; and if you could, you would have got me the push, wouldn't you? But I got on the top floor, didn't I, right into the sanctuary. And now I'm in a position to have anything I want. Did you hear that, Mr. Blenheim? Any-thing-I-want."

"How nice for you." His words were flat, lead-weighted.

"Yes, isn't it? He's balmy about me. At first he just did it to get one over on you. Oh, he knows all about it; I told him. Apparently he knew afore; old Cole had done some snooping and she told Dame Bateman. Oh, I know all about her an' all, Bateman; he's come quite clean with me, he's not a damned hypocrite like you. And he knows how to enjoy himself. And let me tell you something else, he's quite willing to pay for it. Do you know something?"

"I'm in a hurry, Miss Ray; will you excuse me?"

Her fingers came on to his sleeve again, tightly now. "No, I won't excuse you, Mr. Blenheim; you're going to listen. This is the only opportunity I've had." She glanced about her, then said, with mock primness, "It wouldn't be right in the

109

office, to talk like this, I mean. As I was saying, do you know where I'm going on me holidays and for a full month, eh? Do you? Well, I'm going on a cruise, on a first-class liner. He's taking me. All very discreet, of course; we meet up on board. It's a free world. As long as you have the money you can go anywhere, get anything. Me mam's gettin' her car an' all. Isn't that nice, Mr. Blenheim?"

He had the terrible desire to choke her and he closed his eyes as she said, "Dear, dear! Does it shock you? But perhaps if I was a relation it would be all right. How would you like me for a mother-in-law?"

"Huh!" He now allowed a twisted smile to spread over his face, and his voice was a deep sneer as he replied, "If an attractive and first-class businesswoman like Miss Bateman couldn't bring it off, then I hold very little hope for you, Miss Ray."

His tone brought her dark brows together and her lips into a tight straight line and she wagged her head for a moment before hissing back at him, "You'd be surprised! I have me methods. He's waitin' in the car for me."

As they glared at each other, the ballroom door opened and John came through with a girl. He stopped abruptly and looked hard at them, then said, "You're back early."

Harry turned to him. "Get your things, I'll be waiting outside." His voice was thick and shaking. He didn't look at her again but went outside and stood on the top step gulping in great drafts of air in an effort to cool the heat of his anger. Mother-in-law! My God! She could do it, too. Yes, he believed her, she could do it.

It was as the door opened behind him and she came out that he heard the scream. It came from the direction of the cars parked to the side of the hotel. When it came again, he lifted his head like an animal, scenting danger. The scream in a way was recognizable, although he had never heard it before. It wasn't a giggly scream, or the scream of lovers, it was a terrified scream, and now he was running, leaping over the ground.

As he rounded the corner, he saw through the dimness the shape of a man backing out of his car; he was straightening himself up as Harry reached him, and he spluttered, "Sorry, sorry. Thought it was mine. Left it—"

Gail, crouched in the corner of the seat, her hands cupping her face, was making strangled sounds and Harry's mad, fury-filled gaze jerked from her to his father-in-law, taking

110

in his disarrayed clothes. Then with a deep oath he had him by the throat.

He was never clear in his mind about what happened in the first few moments, but he did remember banging the big body against the wall; and when it fell to the ground, he remembered using both his fists and his feet on it, and all the while the screaming went on, not Gail's now, but Betty Ray's as she tried to pull him off. Then other hands came on him and forced him to the ground. But even as they held him, his limbs still reacted to the desire to flay.

When they allowed him to get up, someone sat him on a box and he leaned against the side of a car, but they still held on to him. The place was crowded with people now; their voices were torturing his ears. Dimly through the red haze that seemed all about him he saw John talking to a policeman, and he heard Betty Ray's voice, high, hysterical, yelling, spluttering, jabbering.

When they led him to a car, which was not his car, he thought clearly again and said, "Gail. My daughter," and John said, "She's all right." John did not look at him as he spoke, but kept his head down. He became vitally aware of this and remained aware of it for a long time afterward.

When he reached the police station he passed out, and while they were awaiting the doctor's arrival, they brought him around by dousing him with cold water. It was the sergeant's pet treatment for brawling drunks.

111

Eight

"Keep away! Don't come near me." Esther was standing near the head of her bed and Harry at the foot of it.

"You've got to believe me," he said.

"I'll never believe you. That girl, your . . . mistress"—she hissed the last word—"got round him, like she got round you."

"She only got round him because he wanted her to get round him. And for the tenth time she's not my mistress, and never was my mistress. I've told you, I've explained. It was only that once. It was snow-madness you could say, but I can't expect you to believe that if you won't open your eyes to the fact of what's been going on for years."

"My father's a good man." Her voice was low and trembling. "He always has been; you or no one else will be able to convince me otherwise."

"He's not a good man, Esther; he never has been. The fact that he's been good to you because you were his only child doesn't make him a good man. Nothing will ever make him a good man, in business or anything else."

"Shut up!" Her lips were covered with spittle and she dragged her handkerchief first one way then the other across them. Then she said, "Even if he wasn't a good man was that sufficient reason for you to try to kill him. And you would have killed him if they hadn't torn you off; they all said that."

"It's a pity they succeeded," he said grimly. "But I've told you why I went for him, I've told you. He must have frightened her to death when he tried to—"

"Shut up! Shut up, will you?"

"I won't shut up." His voice rose high now, almost to a shout. "He . . ." when she put her hands tightly across her ears, he bowed his head. Then after a moment he turned about and walked to the window, and from there he said, "The fact that he thought it was the Ray girl makes no difference. And you don't believe he was sodden drunk, even though it might act as an excuse for what happened, but you believe I was drunk." He turned his head now slightly toward his shoulder and said slowly, "And in a way you're

112

to blame for the final incident, because if you hadn't persuaded him to let me have his car, there wouldn't have been two of a kind, and he wouldn't have mistaken it for his own."

When he heard her moan, he turned about to see her sitting on the edge of the bed, her head deep on her chest. He made no attempt to go near her, but from where he stood he said, "I'm sorry, Esther."

Now her head jerked up, and her face cold and tight, she cried at him, "And you'll be sorrier still before you're finished. I don't know where you've been these past three days, so it might be news to you to know that Father's seeing this thing through to the end, and if he's so full of guilt as you infer he is, do you think he would dare do that?"

"Your father is capable of doing anything; he's an expert at chicanery and everything underhand. He was clever enough to keep Miss Bateman hidden for fifteen years."

"I don't believe it, not a word of it."

"Then you'd better go and ask her, hadn't you? And she might introduce you to your half sister."

He was sorry he said that, for her face now looked utterly bloodless.

After a moment of bitter silence she said through clenched teeth, "It isn't my father's misdeeds that've brought us low, it's yours." She gripped her forearms and rocked herself backward and forward now, saying, "We'll not be able to lift our heads in the town again. And what about Gail? And you were supposed to worship Gail, weren't you; she was the apple of your eye. Now who's going to look at her after an incident like that, her name splashed across the papers?"

His neck jerked violently up out of his collar as he said, "There's no need for her to be mentioned." He held out the paper he had been holding the while. "She's not mentioned here, not a word about her. The whole gist of this article is from Betty Ray's point of view, that I was jealous of her leaving me and therefore beat up my rival, that's how it reads. There's no need for Gail to be brought into this at all, although if she was I might be able in future to lift my head up in the town, as you term it, because what I did was in defense of my daughter, not through jealousy. God, no! Yet"—he paused—"I know now that what I did to him was what I've wanted to do for years, and all because of you. You were at the bottom of it."

113

"What! Me? You're blaming me now. You're mad."

"I'm not mad, and you know it. And you also know you've never really been a wife to me. You've given me children, yes, but first and foremost you've remained your father's daughter. You should never have married; you'd have been perfectly happy being Daddy's little girl and after your mother died, keeping other women from him. Yet you'd have had a hard job doing that; he would have beaten you at that. And you know something else? He was jealous of me having you. At first it wasn't apparent, he was being the kind father-in-law; then I knew deep down in me he was out to humble me in your eyes, belittle me; any rise in the world I got must come through him. Even in this house I've had no say, I've never been the master in this house; you've been the master under the direction of your father."

Slowly she rose to her feet, and her eyes looked remarkably like her father's as she stared at him, and her voice held a semblance of her old control as she said, "In that case you won't mind leaving the house. I've thought it all over, and it's quite impossible that we remain under the one roof."

Vaguely he had imagined that this might come about, but as yet he hadn't faced up to it. He had in a way visualized some form of reconciliation; he had imagined that at least she would see her father for what he really was; but now he knew that had been a vain hope. He said, "What if I don't choose to go? This is my home, my children are here."

He watched her draw a deep breath into her flat chest before she answered, "This is my house, it is in my name; all the furniture in it was bought with my money. All your salary has done over the years is maintain it. Everything here is legally mine, including the children."

"Oh, no. No!" He lifted his hand up like a traffic warden. "Hold on, Esther, hold on. Talking of legality. You can have the things and the house, but when it comes to the children, I've got a say there, and the law isn't so rigid that it's going to say that I haven't. Gail is mine."

"Oh, yes," she put in quickly; "Gail is yours, it doesn't matter about the other two. Well, we'll see who Gail belongs to. I'm seeing my solicitors tomorrow with regard to a separation."

"Good, good," he said now; "that suits me. But don't think you're going to separate me from the children because you're not."

"You propose to take them to prison with you? Because

114

if my father's injuries prove to be as extensive as they suspect, you're not going to get off lightly!"

The look on her face, her voice, her manner, all told him that she prayed he wouldn't get off lightly. He felt shaken and suddenly frightened. He looked at her for a moment longer, then went out of the room, along the corridor, and knocking on Gail's door, he waited. When there was no answer, he opened it, but the room was empty. Very tidy, unlived in, it looked as if it had never known Gail.

Within seconds he was back in the bedroom. "Where's Gail?"

Esther had her back to him as she replied, "She's staying with friends."

"Which friends?" He was bawling now.

She was standing in front of the mirror putting her hat on as she said, "I'm not going to tell you." Then swinging around and arching her body toward him, she ground from between her teeth, "And if it's left to me you'll never see her again."

She now whipped up her coat from a chair and made for the door, and when she was abreast of him, she said in a thin, bitter whisper, "You've taken everything I value from me; don't try to take Gail. I'm warning you."

He watched her walking firmly across the landing and down the stairs; then he leaned against the stanchion of the door and closed his eyes. He was like that when a hand came on his arm and Gran O'Toole turned him about and led him into her room; and there she pressed him down into a chair as she said brokenly, "Where've you been? I've nearly been out of me mind."

He screwed up his eyes and placed his fingertips on them. Then after a moment he looked up into her face and asked, "Of my many friends who do you think came forward to support me?"

She shook her head, then said, "Tom Vosey? Mr. Nolan?"

When he still continued to stare at her, she went on, "Mr. Ferndale of the timber yard?" She paused, waiting, then said with a slight impatience, "Then who?"

"Nobody."

"Nobody?"

"I had to get in touch with Peter Thompson, the solicitor, you know, and he bailed me out, but he didn't ask me home. But you can't blame him for that, I suppose, for he'd be under the impression I'd come straight back here."

"Well, where did you go?"

"To Janet's."

"Janet's?" She sat down slowly and joined her hands in her lap and repeated, "Janet's? She was here yesterday and never said a word and knew we were worrying."

"You might have been worrying, Gran."

"No matter, no matter, she should have told us."

"I asked her not to."

"But why Janet's?"

"I felt I couldn't face Esther right away and I had to go somewhere to calm down. If I'd gone into one of the hotels, it would have felt like sitting on a hilltop, I'd have been exposed to everybody. No, it suddenly came to me that the only place I could go and be safe would be Janet's."

Some seconds elapsed before she said, "And what are you going to do now?"

"Wait; that's all I can do."

She now started to nip at one finger after the other as she said, "I was on the landing, I heard what you said about not letting Gail be involved, but don't you realize that's your only hope of getting off lightly. If you tell them what he was up to, they won't touch you, not for trying to defend your daughter, they won't, but if you let things go along the line that the papers are indicating, then I'm afraid you'll be in for it."

"I can't help that, Gran; I don't want Gail dragged through the court. As it is, this is going to have a bad enough effect on her, but if she has to stand up there and say what happened, she'll never get over it. She's in the Galahad state of life and a sponge for impressions, and in that court she'll soak up all the dirt they'll bring up, real and imagined, because no one's going to believe that I was only with Betty Ray that once." He leaned forward now and gripped his grandmother's hands. "You believe me, Gran, when I say this, don't you? I was only with her that once on the day of the office party. I was tight and mad, if you like. Once it was over I knew I'd been mad; I also knew that I wouldn't repeat the madness. I swear to you that it was only that once." He waited, looking into her worried wrinkled face, and when she didn't speak, he asked, "How could all this have come out of one mistake in a man's life?" When still she said nothing, he muttered thickly, "I'm bitter, Gran, bitter, because I'm having to pay for that old bastard's misdeeds; and Gail's having to pay, and Esther's having to pay, the lot of us are having to pay."

"Be quiet! Be quiet!" Her voice came at him low and

116

sharp. "It's no use throwing blame right and left now, you've got to face up to something, Harry. As you say, it was only once, but once was enough. Now look here, lad. You're the only thing in life I've got to live for; I've never said this to you afore, but everybody could drown as long as you could swim. But I'm going to tell you this to your face. It wasn't what the old fellow's done that's caused this, it was just that once you had with that girl, that's what caused it. He's an old swine and you couldn't hate him more than I do, but it was you and that girl that brought this present situation about, and you've got to face that fact."

"Aw, Gran, hold your hand. Don't you go to the other side; I couldn't bear it."

She was on her feet now, holding him by the shoulders, glaring down into his distressed face. "I'm not going to the other side, I'm with you whether you're in the right or wrong, but I want you to see this thing clearly. Don't apportion blame, but at the same time don't carry the whole can yourself. When you're brought up you tell them exactly why you lathered into him, and my God"—her voice dropped and she shook her head—"you did that. I went with her yesterday to see him. Lad, you all but murdered him. I doubt if he'll ever be his self again. Looking at him, I couldn't believe that yours was the hand that had inflicted such punishment on him. It wasn't like you; you must have gone clean mad."

He moved away from her hands and went to the dressing table, and he leaned his body over it as he said, "Yes, I must have gone mad, but it was coming. I'd reached the end of my tether. From the night he came in and stopped my mouth with that directorship I've never known a minute's peace or self-respect. He's played me like a puppet for weeks now; every time he's looked at me that hate has oozed out of him, and it got that way I couldn't bear to face him in case I lashed out. It had to come, it was bound to come; the only thing I'm sorry for is that Gail is involved." He turned to her. "Do you know where she is, Gran?"

"No, lad; Esther wouldn't tell me. And she's right there, because she knew I'd pass it on to you."

He went to her again and took her hands and said, "Will you try to explain the whole thing to her when she comes back? You're the only one that can put it over; she'd listen to you."

"I don't suppose I'll be here when she comes back, lad."

His face stretched. "Where you going?"

117

"I'm not sure yet, but there's one thing certain, when you're gone there'll be no place here for me."

"Now don't be silly, Esther's not like that; this is your home."

"As long as it was your home, it was mine. And I'm quite sure Esther would be willing for me to stay, but I wouldn't want to stay."

"Gran!" He pressed her hands tightly. "Stay, please. I want Gail to have someone to rely on, someone sensible. Well, what I mean is not biased, somebody who can see the two sides. Gail thinks the world of you, she'll listen to you. Stay, please, at least for a while."

She bobbed her head slowly. "Well, don't concern yourself about that. Just leave it, I'll see how things go. That is, until I know what is going to happen to you." Her face now dropped into trembling creases and she asked almost in a whimper, "They wouldn't send you to prison, would they?" and he replied, even heartily, "Don't be silly. No, of course not. A fine, likely, heavy. But prison? Of course not!"

BOOK TWO

ROBBIE DUNN

One

"There, Mam, do you like it?"

"Yes, it's a nice chest."

"Lord! Mam. It's not just a chest, it's a Georgian piece."

"I'll take your word for it. "Janet Dunn smiled fondly at her son.

"Look at the frieze." Robbie ran his finger around the ornamentation below the top of the drawers; then swiftly pressing a button at the top of the lower section of the tallboy, he said excitedly, "And a shelf. Look, a sliding shelf."

"Yes, that's nobby," said Janet; "very unusual."

"I'll say it's unusual. I'll bet you a shilling I've got a find here. Just look at those handles. Original, or I'm a Dutchman. And I'm not, am I?" He poked his face toward her and grinned, and she laughed and pushed him none too gently in the chest. Then she said, "Fancy people parting with things like that. Why do they do it?"

"Because they're daft. But mind, in a way I was sorry when I took these. There was the old girl staring at me and her daughter talking away at her. 'You can't take that old thing into a new house, Mother, it just won't fit in. Anyway, there isn't room for it.' And you know what? She had the nerve to put her hand out for the money, but I turned a blind eye an' handed the fifteen quid to the old girl. I would have made it sixteen—aye, and more, believe me, Mam." He lowered his voice to almost a whisper. "I would have made it twenty-five to get that piece, but whatever I'd made it that madam would have had her hands on it within a minute. God, an' they call us mean." He stared at Janet, and Janet stared back at him, and then they both laughed together.

She turned now from the back room and walked toward the door that led into the shop, and standing there, she said, "The window looks lovely, but why don't you put more in it?"

"Put more in it?" He raised his black eyebrows at her. "Can't you get it into your head that this is a classy shop, little and good. It's not the market, Mam; I'm not having this place chock-à-bloc with rubbish."

121

"No, I didn't mean that, but you've only got that sofa table and that other one. What do you call it?"

"Pembroke."

"Well, that one, and that little couch . . ."

". . . Hepplewhite period settee, Mrs. Dunn."

"Hepplewhite period settee." She bowed her head toward him. "Well, that doesn't seem much to get anyone inside."

"You'd be surprised. There's tricks in every trade as you know, and in this one there's dozens, and that's one of them." He patted her shoulder. "I know what I'm up to, Mrs. Dunn; the last two years or so've been as good as a university education to me."

Janet looked at him, pride in her dark eyes, and shaking her head slowly, she said, "I can't understand how you remember all the names and periods."

"Oh, any fool can do that; it's buying the pieces that's the thing, knowing what to buy, where to look. For instance, who would have thought I would have come across that gem"—he thumbed over his shoulder toward the workroom —"at Bog's End. And it in such good condition." His voice dropping, he said, "That old girl loved that chest. She mightn't have known its value, but she loved it. And you know, Mrs. Dunn"—he grinned at her now—"I love folks what loves furniture."

"How much are you going to ask for it?" asked Janet practically.

"Fifty."

"No, Robbie!"

"Why not?" His chin poked forward. "Put that in a shop in Newcastle and you wouldn't get it under seventy-five. And run it up to London and then the sky could be the limit. I'm getting fifty for that." He wagged his finger at her. "I'll mark it up fifty-five an' I'll get fifty."

"Do you think anyone round here will want it?" she sounded skeptical, and he answered roughly, "No, Mam, nobody around here'll want it, but they come down from Brampton Hill, don't they, an' from Newcastle. And I bet you what you like if I stuck it in the window the morrow I'd have a few hawks after it. It's genuine, it's old, it's got the stamp on it, an' those fellows know what they're after. And boy, so do I."

"All right, all right," she said calmly. She looked fully at him now and her voice dropped to a soft note as she added, "You're a good boy, Robbie."

He blinked rapidly at what was high praise from her, then

122

with an upward thrust of his chin that tossed his lank hair back from his brow, he said, "I'm only startin'," to which she nodded endorsement.

He had turned from her, but quickly looking at her again, he said, "It's close on six. I'll be shutting up. Let's take a run over and look at the house."

"What, again? But we were there yesterday."

"Well, we can go the day an' all, can't we? I'll tell Sid I'm locking up; he can go out the back."

As they drove through the town, they were both silent. Five minutes later they were on the main road running into the country with the fells rolling away on both sides of them, until, turning into a lane, they came upon a slag heap that looked like a huge carbuncle blotting the landscape, and beyond it reared a disused mineshaft and workings. For another five minutes the road wound slowly uphill, terminating in a narrow lane. They crossed a wooden bridge, under which a burn gurgled, then went through a wide aperture in a tangled hedge. And there it was, the wreck of a house.

But when Robbie alighted from the car, he stood gazing up as it as if at a mansion; then turning to Janet, he said, "I was thinking in the night, we'll strip the ceiling in the hall and expose all those beams and soak them with boiled oil."

"But they're all worm-eaten."

"Well"—he nudged her—"don't people pay for worm holes?"

She laughed, and looking upward as they walked toward the door, flanked on each side by glassless windows, she said, "Before you start thinking of boiled oil, it would pay you better to concentrate on slates, with only three of the rooms dry."

"All in good time, all in good time." He pushed her gently up two worn wooden steps and into a hallway, where, in spite of the ventilation coming through the windows, the smell of dry rot met them. The hall, about thirty feet long, had once been half-paneled but all that remained of the original wood were odd pieces which were pegged to the crossbars and had resisted being wrenched off by marauders. A wide flight of stairs, as worn as the outside steps, mounted from the end of the room upward, and the daylight from a gap in the roof showed the broken balustrade, which had once graced the narrow gallery.

It was with something of secret despair that Janet looked about her. She still thought her son stark, staring mad to saddle himself with a two-thousand-pound mortgage for this wreck of a place standing on a piece of barren land. No doubt, once it had been a beautiful house, but it had been empty when she was a child thirty years ago. She remembered her mother and father walking her out here one Sunday and they picnicked on the hill behind the house, and she in her turn had brought Robbie here. And that was a mistake, for the first ride he took on his secondhand bicycle had been to Scarfield Mill. She didn't know why the house was called a mill, for there was no sign of a mill within miles. The only prominent feature on the landscape, and that could only be seen from the hill behind the house, was the pithead. It was a desolate enough place in summer; God knew what it would be like in winter. Up to now everything her lad had touched had turned to money, but she could only see this place eating money, it would take thousands and thousands to put it into shape. When she had put this to him, all he said was "I've got plans," and she hadn't pressed to know what they were because, whereas he could be as open as the fells, he could also be as close as a clam.

She walked across the hall and through a door into what had once been the kitchen. Now it hadn't even the usual iron stove to which it could lay claim; that had been ripped out, as had most of the piping. She saw the task ahead as so formidable that she turned a distressed face to Robbie. "I can't help it," she said, "but the more I look at it, the more hopeless it seems. Why, as I said in the first place, you could have got a nice bungalow for just a bit more if you wanted to get away from Baker Street so badly." The look on his face checked her voice now, and when he stared at her blankly, she ended, "I can't help feeling like this about it. Where are you going to get the money to make this habitable, eh? Where?"

He still continued to stare at her; then with a swift jerky movement characteristic of him, he grabbed her hand and pulled her forward through the back door, across a paved yard thick with weed and grass, over a moldering gate lying where it had once hung, across a narrow field, and up a steep incline, and having arrived at the brow of the hill, he commanded sharply, "Sit down."

She was gasping and half laughing as she obeyed him. Then dropping onto his hunkers by her side, he pointed down to the house, saying slowly and thickly, "From the first time I saw that house I've hated Baker Street." As he watched her face stretch in genuine surprise, he said, "Aye, that's news to you," then went on, "I must have been about twelve when I vowed that one day I'd have a place like this, some place worthy of the mezuzah on the door, but as I grew older I knew that even with things going well I'd have to wait ten, fifteen years or more before that dream could come true, unless I joined the fiddles, an' I could have an' all." He inclined his head toward her. "I've been tapped more than once, but you know me, I never liked little rooms."

She ignored his grin and his jest and said, "But it's going to take you a lifetime to get this place to rights; and how can you do the buying, see to the shop, and do this an' all on your own? It's impossible."

He looked away from her and down on to the broken roofs of the house that was now his, and he said slowly, "I don't intend to do it on me own."

"What!"

He slanted his eyes at her. "You heard what I said, I don't intend to do it on me own."

"You've got somebody to help you?"

"Yes, just that. In two months' time I'll have somebody to help me."

"NO, Robbie! No!" She was on her feet staring down at him, her lips pressed together, her face tight, and he looked up at her and asked harshly, "Where's he going to go then when he comes out? Have you asked yourself that? He wouldn't come back to Baker Street; he knew he was putting us out for the few nights he was there. It'll be a room in some grubby back street until he gets started, and God knows when that'll be in this town. The only chance for him is to move away . . . and you don't want that, do you?" His last words were slow and emphatic, and Janet stared back into his eyes but made no answer. When her face began to work, he got to his feet and said, "Look. I know how things are with you; I've always known."

"Be quiet, Robbie."

"I'll not be quiet. I'm not a kid, I'm not even a young fella, I've never been a young fella, I somehow skipped that stage, I'm a man. I've always had to think as a man because I've had to think for you, so I know how things've been, an' not only the day or yesterday, but for years back."

When she turned from him and stared away over the sloping land, he said, "There's nothing to be ashamed of, woman. And it's funny but I've never been jealous of him, just the opposite. Somehow I've always looked on him as a sort

125

of father. I think it's because he started me up with that ten quid. An' what's more, I knew years ago why you went to the house to help, not for the money but just because he was . . ."

"Robbie!" Her voice was deep and pain-filled, and he drooped his head for a moment against the sound of it. Then his chin was up again and he said, "I've got it all worked out if you'll only listen. He could come an' live here and he could occupy himself with the woodwork. He took up carpentry in there because he wanted to use his hands; well, he can go on using his hands."

She turned her body slowly toward him and her voice held an unusual disdainful note as she said, "You're just using him as cheap labor."

His fists were clenched and his arms were extended to the fullest length as he flung himself first one way and then the other, crying, "God in Heaven! Christ alive!"

"Don't use that term, Robbie!" She was snapping now. "It might mean nothing to us, but I don't like to hear it."

"Well, Mam." He shut his eyes tightly and his head swung as he ground out, "You'd make a rabbi curse. Using him? Of course, I'm using him." He was glaring at her now. "And, aye, for me own benefit, but at the same time it's for his benefit. But besides anything me or him'll get out of it I'm doing it for your benefit, an' you're a fool not to see it."

"Robbie, stop it. Be quiet for a moment and listen to me." She paused until he was looking at her again. "The truth is that Harry Blenheim doesn't know I'm alive except as good old Janet; Janet, who lived upstairs above him for years; Janet, who first took him to school, because I was six and he was five; Janet, who would go into their house and mind him when his mother was out. Then it was Janet who would go and help his wife out." She paused again and wetted her lips before saying quietly, "Never, even as a young girl did I imagine anything could come of it. Harry Blenheim was not only Church of England, he was in the choir and his voice brought him quickly to the fore, to people's notice, and there was us, practicing Jews. Had my father ever thought that I had any private thoughts about Harry Blenheim, he would have had me transported to some far-off place; he was quite capable of it. He picked your father for me; and your father was a good man, yet I might have protested if there had been the slightest hope for me in Harry's direction. But as I've said, he didn't even know I was alive in that way. And he doesn't to this day, so you can save your

126

plans and your schemes, Robbie. And one small point you seem to have overlooked is, he's still married and has a family."

"Huh! Married and his family? If that's marriage, then I'll find me a woman to live with."

"Don't say things like that, Robbie."

"I will say things like that, Mam, and I mean them. He stepped off the white line once and that was enough for her. And his family. God! His family. An' not one of them's been to see him during all this time."

"You forget Terry; he came and asked after him."

"I'd have thought a damn sight more of him if he had made the journey to Durham."

"He's only a boy."

"Boy, me granny's aunt! Anyway, apart from that, what do you think is going to happen when he comes out? Are his friends going to rally round; they were pretty scarce before he went up. As I see it, he's only got us and that Mr. Whelan. But he's in Doncaster now, so where's he going to go . . . prisoners' aid?"

Janet bowed her head and covered her eyes with her hand. "You make it sound so awful."

"It is awful, Mam."

"Couldn't you offer him a job in the shop? You said you wanted somebody presentable, different from Sid, and he could get lodgings in the town."

"I could, but I know damn well he'd refuse; he won't be able to face the town. He'll want time and a place to recover in, and this is it." He pointed down the hill. "Mind." He raised his hand, palm upward, toward her. "I'm not saying I took the house because of him. Oh, no. But the whole thing fell into place, his need an' mine."

"I still think it's making a convenience of him, using him."

"But it's a job for him, Mam, be sensible. And I'll pay him. It won't be builder's rates but I'll pay him, he'll feel independent."

"But he'll be here with me all day and I couldn't bear that."

Her voice was low now and it stopped him from yelling, "Aw, for crying out loud!" Instead, he gripped hold of her arms and shook her slightly, saying, "Well, that's something you'll have to get used to, because if I have anything to do with it, he's coming here; and he can stay until he gets on his feet and then it's up to him."

She looked at him for a long, long moment. Her eyes

127

traveled from his black hair to his equally black eyes, over his big nose and thin mouth, then down his stocky body, and she said slowly as if drawing on familiar thoughts, "You'll marry one day . . ." But she got no further before his chin jerked up and out, and his words came rapidly on brittle laughter as he said, "Don't make plans for me in that direction, Mam; you forget you're talking to Robbie Dunn, who, if he knows nothing else, knows what his assets are in the marrying market. Whoever says 'I will' to me is going to want a fine dowry along of me, such as a big house"—he again nodded down the hill—"furnished with antiques, and a nice fat bankrole. She'll want the prestige money can buy, and as it's goin' to be some little time afore I can offer me beloved that, we'll forget about it, eh?"

"But, Robbie—"

"Look, Mam, I said forget about it. I know what chances I have in that direction." His voice had moved from sarcasm to bitterness now. "Girls I have an eye for look upon me as a Jew boy, fast talking, slick and common. Aye, common. Even those of me own kind don't want to know me. I don't spend enough for some, and the others, like Olive Stein, who you'd think'd be glad to jump at anybody, are waiting to see what I make of things. Aw, Mam, don't, don't cry; for heaven's sake, don't cry."

"Oh, Robbie. Oh, my dear." When she leaned her head against his shoulder, he put his arms around her and stared down the hill to the substitute for loving he had saddled himself with, and there came a swelling in his throat that threatened to choke him, and he beat it off with "Christ alive! Don't you start."

128

Two

The sale, in a private house just outside of Prudhoe, was almost at an end. Robbie was pleased with himself. He had not only got what he came for, an Adam-style wine cooler, but had picked up a couple of good-quality plated cover dishes for almost a song. The last lot of the sale was an outsize clothes basket, full of books and oddments. The oddments were a dented copper kettle and stand, and an old tea caddy, the lid and sides heavily rococoed. The lead had been stripped from the inside and the box lids were missing, yet he thought he might have a find here.

When the lot was knocked down to him for fifteen shillings, he knew he was all right, for the books alone should bring ten bob. He didn't intend to take them back to the shop if he could help it; he didn't go in for books. There was a secondhand bookshop on the main road to Newcastle just beyond Jesmond; he decided to stop there and try to flog them.

At twenty minutes past five he pulled the van up to the curb opposite the shop and saw he was just in time, as a girl was clearing a table of books that stood outside the doorway.

The bookshop had a single window, but this was deceptive, he saw as he entered the shop, because before him was quite a large room with racks down the center and the walls lined with book-filled shelves, and overall the permeating musty smell that is peculiar to secondhand bookshops seemed stronger than usual. It was a depressing place.

The girl was bending down stacking the books on the floor to the side of a rack, and seeing the feet standing a yard or so from her, she turned her head and said, "I'm sorry, we're closing." Her voice trailed away on the last word and she straightened up and stared at Robbie, and he at her. Then he said, "Why, hello. Fancy seeing you here."

He watched the color flood up over her pale face; it was as if she had been caught in some misdemeanor. "You work here?" he now asked. It was obvious that she did, but he could find nothing else to say at the moment.

129

"Yes," she said flatly. "And I'm about to close." The color was receding now.

"Oh, that's awkward." He grinned at her. "I had some books on the van; I wondered if you'd be interested. It says outside you buy them."

"Yes. Yes, we do, but Miss Frazer is out at the moment, she does the buying."

"I'll call back then." He nodded at her.

"Yes, you . . . you could do that."

He stared at her. You couldn't say she was breaking her neck with enthusiasm at the sight of him. She had changed. Well, she would, wouldn't she? It must have changed the entire Blenheim family, that do. It was over two years since he had seen her last. She hadn't grown as tall as he imagined she would. She wasn't much bigger than him, well perhaps an inch or so. He had imagined, at one time, she would turn into a looker, but she hadn't. She still had all the bits and pieces necessary, yet there was something about her face that stopped short at the word "beautiful" or "pretty," or even "attractive." Likely it was due to her expression; it was surly.

She turned away from his stare, saying, "Miss Frazer won't be in until eleven tomorrow."

"Good. I'll call in then. Ta-ra!"

He was making for the door when she said, "How is Janet?"

He looked back at her now with interest. Her question took some of the uppishness out of her manner and he replied, "Oh, she's fine, grand. How's your people?" The short space before she replied conveyed to him that his question wasn't entirely tactful.

"They're very well, thank you."

"Good." He nodded at her. "Be seeing you then." He had turned from her again and reached the door when her voice, hesitant yet hurried, asked, "How . . . how is your business going?"

Slowly now he faced her. His eyes narrowed as he looked at her across the gloomy room and he knew instinctively that she didn't care a damn how his business was going; the question she was asking was "How is my father?" Her expression had changed, the dead look had lifted, and he saw she was agitated because her hands were clasped tightly together on the counter as if to prevent her from spurting something out. He looked from her face to her hands

130

and back to her face again before he said, "It's going like a house on fire."

"I'm glad."

"Thanks." He thought a moment while she dropped her gaze from his, unclasped her hands, and started tidying the counter; then he said, "You going straight back home?"

"Yes."

"By bus?" One of them might come to pick her up, you never knew.

"Yes."

"Well, I've got the van outside. I'm going that way, I could drop you."

"Oh, no. No, thanks." Now she was agitated again. Her fumbling hands upset a stack of paperbacks, and as she reassembled them, she repeated, "Thank you," then added, "I wouldn't want to trouble you, I might be some time."

"The evening's me own, I can wait."

"Thank you all the same."

As he continued to stare at her, fumbling with one thing after another, the old animosity welled up in him, until he was not seeing her anymore but was looking at John Blenheim. Had his real education been garnered from school, he would, because of the pride that was inherent in him, have smothered his feelings, taken no for an answer and left, seeing he had no personal interest in her. But his education had come mostly from the market and from men without inhibitions who said what they thought, more often than not without thinking. Daily contact with such types had also ousted in part the inborn reticence that was his, and so he said now, "Are you frightened of being seen with me?"

She jerked her head up and for a moment she looked like the Gail he remembered before the affair, and she sounded like her too, impetuous, kind, as she said, "Of course not, Robbie. Why do you say such a thing?"

"Well then, what's stopping you riding back with me in the van?"

Her gaze dropped again and she said, "It's . . . it's only that . . ."

He finished the sentence for her. "Some of your family might see you, your John, for instance."

She was looking him full in the face now and she answered him truthfully, "Yes, it could be that."

"Huh!" He laughed, then said, "Well, what if I drop you this end of the town? You could pick up a bus there and

131

you won't have half an hour to stand in the queue, like down here."

He watched her wet her lips, fumble with the books again, droop her head, and think, before saying, "Very well, I'll ... I'll be out in a few minutes."

"Good enough." He turned without further words, went out, and got into the van, and as he sat waiting, he thought, "It'll give her the opportunity to ask; but she's got to ask, I'm not tellin' her else ..."

But she didn't ask; she hardly opened her mouth during the whole of the journey except to say yes or no, until they reached the outskirts of Fellburn, and then she said, "Would you mind dropping me here, please."

"O.K." He pulled in abruptly to the curb, then leaned across her to open the door and pushed it wide and when she stepped onto the pavement, he said, "See you the morrow then." As he watched her eyes widen for a moment, he put in, "I'll be bringing the books."

"Oh, yes. And thank you for the lift, Robbie."

"Anytime." He nodded his head at her, pulling the door closed, then started the van off with the same abrupt movement as he had stopped it. As he drove along the road, he watched her in the driving mirror until he turned the corner, and then he muttered aloud, asking himself, "Did you see her face when I said I'll see you the morrow? She had forgotten about the books, but the look on her face. Well! She needn't worry." He swung around another corner, and spitting out one word now, he said, "John!" Then he added, "To blazes with John, and all his breed."

As soon as he entered the house, and before Janet could ask her usual question, "Well, how did you get on?" he said flatly, "Who do you think I saw the day?"

"Someone you're not used to seeing, evidently," she answered him, smiling and waiting.

"Gail."

"Gail! Where?"

In a few brief words he told her where, and as he ended, he was unable to keep the bitterness out of his voice, "She was scared to death to be seen with me."

"Don't be silly."

"I'm not silly, Mam. Most people can see through curtains, but I can see through brick walls; it's been me trainin'."

"Oh, Robbie."

"Anyway, she said she was."

132

"Gail said that! No, she would never say that. I wouldn't believe it."

"Well, I'm telling you she did, and on account of Master John."

"Oh . . . well, now, that's possible and understandable."

"Is it?" His voice was aggressive.

"Well, you know you couldn't stand the sight of each other before all this happened, and he's bound to know you've been to see his father."

"How's he bound to know? Not one of them've been within a mile of Durham in case they would get the smit."

"That may be true, but news travels and by very odd pathways. Did she ask after him?"

"No, she didn't." He pushed his eyebrows almost up to his hairline. "That's the point, she didn't, and the only reason she came in the van with me was to find out something about him."

"Well, why didn't you tell her?"

"What! Not on your life. Look, Mam; she's not dear little Gail anymore, she's a girl of eighteen, and if she had any spunk, she would have gone and seen him. You haven't to be told that he thought the sun shone out of her, and she was supposed to be clean mad about him. It wouldn't really have mattered so much about the lads. Master John—well, he'll never live the stigma down, one couldn't expect him to go visiting at a prison. And Terry, after all, as you pointed out, he did come and ask how his father was faring. And the old grannie would have been there like a shot if she hadn't had that fall. But our Miss Gail was the one he cared about. I know this much; he wouldn't have cared a damn about the others as long as she had gone, if only once."

"She had a very bad experience, you must remember that," said Janet calmly. "It was bound to leave an impression on her mind."

Robbie turned away from her and went into the scullery, and as he took off his coat, he called, "It hasn't only left it on her mind, it's left it on her face. She gave you the idea years ago she was going to look something."

"Well, doesn't she?" Janet came to the scullery door and he said, "No. It was a kind of a shock when I saw her; it was her and yet it wasn't her, she's plain."

"Gail plain?" Janet gave a laugh. "You don't lose beauty overnight."

"It's been a long night, nearly two years, and I tell you

133

any looks she promised have given her the slip. Her face is dead, blank-looking, no life in it."

Janet stood looking at him as he washed himself and she said quietly, "Well, if you're right that's one of the worst things that could have happened, for she did promise to be beautiful, and he was so proud of her. But perhaps she'll still look beautiful to him when he sees her."

He blew into the towel, dried his face hurriedly, then said, "If he sees her."

"Well, if she won't come to him, he could go to her now you know where she works."

"That remains to be seen because he's altered an' all. You know he has. He was never a boisterous fellow, but he's so quiet now he could be dumb."

"It's the place," she said; "it doesn't induce conversation."

"No? Well, the others talk and seem glad to talk."

Later, as they sat down at the table, she said, "It's only six weeks and I'm dreading it in a way. Oh, not for me." She shook her head. "For him."

"Yes." He paused before picking up his knife and fork. "You know, you could be right; I think he's dreading it an' all. Last time, when I said to him, 'It won't be long now,' he just looked at me. And it was as much that look as anything, I might as well tell you, that settled the question of the house, me taking it."

She was holding his glance, and now she reached her hand across the table and touched his, saying, "You're a good boy, Robbie, a good boy."

He attacked his meal, and after bolting a mouthful of food, he said roughly, "Don't give me credit for being . . . altruistic." He jerked his head at her now and laughed out loud. "That's a good 'un, isn't it? I read it somewhere, but I'd like to bet I haven't pronounced it properly. Anyroad, you know what I mean, 'cos what I do, Mam, first, middle, and last is to look after number one because if I don't nobody else will."

She nodded at him solemnly now, saying, "Yes, I know you're full of vices, but being your mother, I'm blind to them, so to me you're a good boy." When he spluttered on his food and burst out laughing again, she laughed with him.

Three

The following afternoon Robbie took the books along to the shop and was met by Miss Frazer. Miss Frazer was a woman in her fifties. She was tall, lean, and sparing of words. She quickly looked through the assortment of books, then said, "There's only two I'd buy but I'll give you seven and six for the lot."

His natural response to this would have been "You won't. Twelve and six or nothing"; then following a little bargaining, he would have walked out with ten shillings, but Gail was standing at a bookcase with her back to him and he knew she was listening, and although he thought, "It's going to cost me that much for petrol," he said, "All right; I just want to get rid of them, I don't deal in them."

"You're a dealer?" Miss Frazer raised her eyebrows just the slightest, but even so they expressed disbelief, and he stared hard at her as he said stiffly, "Aye. Yes, I'm a dealer."

"In what?"

"Antiques." His voice was much louder than the answer in the ordinary way would have necessitated, but this old dame didn't believe him. For a moment he almost turned to Gail and said, "Tell her what I deal in," but Miss Frazer was handing him the seven and sixpence, and although his maxim had always been pennies make shillings and shillings make pounds, he almost said grandiosely, "Keep it; you need it more than me."

During the time he was in the shop Gail did not acknowledge him in any way; she did not even turn and look at him, and when he was in the car once more, he found himself swelling with anger and, as usual, talking to himself. "God! Some people. Who the hell do they imagine they are! Royalty? The Aga Khan's lot? Or what?" But it wasn't quite evident whether he was referring to Gail or to Miss Frazer, or to both.

It was three weeks later when he met Gail again, and in an unusual place, the Roxley Eventide Home.

It happened that he received a letter from a Mrs. Bailey saying that her friend, Mrs. Scott, had sold him some pieces

135

of furniture and had recommended him to her. She herself had a few articles at her son-in-law's, but he was moving away and didn't want the things, so would Mr. Dunn care to look at them, then come and see her?

So, after he had found among Mrs. Bailey's old-fashioned furniture a beautiful eighteenth-century grandfather clock, and an envelope card table, he gladly went to talk terms with her at the Eventide Home.

It was as he was crossing the main hall that he saw Gail; she was going out of the front door. He stopped in his stride for a moment, then hurried after her, and when he came up to her, he said airily, "You retiring?"

For a moment she looked startled, then she said stiffly, "Well, hardly." When she walked on, her gaze directed ahead, he felt, as he put it later to Janet, a bit daft her taking it like that.

Before he reached the main gates, he had decided to let her get on with it. If she wanted to play the madam and remain aloof, it was O.K. by him; but then she took the wind out of his sails, for when they reached the street she stood in front of him and, with her head slightly lowered said, "I'm sorry."

"Oh, that's all right; I was only meaning to be funny."

"Yes, I know, Robbie." She was looking straight into his face now. "And you must think me awful. And the other day when you came into the shop. And I know what you meant just a minute ago, but . . . but with one thing and another I get upset."

"Don't we all?" He grinned at her.

"Yes, I suppose so." She looked away from him. "You get it into your head that you're the only one who's got troubles, but to see Gran in there upsets me."

"Your Gran in there?" His voice was loud, his arm extended back toward the gate. "Mrs. O'Toole, you mean?"

"Yes."

"Good God, no!"

Immediately her manner was on the defensive again. "It isn't our fault, you can't blame us, she insisted on going. My mother tried to stop her. She did . . ."

He didn't say, "I'll take your word for it," but something in his expression must have said it for him, for she insisted harshly, "I'm telling you she did, she tried everything to stop her going in."

"How long has she been there?" The question was quiet, and she gulped in her throat before she answered, "Eigh-

136

teen . . . nineteen months or so. She arranged it all herself after she fell and hurt her hip. We didn't know anything about it until it was done."

He now said, "Your father's had letters from her, but he doesn't know about this. He's going to go mad." Without thinking, he had given her an opening. He watched her now as she turned her head right around to her shoulder, and his brows beetling, he said, "Turnin' your head away won't rid you of the fact that he's still your father. And I'll tell you this. No matter what you or anybody else says, he's a decent bloke; just unfortunate, that's all, and them with sense see it that way."

When she put her hand up to her mouth and pressed it tightly, he thought, "She's going to cry"; but she didn't, and after a moment he asked, "Would you like a cup of tea, I'm parched meself? There's a nice café along there by the river . . . pleasant."

Her ready acceptance surprised him, so much so that when she said, "Thanks," and stepped off the pavement onto the road in the direction of the green, he walked by her side until they reached the café without again opening his mouth.

When he ordered a pot of tea for two and a plate of cakes, she did not go and take a seat at one of the tables outside but stood waiting until he was served; then carrying the plate of cakes, she followed him as he made his way to the far end of the garden. "There," he said as they sat down. "Isn't this nice?"

"Yes." She looked about her. "It's lovely. I never knew this café was here."

"Well, I didn't meself until last year. I go to the home sometimes because the old ladies want to sell bits and pieces. I've got the name for givin' them a fair crack of the whip; they trust me not to diddle 'em. Balmy, aren't they?"

When she made no answer to this but continued to stare at him, he said, "Well, aren't you going to pour out?"

"Yes, of course." She seemed flustered.

This was new too, because the girl he had met in the bookshop wouldn't, he had imagined, know how to be flustered. Agitated yes, but not flustered. He watched her from under lowered lids as she poured out the tea. He couldn't get over the fact that she seemed to have lost her looks. He wondered what her father would think when he saw her. Get a bit of a gliff, he supposed, and blame himself for the change in her. He had been determined he wasn't going to mention her

137

father to her, but he had, and now he found himself saying, "Your father'll be free in a fortnight's time. Do you know that?"

"A fortnight?" Her lips moved with the words but made no sound.

"Have you thought what's going to happen to him when he's out?"

"Yes, yes, I have. All the time."

He took no heed of the terseness of the words or the pain in her voice, but leaning across the little round table toward her, said harshly, "Well, why didn't you go and see him and try and find out?"

Gail stared at him. His face was not more than six inches from hers. His eyes were coal black, and his short lashes so dark and thick one could imagine they had been touched up. In the twice they had met, not counting the day he had sold the books to Miss Frazer, he had been kind to her. She could, in a way, understand him sympathizing with people's problems, as he did with the old ladies in the home, but she couldn't imagine him understanding if she said, "I was afraid to," for he would come back smartly, asking, "Afraid of being seen visiting him in prison?" And the truth was just that, she would have been afraid of being seen visiting the prison. Nevertheless, she would have gone if it hadn't have been for her mother.

At one time it could have been said that she adored her father and loved her mother, it could have been said up to the night in the car park; since then she had ceased to question her feelings toward her father, but her feelings toward her mother she knew were no longer of love but of deep resentment, even of fear, and, at times lately, kindled an emotion she dared not face up to. Although she no longer attended church, she still considered it a terrible thing to hate one's parent.

At times she thought it was unfair to blame her mother for her attitude because she hadn't started all this; yet when her thoughts touched on the person who had been the instigator of all the trouble that had come upon them, she directed them hastily away, for she couldn't blame him, not really, except when awaking from dreams in which she imagined herself screaming at a girl who kept talking and talking and talking. In the dark she could always see Betty Ray as she had that night, and hear her yelling at her father as she struck out at him, "You didn't want the cake, but you didn't

138

want anybody else to have it." She hadn't understood about the cake then, but she had the next day when her mother made it plain to her. It was odd the things that stuck in your mind. For days afterward she could only think that the girl was the same size as she was. She had kept her mind dwelling on the girl at that period, not letting it touch on her father . . . or her grandfather; no, certainly not on her grandfather. The thought of her grandfather made her physically sick, even now, and at that time she hadn't cared whether he died or not. It was only when she realized the consequences to her father should this happen that she began to pray that her grandfather might live.

She had never seen her grandfather since that night. Her mother had said to her, "You mustn't blame your grandfather; he wasn't a married man with a family, he was a free agent." At first Gail couldn't understand her mother's differing attitude toward the two men. She had put her husband out of her life altogether, yet every day for two months she went to the nursing home and visited her father, and after he returned home, hardly a day passed when she didn't go and see him; this was when he wasn't taking one of his long holidays. Gail wondered for a long time whether her grandfather went on these holidays alone, and as recently as two weeks ago, when having another verbal battle with her mother she had dared to hint of such a thing, she thought for a moment that Esther was going to strike her. But instead she had stood with her back to the door and told her for the countless time in that cold monotonous penetrating way what a changed man her grandfather was. How he was still quite incapable of carrying on his business, and never again would he be able to work as he had once done, and it was only thanks to his past industry that he could exist now.

She had dared her mother's wrath again by saying, cynically, that his past industry must have been very lucrative because his way of living went on as before; added to which, he now kept them. At least he kept her mother and the boys, together with the house and car; he did not keep her.

Nothing would induce her to go back to school after she had returned from the protracted holiday her mother had forced on her. She had been lucky to get the job with Miss Frazer almost right away. The other thing she had wanted to do at this time was to leave home, but that had been a hopeless desire. Even now, at eighteen, it was still hopeless.

Whereas the boys were free to go where they liked, her mother almost timed her movements. And this was while her father was in prison; what it would be like when he came out she dare not think. She'd likely send John with the car to pick her up. But it couldn't go on forever. No, it couldn't go on forever.

"Did you hear what I said?"

"Yes. You asked me why I didn't go and see him and find out what he's going to do?"

"Well, why didn't you?"

"Because I couldn't." Her head was drooped now, and he looked at the crown of it for some time before he said, "Your mother wouldn't let you, is that it?" When she didn't answer, he sat back, picked up his cup and saucer, sipped at the tea, then said, "This's got cold, is there a drop more hot in there?"

After she had poured him out another cup, he pushed the plate of cakes toward her, saying, "Aren't you going to have one?"

When she took a cake from the plate, he helped himself also and they both ate in silence for a few minutes, until he asked quietly, "Will you come and see him when he comes out?"

She looked up at him now. "I don't think I'll be able to. I mean . . ."

He was leaning toward her again. "Well, if you could, I mean if there was nobody stoppin' you, would you then?"

She stared at him, then said softly, "But where would I see him?"

"Our place."

"He's going to stay with you at your house?" Her mouth remained slightly agape.

"Yes, but not at Baker Street. We're movin' on Monday."

"Oh."

"Do you know Scarfield Mill? It's about three miles out beyond the old Beular mine." When she shook her head, he went on, "It's a big old house, not much to look at now, with only three rooms habitable, all the rest let in water, but wait till I get it finished. My! It'll be a grand place. I've had me eye on it since I was a lad." His voice was laden with pride.

"Really!" And you've bought it?" She was smiling. It was the first time he had seen her smile, and for a brief instance he saw the young Gail again. Her eyes looked warm, her

140

face alive. She said now, "That's wonderful for you, a great achievement. Janet must be pleased."

He pulled a wry face at her. "Not as much as me. There's about ten years' work ahead of us, and she's not really taken with that."

The smile faded as she said, "And my father's going to live with you?"

"Well, that's the idea, sort of. At least"—he wagged his head—"until he gets on his feet. He'll need time to find himself. You know what I mean."

"Yes." Her voice was a mere whisper. She hung her head again and remained silent, then surprised him somewhat by almost jumping to her feet, saying, "I'll have to be getting back." She glanced at her watch. "A bus goes in five minutes."

"Why not save the fare?" He was grinning up at her. "All right, all right, I know. But like afore, I could drop you off outside the town."

"It's very kind of you."

"Kind, nothing." He jerked his chin up. "Same amount of petrol, won't cost me any more." When he saw the smile creep into her face again, he urged it outward by saying, "I never do anything that's goin' to cost me money. Now it's a different story if I'm going to make a bit. Oh, I'd even tackle climbing up a gum tree if I thought there was sixpence at the top."

"Oh, Robbie."

He had succeeded and the smile was on her face again, and when she said, "Thank you for the tea and everything," he put in brusquely, "Well, come on; we'd better take these things back, else they'll charge us for being waited on."

When they put the tray of dirty crocks on the counter, the woman behind the tea urn said brightly, "Oh, that's kind of you; thanks." And after he had said, "You're welcome," he muttered under his breath as they made their way outside, "Now if I'd known that you weren't expected to bring the empties back, I wouldn't have wasted me strength on them."

She cast a sidelong glance at him. Her eyes were still laughing, but her voice was touched with sadness as she said, "You're the one person who hasn't changed in all these years, Robbie."

He put on a long face. "Well, that's bucked me up. Here's me reached the state of manhood, owner of the best an-

141

tique shop in town, not forgetting the stately mansion, drafty as yet but nevertheless stately, and you tell me I haven't changed."

When she laughed outright, he felt a sense of real achievement and he said eagerly, "How would you like to run out and see the place, it'll only take about twenty minutes?"

"Thank you, Robbie, but I can't today. I'll . . . I'll have to be getting back. I . . ." When she hesitated, he put in quickly, "Fair enough, fair enough. Well, here we are." When he stopped in front of the Cortina, she seemed surprised and said, "I . . . I thought it would be the van."

"The van?" His tone was haughty. "The van on a Saturday afternoon! No, ma'am, no van on a Saturday afternoon. Nor for weddings an' funerals."

She was still smiling as she took her seat and asked him, "Is this the one you first bought?"

"Good Lord, no. You mean that Christmas?"

"Yes."

"I've had three since. No, no, this is the fourth, all second-hand and all bargains. And they were still bargains when I sold them again an' all."

Gail sat back in the seat. She couldn't tell how long ago it was since she felt so relaxed. Her body felt free; it was as if it had been encased for years in something tight and she had at last unloosened it, or Robbie had. He was nice, kind and nice. But it was true what she had said, he hadn't changed at all. He still acted like a smart alec, that was John's term for him, among others less complimentary. She knew a moment's stiffening of her body again. If John were to see her with him, there would be trouble. He had nearly gone mad when he knew that her dad had stayed with them after he had left the house. She understood it was only for a few days, but that was enough to make John go almost berserk. The fact that their father had gone to the Dunns seemed to concern him more than the reason for him to go to the Dunns. Her mother had not sent for Janet from that time, and neither of the Dunns had been mentioned since, not in her hearing anyway.

What would happen at home when John found out that his father was going to live with the Dunns again? Her mother's reactions, she felt, would be that her father was dropping to his original level and she'd likely leave it at that, but John's reaction would likely take an active form. She

142

had known for a long time now that John was vicious; if he didn't see eye to eye with you, he'd take it out of you in one way or another. Perhaps it was merely passing you day after day in the house without speaking until you were forced to make a move toward reconciliation. Or his retaliation might take the form of light table chat around the doings of Paul Birkett, who was now at Technical College.

The Birketts, like most of their friends, had faded away when the scandal hit the town. Not continuing at school, she lost touch with Anna, and Paul, the recipient of her adolescent painful love, slid from her horizon like a ship to an unknown destination. Only at times when she had incurred John's displeasure would she hear with whom Paul was now voyaging. First it was Tracy Meekan, an art student; next it was Gwen Stapeley; then one evening at supper he told his mother of Paul's engagement to a Miss Linda Ratcliffe, whose uncle was a lord. This was the night that Terry had bounced up from the table, exclaiming, "You make me sick!" Terry didn't like rows and it meant a lot that he had stood up to John, and on her behalf, on this occasion.

"Do you go to see your grannie every Saturday?"

"No, one week I'm on duty in the shop until six; that week I go to see her on Sunday."

"Well then, I'll work that out," he said, "and pop over and let you know how things are. What about that?"

"Thank you."

"What's your usual time for coming?"

"Around two-thirty."

"O.K. then. When he's settled in, I'll come and let you know. That's if we don't run into each other afore then." He cast a swift glance at her, but she was looking ahead. Her face was straight and he thought, "Aw, we're back to square one."

When he dropped her on the outskirts of the town, she stood on the pavement looking down at him as he sat with his hands on the wheel, and again he had the glimpse of the young Gail, for she smiled widely now and said, "Thanks, Robbie. I've . . . I've enjoyed this afternoon."

"Me, too." He grinned up at her. "Well, be seeing you."

"Yes, Robbie. Good-bye."

" 'Bye."

He set the car off with a zoom. My, my! Would you believe that? Wonders would never cease; she was quite human. Wait till he told his mam he'd had Miss Gail Blen-

143

heim out to tea, and she had promised to come and see Harry. What would she say to that? She'd say her son was a clever lad, that's what she'd say, and he felt a clever lad. In this moment he felt powerful, capable of achieving anything he set his mind to, anything.

Four

Robbie was waiting when Harry stepped through the prison gate. He did not immediately speak to him because for once he felt embarrassed. It was Harry who said quietly, "This is good of you, Robbie."

"Me mam's waiting along the road." He jerked his head toward the car and they both turned and walked toward it.

Janet was sitting in the back of the car. She looked up as Harry looked through the window; then when Robbie opened the door for him, he bent down, and when he was half in, he twisted around as if he was going to speak to her, but he turned away again and settled in his seat, and no one spoke until they were well out of town. Then Robbie came out with the only thing his mind gave to him. "It's a grand day," he said.

There was a moment's pause; then Harry repeated his words, "Yes, it's a grand day, Robbie."

As if Janet had been released by a spring, she now bent forward and, touching Harry's shoulder, said eagerly, "Oh, it's good to see you, Harry." She had just prevented herself from adding, "Out."

He put up his hand and placed it over hers and turned his face toward her. "It's good to see you, Janet." He looked into her face, then turned his eyes to Robbie, and said huskily, "What would I have done without you both?"

"God provides," said Janet.

"Huh!" Harry's laugh was quiet, even gentle, but mirthless, and he swung his head for a moment, then stopped suddenly, and bringing his eyes back to her, he said, "Well, there may be something in it after all, He provided the both of you."

Robbie now broke in, his voice holding an excited note, "I've got a surprise for you, Harry."

"Yes."

"I've bought a mansion."

"Oh, our Robbie!" Janet clicked her tongue. "Don't exaggerate so."

"Who's exaggeratin'?" When he turned around as he spoke

145

to her, she cried, "Look where you're going, you'll have us in the ditch."

"Well, that will learn you not to contradict me. As I said, I've bought a mansion, Harry."

"Dropping to bits with woodworm and dry rot," said Janet under her breath.

"Do you know Scarfield Mill, Harry?"

"Yes, Robbie. Yes, I know Scarfield Mill."

"Well, that's the place I've brought, and isn't that a mansion?"

"You've bought . . . Scarfield Mill? But wasn't it derelict? Is that the same place?"

"That's the same place," put in Janet. "He's mad, but I couldn't talk him into sanity."

"You don't live in Baker Street any longer?"

"We don't live in Baker Street anymore, Harry."

There was a pause before Harry said, "It sounds interesting, Robbie."

"It is. Just you wait until you see it, Harry. The prospects are endless."

"You've said something there," muttered Janet.

"I wish you'd shut up, woman; if I have any more of your old buck, I'll put you in lodgings."

"Anytime, anytime," said Janet, laughing now. "It would suit me. Life would be much easier, I'll tell you that."

And so they talked, trying to lighten Harry's first hour of freedom. And it was almost an hour to the minute when they passed the pithead, turned down the road and up the narrow high-banked lane toward the house.

"There! What do you think?" Robbie swept his hands from one corner of the house to the other, and as he did so Janet went in through the front door, saying over his shoulder,

"Don't tell him all at once, Harry; it might be too much for him."

Harry looked at the paneless windows, the gaping roofs, the damp mildewed walls, and what he thought was "He's joking." Then he looked at Robbie's face and he knew it was no joke. He knew that young Robbie Dunn had taken it on and was proud of it. He nodded at him now, saying, "As you say, I think it has prospects, although it will require a lot of work."

"Oh, that will get done with the years. But isn't it in a lovely setting? There's three acres of land with it and open country all around, and you can't see the pithead unless

146

you go up the hill beyond there; and then even that looks good. But come on in, I'll show you your room."

"You've got it furnished?" Harry sounded surprised as he walked slowly toward the front door, and Robbie said over his shoulder, "Just the stuff from Baker Street. But that won't have house room once I really get going. I mean to have the place lined with antiques. Mam laughs, but I'm serious."

In the hall Harry looked about him and said, "It must have been a beautiful place at one time."

"Aye, an' it will again. Come on through this way." Robbie led him down a passage and into a room that was cluttered with furniture and full of sunshine, and there Janet, busying herself at a gas stove, said, "We're in an awful mess, Harry, but I'll get straightened up within the next few days. Sit down, sit down and have a cup of tea and a bite."

Harry sat down and forced himself to eat the beef and tongue and salad that Janet heaped on his plate. It was odd, but he missed the clatter of the tin plates and the distinctive smell of men, imprisoned men. During the whole course of the meal he hardly spoke, leaving the talking to Robbie and Janet, who both, in their own particular ways, were trying to make things easy for him. He knew that he should say something off his own bat, but he couldn't. That was one of the things he'd have to get used to again, talking, starting a conversation. Yet there were words gnawing at his mind, forming a simple question, "Have you seen anything of Gail?" But they were impossible to get out. Then Robbie gave him the answer without the question having to be asked. Leaning toward him, he said, "I've got some good news for you."

His face moved into what should have been a smile as he waited.

"I've seen Gail a couple of times lately . . . an' she's going to come an' see you."

Harry put his cup slowly down on to his saucer and stared at it; then he rubbed one lip over the other several times before he asked simply, "When?".

"Well, it could be next Saturday or Sunday, Sunday likely. Yes, it'll be Sunday."

"But where will I meet her?"

"I told you, she's coming to see you here."

"Oh." Harry straightened his shoulders, and his voice slow, he said, "That's almost a week ahead; I couldn't put you out like that."

147

"What you talkin' about?" Robbie's voice was high now. "You're going to stay along of us."

"Oh, no. No!" Harry looked at Janet, who was sitting quietly at the end of the table crumbling some bread on her plate, and he added, "It's more than good of you, but . . . but I just couldn't."

"Well, where do you intend to go?" Robbie's voice was rough and Harry turned toward him, saying, "Well, I'll . . . I'll get a room, and a job of sorts."

"You've said it, Harry. And it'll be a job of sorts."

"Robbie!"

"You be quiet, Mam." He wagged his finger at her. "Harry knows what I'm talkin' about. He's got no more chance in this town than snow in hell and he knows it. Now look." He was bending toward Harry. "I've got all this planned out. I've got a job for you, an' it'll keep you going for years."

Harry was looking at him now as he asked, "What sort of a job?" There was no interest in his face; the only name you could put to his expression was blankness.

Robbie glanced at his mother and the glance said again, "Now you be quiet." Then looking back at Harry, he said slowly, "Rebuilding this house."

"What!"

"You heard. Rebuilding this house. Now look at it this way, Harry. I've got to pay a man to help me, I can't do this all by meself; in any case, it's going to take years, and if I employed a bloke regularly, let's face it, it would be union wages. Now I'm not going to offer you union wages, all I can offer you is board and lodgings and six quid a week to start. As I make a go of it in the shop, I'll put it up. I promise you that."

Harry was shaking his head in small movements. "It's very kind of you, Robbie, but . . ."

"It's not very kind of me," put in Robbie swiftly. "As usual I'm thinkin' of number one. I'm asking you to do me a good turn, an' I look at it as this way. Take it on just for a few months until you feel your feet, until you get yourself sort of acclimatized again, an' then if you find you don't want to stick, well and good, there'll be no harm done. I'll be thankful for what you've done by then."

"But, Robbie, I know nothing whatever about building. I did a bit of carpentry . . . in, in there, and that's all."

"That's all you need to know, man. It's carpentry that's needed here: window frames, door frames, paneling, roof raf-

148

ters, the lot. When it comes to bricklaying and plastering, we'll both learn as we go, but it's the woodwork that's important."

Harry looked from Robbie to Janet, but Janet had her eyes lowered. Her hands were still now on her lap. It was as if she was saying, "I'm having nothing to do with this."

"Janet." She looked up as he spoke. "What do you think about all this? I've got the impression that it's all being done for my benefit and I don't want that; I don't want to be carried, not by anyone."

"Oh, it isn't like that," Janet put in quickly now, and her voice was earnest because in this she knew she was speaking the truth. "You'll be helping Robbie, doing him a good turn, doing us both a good turn. But one thing"—her voice dropped—"if you want to go, you do that, Harry. Don't let either of us stop you."

Again he looked from one to the other, then said helplessly, "But where would I go at the present moment? I . . . I feel lost, all at sea so to speak. The funny thing is"—he looked down at the table, and taking up his knife, he began to move it around the plate like a man doodling with a pencil—"I've been thinking for some time that the best thing to do would be to get as far away from the town as possible, yet I knew I wouldn't be able to. As long as Gail's here, I knew I'd hang around, take anything just to see her and try to explain, if that's possible. She might understand, now she's older, that is unless her mind's been completely turned against me." He slanted his tired gaze toward Robbie. His eyes looked like those of a man who had gone a long time with little sleep, and Robbie, looking into them, said quietly, "I don't think you'll find that."

"No." Harry looked thoughtful now. "Whatever brainwashing was done, Gran would counteract it. That's the only thing that's given me comfort all this time."

Gran. Robbie looked swiftly at Janet, and she made a small motion with her head and he thought, "Aye, best leave that for a time; he's got enough to get on with at present."

But everything else was going according to plan. He felt he could congratulate himself. He had done Harry a good turn and he had no doubts about that, but at the same time he had done himself one outsize good turn, for give Harry a year or two on the house and with what he could do himself and perhaps a bit of help on a Sunday from Sid, and the place would be ready enough for him to put his big idea into practice. Boy! Yes, that would be something, his big idea.

He had forgotten for a moment why his mother wanted Harry to stay.

It was twenty-past three on Sunday afternoon and Robbie said they would be back around half-past. Harry was standing in front of the house near a ladder that was leaning against the rough scaffolding. He was on edge, apprehensive. He thought that if it was Esther who had been coming, he wouldn't have felt worked up like this, for now he had no feelings for or against Esther; where she was concerned there was a neutrality in his life. There was only one thing he blamed Esther for, and that was keeping Gail away from him during those weeks before the trial.

The past week had been surprisingly pleasant. He had worked ten hours a day and would have been willing to go on, only Janet had put her foot down. Janet, he found, was a surprising woman; apart from his knowledge of her as a child, and a young girl, when he remembered her being full of chitchat, and merry, and then during her visits to help in the house when she had appeared slightly reserved, he had really known nothing about her. Yet this week he had found out a lot about her. She was sympathetic and kind. But he had always known that much, that had been made clear in the black days two years ago. But during the past week he had come to recognize her as an intelligent woman. Her conversation was bracing; she even made the future appear bright. And that was something, for his future was a dark patch of which he was afraid.

As he stared toward the road he thought, "If everything goes right this afternoon, I'll be as happy as ever I'll be."

When he heard the car turn into the lane, he went hastily indoors, across the hall and into the kitchen, where Janet had a substantial tea all ready spread out, and he said to her, "I heard the car, Janet. Do you mind if I see her in my room?"

"Of course not. You go on and I'll send her in." He nodded and, turning hastily about, went down a passage and into a small room that held, along one side of it, a single bed, a chair, and a chest of drawers. On the bare floor at the other side were two tin baths and a large earthenware dish, the last hole in the rafters of that section of the roof explaining their presence.

He sat down on the edge of the bed and put his joined

150

hands between his knees. He could hear Robbie's voice now and Janet's muted tones, but he heard no sound of a third voice. His teeth were gritting against each other when the tap came on the door.

He only had to rise and take one step to open it and there she stood, his daughter, and he hardly recognized her. She was thinner, as he knew she would be, and her features were the same as he remembered them, but when he remembered them they had promised beauty, exceptional beauty, yet the girl before him was almost plain. Her fair hair, which had flowed like sunlit water down onto her shoulders, was pulled tightly back over her head. She was eighteen, yet she could have passed for any age up to twenty-five.

"My dear." The words were thick. He extended his hands tentatively toward her, but she didn't take them and she didn't speak. He gulped in his throat before he stepped back to let her enter the room; then he placed a chair for her and she sat down, and he sat on the bed again, facing her.

His hands gripped on his knees now, he said softly, "Oh, Gail, it's good to see you." He waited for her to speak, and when she didn't, he said formally, "How are you?"

She was staring at him, her eyes wide, her whole face tense. He watched her lips part as if she were about to speak; then there came a sound from her throat as if a balloon had burst inside. The eruption was painful, for she gripped her neck, closed her eyes tightly, and swallowed. His hands were moving out to her again when, as if the past two years had never been, she flung herself forward and into his arms, and sobbing loudly, she cried, "Oh, Dad! Dad!" And he held her as he used to do and rocked her silently, his own eyes tightly screwed up now against the pain and happiness that was filling him. He hadn't lost her, she was still his.

151

Five

"Why are you doing your hair like that?"

Gail looked through the mirror at her mother, then said, "Because I want a change."

"It suited you better drawn straight back."

"It didn't."

"Don't answer me in that fashion, Gail; I've told you before."

"Well, it didn't. And you know it didn't."

Esther looked at her daughter, her eyes narrowed. The change in her was more startling today. Could it be she had a boy? No, that was impossible. She had rejected the idea before. But she was different. Something had happened. Could it be that she had seen him? No, that was impossible, too; John picked her up from work most evenings, and when she went to the pictures, she herself accompanied her. The only place she went to alone was the Old People's Home. Well, she would find out today if there was anything going on there.

As Gail pushed past her to go out of the room, she said, "Terry's going with you to see Gran."

"What!" Gail stopped dead. "Terry? Why? Not one of you's bothered to go and see Gran before, so why is Terry starting now? . . . Oh, don't tell me." She thrust her head forward. "I know."

"What are you talking about?"

"You know what I'm talking about." She marched out of the room, across the landing and down the stairs, to see Terry standing in the hall looking somewhat shamefaced.

She paused on the bottom step and stared at him, and he lifted his gaze quickly from hers and looked upward to his mother standing on the stair head. Then turning abruptly, he went to the front door, jerked it open, and hurried out.

Gail followed more slowly, and she resisted coming abreast of him until they reached the street, but as soon as she came to his side, he muttered under his breath, "Don't blame me, I didn't want this. It isn't my idea of a Saturday afternoon out."

"Then why didn't you tell her?" she snapped at him, but

152

kept her gaze directly ahead. And he came back, his tone equaling hers, "Well, it was either me or John, and I thought I was the lesser of two evils for you."

"John would never give up his rugger."

"That's all you know. He was quite prepared to do it if I hadn't said I would come with you."

They were looking at each other now and she said, as if the knowledge was new to her, "He hates Dad more than she does."

Terry made no answer to this, but he looked ahead again as he asked softly, "Have you seen him?"

"Yes."

"Is that why you've been late this last couple of times?"

"Yes."

"Where is he?"

"He's staying with Janet."

"Janet Dunn?"

Again they were looking at each other. "Yes, Janet Dunn. Why do you sound shocked, he's got to stay somewhere?"

"But that place in Baker Street."

"They don't live in Baker Street anymore."

"Where then?"

"Robbie's taken a big old house out beyond the Beular Mine, it's called Scarfield Mill. Dad's helping to rebuild it."

"Dad helping to rebuild a house?" His voice trailed away.

"Yes." Her head was thrust out toward him now, her voice cold again. "He learned to do it in prison."

"All right, all right, you needn't shout." He looked about him. "There's enough people know already."

They were waiting for the bus when Gail, looking pleadingly at him, asked, "What are you going to do? I mean, are you going to tell her?"

"What do you take me for?"

She smiled faintly at him, then said, "Thanks, Terry."

He hung his head until she asked, "Would you like to come along with me and see him?"

His head still remained bowed as he muttered, "There'd be the devil to pay if she found out, or worse still if John found out, and especially as it's Robbie Dunn he's with. You know what he thinks of him. There'd be murder."

"They need know nothing if we're back in time."

He raised his head. "You think it'll be all right?"

"Yes."

"O.K. I'd . . . I'd like to see him. How is he?"

153

"He's, he's fine, but sort of quiet. It'll make him happy to see you."

He drooped his head again and they remained silent; but when the bus came she said, "Let's go on top." For a moment she was a young girl again, eager for excitement, even if it was only riding on top of a bus. Life wasn't so awful. She had her dad again and Terry was on their side.

Six

The days drifted into weeks and the weeks into months, during which life seemed to stand still for Harry. He felt he was marking time; as a prelude to what he didn't know. There was enough work on the house to keep him busy for another two years, but was that what he wanted? He just didn't know. What he did know was that if he had wanted to leave tomorrow, he wouldn't have done so, because his gratitude to Robbie and Janet would have compelled him to stay as long as they required him.

When thinking of gratitude, he put Robbie first, for he knew it was he who had made this quiet retreat possible. And living here was like a retreat. Except for the picnickers who came onto the hill behind the house on a sunny day, and Gail, who came every Saturday or Sunday, accompanied by Terry, he saw no one other than Janet and Robbie, that is, except on a Sunday or a Wednesday when Robbie would drive him out to see his grandmother. And if it would have been possible to get out of these visits he would have done so, for the sight of that high-spirited old woman sitting among thirty older old women was one of the worst things he had been called upon to bear, equal in its way to his early estrangement from Gail.

There had been suggestions from both Gail and Robbie to alter the situation. Robbie suggested bringing her out as soon as he got a room ready. Well, he had got a room ready, but she wouldn't come. And then there was Gail's suggestion that they should find a little place and the three of them live together. He hadn't given his grandmother the opportunity to refuse this suggestion because he had never put it to her. He knew that his lack of enthusiasm for her proposal had upset Gail. She couldn't understand why he wasn't for it and he couldn't tell her. How explain that he didn't feel capable of taking on responsibility of a home ever again? How to explain that he felt so unsure of himself that at times he wished he was back in that small room where he had no control over his own life, where his every action was set to a timetable?

When he allowed himself to think, he likened his present

155

existence to the life in an open prison; he knew what work he had to do, his meals were put before him, and in the evening he could read or look at television, and for privileges there was the occasional jaunt in the car. It was all he wanted.

And then came the morning that Robbie said, "I've got an idea, Harry. Like to hear it?"

"Fire away." Harry smiled, picked up a piece of toast, put some marmalade on it, bit into it, then looked across the table at Robbie, who was leaning back in his chair with a cup of tea in his hand.

"Well, before I start," said Robbie, now looking at Janet, "I want you to be quiet, Mam, because before I open me mouth I can hear you say, 'Oh, no, you don't'; so will you oblige me, Mrs. Dunn, by keeping yours closed?"

"That all depends." Janet nodded at him. "If it's anything harebrained—"

"Harebrained, tatty-haired, long-haired, it doesn't matter, it's something I've been chewing on for months. I thought I'd have a chew on it for another year or so, but because Harry there has done such a good job, I could get going anytime."

"Something about the house?" asked Harry now.

"Something about the house, Harry. . . . The roof's all done, all the windows in the front are done, the whole front's presentable and the front's what I want. The long room's done—"

"Look! I don't know what you've got in mind but you said that was going to be our sitting—"

"It will be, it will be. Didn't I tell you to keep it shut." He leaned toward Janet. Then looking at Harry again, he went on, "As I said, the long room's done and you've done more than half the paneling on the hall. Now how long will it take you to finish the woodwork there?"

"Oh"—Harry paused, thinking—"another month I should say. Perhaps a bit longer."

"Four weeks, five weeks, six weeks, that'll be fine. Now this is what I propose." He put his cup on the table and laid a hand palm downward at each side of it. "I aim to furnish the hall, an' the long room as showrooms, period rooms, and that'll only be a start." He now lifted one hand sharply in Janet's direction, saying, "What did I tell you? Now keep it quiet for a minute until I'm finished." He drew in a deep breath, then addressed Harry again. "It could be asked

156

who's going to come out here from Fellburn to buy antiques, they're not an antique-minded lot, except those on Brampton Hill and they're thinning out fast. Well, I'm not going to look for my market in Fellburn. I have four good customers in Newcastle and I'm sending stuff the morrow to a house in Doncaster. Now what I propose when these Newcastle lot come into the shop is to bring them out here. They're moneyed people, two in shipping, one in oil, and one running a chain of shops, so many now he can't count them. Nor can he speak English; and his wife's even worse. I could give them some pointers, that'll tell you how bad they are." He nodded and grinned at Harry. "But they've got this thing about furnishing the house with antiques and he, being a businessman, got the idea that if he can pick up bargains locally why go farther afield. Now from people like them it's only a step to the American market, and that's where I'm going, and not through half-a-dozen middlemen either. Well, what do you think, Harry?"

Harry stared at Robbie; then he looked at Janet, and he said, "Well, it isn't what I think surely, it's your mother, isn't it?"

"Look, I can manage her, I always have." His grin in Janet's direction was wide now. Then again he said, "Well, tell me what you think?"

"I think it's a very astute business idea and I can see you making it work."

"I can't on me own."

"No?"

"No. I can't be in two places, or three places for that matter, at once, at the sales, at the shop, and here. Sid is not bad in the shop, but then he's not good. I've got to put up with Sid and pray to God he won't give the things away while I'm out. But here I want not only a salesman, but . . . well. Well, to put it bluntly someone with a bit of class like yourself."

"Aw, Robbie." Harry shook his head heavily.

"Now don't aw Robbie me in that way, I mean it. What I'm offering you is a partnership."

Harry's head came up with a jerk. "A partnership? But you know how I stand, I've got—"

"You've got everything I want. You've got the ability to build this place, which you're practically doing on your own an', as I've said, you've got a presence, you'll be able to talk to people."

157

"Oh, no, no." Harry's tone was definite now. "I don't want to talk to people, Robbie."

"But you've got to talk to people sometimes, Harry. Look, I've been wanting to have this out with you. You've got to talk to people, you've got to get out and mix. You've done a marvelous job here and you'll go on doing a marvelous job, but you're not in a monastery, man. And that's how you've been living except for the one female here." He nodded toward his mother.

"He's right, Harry." Janet's voice was soft, and Harry turned and looked at her, and she said again, "He's right in all he says. He nearly always is. He knows what he wants, but he can't do it on his own. If you turn it down, it won't mean that he'll give up the idea, he'll only have to get somebody else, and they won't be one quarter as good as you."

Harry's chin was now deep on his chest and his voice was a thick mutter as he said, "It's all so one-sided."

"One-sided, be damned!" Robbie rose to his feet. "I never do anything unless I think there's a good profit in it for me." He stabbed his finger across the table. "Make no mistake about that. Anyway, man, your own sense should tell you I've been making a profit out of you for weeks; where would I get anybody to do the work you've done for six quid a week? You've put thousands on this place. Wait till that little squirt, Pearson, comes to value it the next time; he won't see it being two thousand down the drain, bet your life he won't, he'll be falling over himself to put up the premium. Well now, what do you say?"

"What can I say, Robbie?"

"It's settled then. Everything you sell here we split the profit."

"But I know nothing about period furniture, Robbie."

"I've thought of that, and I bet when you get through the two dozen *Apollo*'s I've got in the back shop you'll know twice as much as I do; then you can come to one or two sales with me just to get the feeling. Look, what about coming down to the shop this mornin'? I got a load of stuff in on Friday. It's been knocked about a bit, but I'd like you to see it as it is afore it's done up. What d'you say?"

"There's the hall; if you want it finished, I should be getting on with it."

"Look, the hall can wait for one morning." Then, his voice dropping, he added, "You've got to come into town sometime, Harry, and this morning's as good as any."

158

Harry looked from Robbie to Janet, and she said quietly, "He's right, Harry."

An hour later when Harry, standing in the back shop, looked down on a jumble of chests of drawers, Victorian chairs with the stuffing sticking out, old-fashioned couches, and battered card tables, he thought, "I wouldn't give them house room."

Pointing to a couch, Robbie said, "You won't recognize that piece when you see it again, it'll be done in Regency stripe and be known as a chaise longue. Thirty pounds, madam, very reasonable."

"Never!" said Harry on a small laugh.

"It's a fact. I'm tellin' you."

Harry shook his head.

"And wait until you see it against the dark paneling of that hall. That's the setting for it. An' you needn't believe me, only time will tell, but in some cases that setting will double the price."

Again Harry shook his head. It was all he could do.

It was just after twelve when they left the shop and crossed the market, and it wasn't until they turned the corner by the bank that Harry realized that he must pass Peamarsh's and the thought checked his step. It wasn't that he hadn't been aware of how close he was to the office; all the way to town he had thought of the possibility of running into one of them; but listening to Robbie in the shop and sharing, in a way, his enthusiasm for the new venture had for the moment pushed Peamarsh's to the back of his mind. But now, there it was across the road, big letters heading a stone facade, and down the steps into the street almost opposite to him were walking three men, Arthur McMullan, Tom Vosey, and a man who was a stranger to him.

Arthur McMullan stopped for a perceivable second, looked at him, then walked on; Tom Vosey paused a little longer, then he joined the other two.

Robbie looked at Harry. He was standing as if glued to the pavement. If he had been facing the other way, he could have pretended he was looking into the windows of Howard's, the jeweler's, but he was standing half facing the steps across the road. "Come on, man." Robbie touched his arm, and Harry allowed himself to be led away like a blind man.

They had gone but a short distance when there came hurried steps behind them and a voice said, "Just a minute."

They both stopped and Robbie turned, but Harry stood looking straight ahead.

"How are you, Harry?" Tom Vosey stood to Harry's side and Harry, moving his neck slowly around, looked at him and said, "Oh, I'm all right, Tom. How's yourself?"

"Fine, Harry, fine." Tom Vosey now glanced at Robbie, then back to Harry, and his voice was tentative as he said, "Would . . . would you care to come for a drink?"

"No, thanks. Tom. I'm . . . I'm on a piece of business."

"Oh!" Tom nodded, again glancing at Robbie. Then he said, "Everything all right with you, Harry?"

"Splendid, Tom."

"That's good. I'll be seeing you around some time then?"

"Yes, Tom, be seeing you some time. Good-bye."

"Good-bye, Harry."

Tom Vosey went one way, Harry, accompanied by Robbie the other, and when they reached the end of the street and Harry hadn't opened his mouth, Robbie said, "What about having a bite to eat in town?"

It was some seconds before Harry replied, "If it's all the same to you, Robbie, I'd rather get home."

"It's O.K. with me; I always like me mam's cooking better than anything they give you in a restaurant." He made the remark sound light, but it fell flat.

In the car Robbie began to talk. He talked rapidly, asking himself questions and giving himself the answers, and all the while Harry sat silent, until they came within half a mile of where they turned off the main road into the lane. This stretch of the road was on an incline and had a sharp bend in it. It was when they were approaching the bend that Robbie cut off what he was saying to exclaim loudly, "Look at this madman tearing up here; he's passing two cars behind me and we're almost on the bend. God! Will they never learn? You could wish somethin' would happen to teach him a lesson. An' look!" His voice was even higher now, drawing Harry's attention to the passing car. "It's full of kids."

As the car passed him within yards of the bend, Robbie blasted his horn once. He was about to do it a second time when his hand became still and he almost closed his eyes as he saw the car swerve quickly in front of him to avoid the oncoming bus. If he put on his brakes, he knew the cars behind would pile up into him. He held his breath, kept

160

his pace steady, and they were around the corner, the car full of children speeding away in front.

Harry was sitting on the edge of the seat now and he asked quietly, "You all right, Robbie?"

"Aye. Yes, just." There was a slight quiver in his voice. "But only just I'm tellin' you. That bloody, mad swine. God! If only I could get me hands on him. And the car full of kids. You saw them, there must have been six."

As they turned into the lane, he drew in another long breath; then relaxing in his seat, he said, "You know what? I can tell you what's going to happen to that lot. Very shortly those kids are going to say, 'Why are we wearing haloes, Daddy?' and Daddy'll say, 'Because I was a clever bugger.'"

Why are we wearing haloes, Daddy? Because I was a clever bugger. That was funny. And the way Robbie had said it. Oh, that was funny. Why are we wearing haloes, Daddy? Because I was a clever bugger. Slowly Harry's shoulders began to shake, his head drooped and he put his fingers to his brow. The chuckle came into his throat, and when it passed through his lips, it had turned into a laugh; and then it grew louder and louder.

When Robbie had seen that Harry was amused, he had laughed too, but now his laughter had faded away because Harry's laughter wasn't merriment. He wanted to say to him, "Give over, man." The sound was embarrassing, it was sort of hysterical. When Harry's hand groped out toward him and touched the wheel, he stopped the car. And now, to his concern, he saw Harry was no longer laughing, he was crying; the tears were spurting from his eyes and running over his spread fingers. His shoulders were hunched and his body was curved downward. Robbie said quietly, "Aw, man, don't take on like that. Nothing's worth feeling that much over." He ended harshly, "You'll see your day with the lot of them yet, you mark my words."

When Harry groped at the handle of the door and, pushing it open, got out, he leaned across the seat and said, "Where you going?" And Harry, unable to speak, pointed to the hill behind the house, and at this Robbie nodded to him, then watched him go around behind the car, jump the ditch into the field, then cross it.

When he drove up to the house, Janet came to the door and, seeing him alone, asked anxiously, "Where's Harry?"

He pointed upward over the house, saying briefly, "He's gone up the hill."

"Up the hill?" Janet followed him closely indoors. "Why's he gone up the hill?"

"He ran into some of his old pals near the market and they cut him, except one. He came back, but he made it as awkward as hell. I think it was the last straw. He broke down just along the road; I'd leave him until he gets over it."

Janet walked slowly across the hall, down the passage and into her own room, and there, sitting on the foot of her bed, she gripped the rail and laid her head against the wooden post. Would this make him leave? Go away somewhere by himself, or perhaps with Gail and Mrs. O'Toole? Either way it would be like death to her. She had never been so happy in her life as she had been during these last five months, but at this moment she was sick deep down in her soul, sick with fear that this wonderful existence—and to her it was a wonderful existence—was about to end.

She didn't know if Harry had any idea of her true feelings for him; she doubted whether he had, because some men, good men like him, couldn't see what was under their noses. She lifted her head and stared at the wall and, like a moving picture, she saw her life in it; all her young days subject to her parents' religious bias, her married life without joy, except when her son was born. He had been the only comfort she had had, but it had never been enough, there was always a gap in her, and only one person could fill it.

She rose to her feet, opened the window, and stepped over the low sill into the courtyard—she didn't want to run into Robbie at this moment. She walked across the yard, through a gate in the rough fence, across the field, and mounted the hill.

He was lying on the grass in the shelter of an outcrop of rock when she saw him, and she knelt by his side and touched his shoulder. It was a moment before he raised his head, and she was surprised by the look on his face. She had expected anguish, bitterness, anything but the calmness she saw there, and his voice too was calm when he said, "It's all right, Janet, it's over."

"They're nothing but a lot of nowts," she said.

"Aw, it wasn't only that. It had to come. It's as well it did. I feel better." He brought himself into a sitting position by her side and he stared across the valley for a moment before he said, "It's as if I've been swimming underwater for years and at last broke surface. I feel free, freer than I ever remember being before. Yet nothing has

162

changed. It's funny, but I know this is another starting point and I won't go back. As Robbie said, I'll see me day with most of them. Not that I want that but . . . but I want to get moving, do something." He looked at her and she asked in a voice scarcely above a whisper, "Does that mean you're going?"

"No, no." His reply came quickly. "Robbie's given me a chance; I'm going to take it up, but in an entirely different way from what I expected to do this morning." He put out his hand and covered hers now, saying, "I don't know what I would have done without you both. It frightens me remembering the state I was in a few months back and where I might have drifted if you hadn't been there that morning. You've been a good friend, Janet."

They were looking straight into each other's eyes as she said, "I'll always be ready to be whatever you want me to be, Harry."

There was no mistaking the implication of her words. His eyes widened slightly. Janet and him. He'd never thought. Well, yes; years ago, his mam and dad used to chip him about Janet because he could never go out back or front without he ran into her, but he only took that as the result of the proximity of Janet living upstairs and they down and of sharing the same backyard. Anyway, she had married before him, and to an orthodox Jew. As he looked at her he saw her as she was when a young girl. There was the same look in her eyes. Poor Janet. And all these years coming back and forward to the house helping; he had never even guessed. Well, now that he had, what about it? He was still married, wasn't he? But say he wasn't, then what about it? He received no answer to this, only another question. How would he like living without Janet now? And to this the answer came promptly, he wouldn't. No, no, he wouldn't. Janet brought him a sort of peace, security; yes, that was the word, security, for although in the last half hour he had come to know where he was going, he also knew he was a man who would always need security, the security of a home and a woman.

Apart from Gail it was almost three years since he had touched a woman, and when Janet fell against him, he held her stiffly until she began to tremble and to mutter his name over and over again. Then his arms tightened about her and he buried his face in her black shining hair, and there returned to him a feeling he hadn't known since the early

163

days of his marriage. But the feeling was immediately punctured by the thought of Esther, and her moral point of view rose before him like a battlement through which a divorce would never penetrate.

Seven

For the second time within four days Esther Blenheim was experiencing a feeling that really terrified her, for she was being consumed by a rage that urged her to get something into her hands and smash it. All her life she had assumed a calm exterior. Daily small tribulations had never ruffled her; the greater issues occasioned by family life might have disturbed her inwardly, but on the surface she appeared in control. Her mother had once said to her that emotions not only tear you to shreds inside but they aged you, and you could say that on this advice Esther had based her life, because deep down she was a vain woman, and this had been proved, if only to herself, within the past few days.

When she had received the letter from the solicitor stating that her husband was seeking a divorce, the facade of years had cracked. She had read the letter at breakfast and she didn't remember leaving the table and getting upstairs into her room, but she did remember picking up the first thing she saw, which was a petticoat, and rending it from top to bottom.

The coaching of years had quickly cried a halt to the fury of her hands, but not to her mind. She had sat pulling one finger after another listening to the knuckles cracking like castanets while startling vituperations frothed from her lips. Six months out of prison and he had found another woman! And in Fellburn—he had gone back to that girl, that dirty slut. She had imagined he hadn't come back to the town after he had come out of prison or he would in some way have tried to get in touch with Gail. But the solicitor's letter was from Fellburn, so from that she gathered he was still here. And this fact alone disturbed her, for she couldn't imagine him being in the town all this time and not trying to contact Gail.

It wasn't until this morning she had answered the letter, and to the effect that her husband knew her views on divorce and she wished to receive no further communication on the subject.

She had mentioned the matter to no one, not even her father, for she told herself there was no need, as nothing

165

was going to come of it, and since the letter was posted, her calm demeanor had taken control again, at least on the surface.

But now, here was John telling her something that was engendering rage even more fierce than the previous bout. She wouldn't believe it. When she could speak, she said just that to him, stuttering on the words. "I-I don't believe it. You've—you've made a mistake. No, I can't believe it. I won't, I won't."

"Mother! Sit down." He took her by the shoulders and pressed her into a chair; then bending over her and staring into her face, he said, "It's true, I've told you. For weeks now I've suspected our Terry was up to something because he's gone with her on Saturday afternoons without a murmur; and you said yourself she'd changed."

The perspiration was hanging in beads on her brow and around her lips, even her neck was running sweat, yet her flesh felt cold. She gulped as she said, "Robbie Dunn?"

"Robbie Dunn." John gritted his teeth on the name. "There he was, waiting outside the home, and out they came and got into his car and drove away."

"But—but your father? You're sure?"

"Of course I'm sure. Didn't I follow them? When they turned up Cooper's Lane, I knew it led to a dead end to that old derelict house. It used to be derelict, you should see it now."

"And you're sure it was Janet?"

He bared his teeth and the words sounded like a hiss. "Yes. Yes, I've told you. She was standing with him watching the others sliding down the hill; the three of them were laughing and acting like lunatics."

She closed her eyes and began to pray, beseeching God to take this terrible anger away from her. Her fingers were plucking at each other, desirous again of rending something. With her eyes still closed she said, her voice beseeching now, "But—but about the other. You're not just making it up about Gail and him . . . be-because you don't like him?"

"That's stupid reasoning." He straightened himself, pushed his shoulders back, and drew his chin in. "I told you, when they were going back to the house they kept way behind the others. I lost sight of them for a bit because I had to move along the hedge, but when I next saw them they had their arms around each other." Again he was talking through his teeth. "If ever there was a two-faced little brat it's her. She goes around here looking like someone in a closed

166

order, but if you could have seen her today, snuggling up to that filthy little Jew. Ugh! I wanted to vomit. It was all I could do to stop myself from dashing out and knocking him silly."

"What—what time is it?" She had her head down.

"Ten to five."

"They should be here any minute; leave it to me." She raised her head now. "Do you hear? Leave it to me." As she finished speaking, there came to them the sound of the front door opening and she rose from the chair and walked around the couch toward the fire and, turning, she stood with her back to it. She could always manage situations better standing on her feet.

Gail and Terry had learned to alter their expressions as soon as they entered the drive. They always came into the house soberly, Terry assuming an air of slight resentment, while Gail's expression suggested acceptance, if begrudgingly. They hadn't planned their attitudes, but they knew they were a necessary extension of the whole deception.

Today they found it harder than usual to put on their masks. Gail couldn't remember enjoying herself so much for years. That slide, and them all laughing, and the wonderful tea after, and Terry being amusing and her father looking happy. Yes, he had looked happy. She must remember that, he was happy.

When he had first told her he wanted to marry Janet, she had been amazed and frankly a little shocked. Janet, who had worked for them; Janet, who was a Jewess; Janet, who was the mother of Robbie, and Robbie was— Well, what was Robbie? A typical Jew, a market Jew, as John called him, brash, go-getting, common—but behind it all, kind, thoughtful, a good friend, as he had proved to be to her father. If her dad married Janet, it would make him Robbie's stepfather and Robbie and her stepbrother and sister. Neither of these facts appealed to her. That was until her dad had taken her up the hill and had talked to her about things that she had never heard mention before: his early life, when he had lived almost in the same house as Janet, and her devotion to him, which he had been too blind to notice.

"Are you going to ask Mother for a divorce?" she had said, and he answered, "Yes."

"Do you think she will?"

"I don't know; I doubt it."

"Then—then what'll you do?"

167

When he had said bluntly, "I'll live with Janet," she hadn't been shocked.

She knew that her mother must have received her father's application for the divorce earlier in the week, but she had made no reference to it, she wouldn't. It was another shame-tinged secret to add to her martyrdom.

They had hung their things in the cloakroom and together they entered the sitting room and together they stopped just within the door and looked to where Esther was standing on the hearth rug, and John at the head of the couch, both apparently waiting for them.

"Well, what are you standing there for? Are you afraid to come in?"

Terry blinked and glanced quickly at Gail but Gail was staring across the room at her mother.

"Where've you been?" The question was addressed directly to Gail, and before she answered it, she felt Terry moving away from her side. If there was any lying to do, he was going to let her do it; Terry hated upsets. "You know where I've been, to see Gran," she said.

"And after?"

Gail slowly turned her gaze from her mother to John. So that was it, they knew. John had been snooping. Looking back at her mother, she said boldly, "You know all about it, so why ask?"

"I want to hear you tell me where you went after visiting the home."

Gail lifted her shoulders high up around her neck; it was an attitude, she knew, that always angered her mother, but that was a small issue now. And she walked toward the other end of the couch from John before saying, "Well, I don't suppose I can enlarge on what my dear brother has told you, but I've been to see Dad." As she looked into her mother's face, she saw the bitterness swamp it like a tidal wave.

"You lying, cheating, little—" As Esther clenched her hands together, her flow of words trailed away and Gail put in harshly, "Who made me lie and cheat? You did, you! Anyway, I've a right to see him, he's my father."

"You have no rights, as you say, you're under my care and protection."

"Don't be silly." The tone was scornful. "You're talking as if we were early Victorians."

"Don't dare speak to me like that, do you hear?" Esther

168

moved to the front of the couch, her body arched. "I will not be spoken to in that manner."

"Well, don't talk nonsense. You can't tie me up, although you've had a jolly good try."

"Don't you make any mistake, my girl, I can tie you up; there's ways and means of tying silly girls like you up to protect them from men like him."

"Men like him! What do you mean? Men like him." Gail's eyes slowly widened. "You talk as if he was a mad beast or something. It's as if you had never known him. Anyway, I know now that if he had told the truth about why he hit grandfather he would never have been given the outrageous sentence. He let them put the wrong construction on it to save me any more worry and embarrassment. Yes, and to save your face from getting red. And it would have been red, wouldn't it, if the truth had come out about your dear father?"

Esther was beyond words; she could only stare at this daughter, who dared to recall the shocking incident that had wrecked their lives. Even when Gail went on harshly, "But I know what's getting you now, it's the divorce, isn't it? You don't want him yourself and you don't want anyone else to have him, least of all Janet."

Esther couldn't speak, that was until John, looking at her, repeated, "Divorce?" Then she stepped back from the couch, put her hand to her cheek, and muttered, "What did you say? Janet?"

It was evident to Gail that the matter of the divorce had come as a surprise to John, but the association of Janet's name with her father was acting as an even greater shock to her mother. When Esther exclaimed again in a low voice, "Janet! Janet Dunn?" Gail felt a momentary feeling of pity for her because she was remembering how she felt when her father had broken the news to her.

"Is this true? He's asked for a divorce?" John's hand was out touching his mother's arm, trying to draw her attention toward him; but she didn't look at him as she said dully, "Yes, yes, it's true." And now her face moved into a mirthless smile, her upper lip showing all her even teeth, and she nodded at Gail as she said, "And so he wants to marry Janet Dunn. Your father wants to marry Janet Dunn. Well, he's sunk to the right level, but he'll never marry Janet Dunn, not while I'm alive."

Gail was staring at her mother as if hypnotized. The room was utterly quiet now until, her voice breaking the silence

169

like a high whistle, she almost screamed, "Then he'll live with her. You can't stop him doing that."

The silence fell on them again, and during it Esther drew herself to her full height; she moistened her lips while the muscles of her face twitched and those in her neck stood out like cords. She was letting the silence say that the matter was closed. She had for the moment forgotten Robbie Dunn, but John hadn't, for now, moving toward Gail, he demanded, "And what about you and that Robbie Dunn, eh?"

Gail stared at him. She was in no way intimidated by his attitude. "And what about me and Robbie Dunn?" she asked, her eyes widening.

"You must be hard up for a fellow, cheapening yourself with a dirty little Jew like him."

"Don't you dare call him a dirty little Jew." She even advanced a step toward him. "He's got more in his little finger than you've got in your whole body. It's jealousy that's always hit you with regards to Robbie, you're jealous of him."

"Oh, my God!"

Esther didn't chastise her son for blasphemy at this stage, and John went on laughing scornfully now, "You must be joking, jealous of that! The point is, I won't stand for a sister of mine necking in public with a little runt like—"

"You're lying! I've never"—she had to force herself to say the word—"necked in public with him, or anyone else."

"Look." He was yelling now. "Face the fact that I saw you. I saw you with my own eyes today. My dear brother there"—he cast a swift threatening glance to where Terry was standing at the far side of the window—"my father and"—he paused—"his mistress were trotting on in front, but you two stayed behind, remember? And don't tell me you weren't necking."

Gail's mouth was hanging wide, her eyes stretched. She was remembering that she had stepped onto a frozen puddle in the field and had slipped, and Robbie had put his arm out and caught her, and they had stood laughing together for a moment. She had felt odd, sort of excited at the close contact with him; it was the first time he had touched her, he had never even helped her in or out of the car; and then, all of a sudden she had been close to him, pressed to his chest, her cheek near his chin, his breath, like white smoke, fanning her face. When he had released her, she had been unable to speak, and he hadn't said anything either.

But, necking! She defended herself harshly now, "I slipped; he stopped me from falling, that was all. Do you hear. THAT WAS ALL!"

"Oh, Lord, with the experience you've had lately I would have thought you'd have come up with a better one than that." His tone was derisive, his eyes blazing. "Who do you think you're talking to?"

"I know who I'm talking to, a low-down sneak, that's who I'm talking to. You've always been a sneak, you always will, you couldn't be straight if you tried, even since you were small."

"That's enough! That's enough!" Esther was holding up her hand, and once more she addressed herself solely to Gail. "Listen to me," she said, her voice sounding strangely calm. "I forbid you to see that boy. Do you hear? You are not to associate with him in any way. If you do, I'll take steps, legal steps to put a stop to it. I suppose you've heard of being made a ward of court?"

"Ward of court!" Gail's voice was full scorn. "Don't be so ridiculous. You know what you are? You're ludicrous. Now listen, 'cos I'm going to tell you something." She was bending over the end of the couch, her body strained forward as if she was aiming to bring her face in contact with her mother's. "And listen carefully, because I mean it. I'm going to marry Robbie Dunn, so what do you think of that, eh? Whether you divorce Dad or not, I'm going to marry Robbie Dunn." She swung her angry gaze from her mother to John, and bouncing her head at him, she cried, "And you can do what you damn well like about that." The silence fell heavily on the room again and no one broke it as she turned and rushed out.

She almost fell into her bedroom, such was the speed with which she ran across the landing and flung herself at the door. Once inside, she didn't put on the light but groped her way to the window and, extending her arms, gripped each side of the framework. Her whole body was shaking with a mixture of amazement, fear, and cold. What on earth! What in the name of heavens! What . . . WHAT had possessed her to say such a thing? Marry Robbie Dunn, when he had never even looked at her in that way, never even as much as touched her hand until this afternoon? She must have gone stark staring mad. What if John went to him? What if her mother wrote? Her head sank deep onto her chest. She would die of shame. She didn't love him, he didn't love her, then why, why had she said that?

Oh, God! She turned about and threw herself face downward on the bed and she bit tightly on the corner of the pillow, but she didn't cry. She mustn't cry, she told herself bitterly; what she must do was to think, and think clearly of what she was going to say to Robbie when he asked her for an explanation.

It was about seven o'clock on the Monday evening when Esther, without announcing herself in any way, went into Gail's room and, closing the door behind her, looked at her daughter and said quietly, "I want to talk to you."

Gail was sitting at the dressing table, and after one quick glance in her mother's direction, she lowered her head and started to sort among some oddments on the tray in front of her.

While Esther Blenheim stood looking at the back of her daughter's head, she told herself that she must keep calm. She couldn't believe that only two days had elapsed since Saturday, for she had crowded so much painful thinking into them that they appeared like months. The outcome of this cathartic process was that she was about to waive her moral principles in order to save her daughter years of unhappiness; she was choosing the lesser of two very real evils. At least that's how it appeared to her.

"Look at me, Gail."

Gail slowly raised her eyes from the tray and looked at her mother's reflection through the mirror. She didn't know what she was up to now, but undoubtedly it would be something twisted; she didn't really care what it was as long as she didn't hear her say, "I've written to Robbie Dunn." Her mother hadn't spoken to her during the past two days and she'd been afraid to break her silence.

Esther, looking at the young tight drawn face, said, "I want to make a bargain with you." She paused, then went on slowly, "I don't believe in divorce. Your father has always known that; I've—I've already refused his request but" —she swallowed twice and nodded her head a number of times before ending—"I'd be willing to give him what he wants if you'll give up all idea of marrying that boy."

Gail was facing her now, having swung swiftly around on the stool, and Esther, taking this as a prelude to a verbal onslaught and a refusal, held up her hand and cried, "Now listen, listen. In the first place, and I mean this, it's you I'm thinking of. That boy—that boy's not in your class, you know he's not. You wouldn't be married to him five minutes

172

before you were ashamed of him. I know what I'm talking about. He's— I'm going to say it, he's a Jew, he looks a Jew of Jews, he thinks like a Jew, he acts like a Jew. You would be more likely to be at ease with a Negro than you would with him after a while. You have nothing in common." She paused again while she stared down into her daughter's face, and her voice dropping to a whisper, she said, "There it is, it's in your hands. I'll give your father the divorce if you'll do this, break off—break off all connections with Robbie Dunn."

Gail slowly lowered her gaze from her mother's face, then her head moved downward. She had the desire to laugh. It was gurgling in her. She felt sick with relief. She kept her head bent as her mother went on talking, almost pleadingly now, saying, "You think me cruel, but you'll thank me later on."

Esther stopped and stood staring down at the center of the bent head. The fair hair looked beautiful, alive and springing, and she remembered that at one time all of her daughter had promised to be beautiful. And she could be yet. But whether she changed or remained as she was, the thought of flesh of hers being associated with that low, common individual was unbearable. She said now, "I'll give you time to think it over."

She was turning away when Gail muttered from under her breath, "If—if I do it, will you let me do it in my own way; you—you won't approach Robbie, or let John?"

There was a pause before Esther said, "Very well."

"When will you see to it? I mean, about Dad." Her head was still bowed.

"As soon as possible."

"I won't stop seeing Robbie until they've got it in writing."

"Gail! I've given you my word." Esther was bristling.

Gail's head was up now and she was staring at her mother. "That's how it must be. When the solicitor says it's all right, then I'll tell Robbie, not until. Take it or leave it."

Esther let out a long drawn breath, then went swiftly out of the room.

Staring at the closed door, Gail cupped her face in her hands and pressed her cheeks so tightly that her lips pouted. Then, her hands dropping into her lap, she turned to the mirror again and watched her eyes cloud over and her face crumple as if she was about to burst into tears. A few minutes ago the whole situation had seemed marvelous, even

173

funny. Her father was getting what he wanted because she was giving up something that she'd never had, Robbie Dunn's love, but now she had signed that something irrevocably away. Once the divorce proceedings started, she wouldn't be able to see Robbie again.

Eight

Robbie lay, his hands behind his head, staring up at the ceiling. It was Sunday morning and Sunday morning as a rule meant a long sound sleep until Janet would shake him by the shoulder, saying, "Come on, have this cup of tea. Do you know what time it is?" But this morning he had awakened around four o'clock and couldn't get off again; it was all the talking last night before they had gone to bed. They were all worried. Well, for himself he couldn't say he was worried, not really worried. If that's the way she wanted it, well, there wasn't much he could do about it, was there? If her dad couldn't get her to come out here, then he hadn't much chance had he? But why had it happened all of a sudden like that? Was it because the social gap had just struck her? No! No! It wasn't that. Then what? Aw, why was he bothering his head? What did it matter? Now let him get this straight and not kid himself anymore. In his own way he was as much concerned about her change of attitude as the other two, although he hadn't let on to them. And it wasn't that he had fallen for her, Lord, no! That would have been something, wouldn't it? The reception she would have given to any advance from him would have knocked his ego so far down that he would be getting his pension by the time he retrieved it. Oh, no, he was too cute to let himself in for anything like that. It was just that they seemed to get on well together, pally like. And then she writes that letter to her father, saying that she wouldn't be able to come on a Saturday anymore and perhaps she could see him in town sometime. Just like that, cool like, as if she owed them nothing. But don't let her forget it, she did owe them something; she, in a way, owed them her father, for where would he be now if they hadn't stood by him? Aye, that was a question he'd like to ask Miss Blenheim.

He moved restlessly in the bed now, turned on his side, brought his knees well up and his head down toward them, and he lay like this for some time before he muttered aloud, "It's me. It's not Mam, it's me. Let's face it, it's me, because she accepted the fact that her father wanted to marry Mam all right, and when Harry put in for the divorce,

175

she was as anxious as any of us to know what her mother would say. It was from that Tuesday night when she came unexpected; she was changed then, acting like she did at first, quiet, offhand; yet on the Saturday she'd been gay like I'd never seen her afore. Then what happened in between? I did nothing. Aw, no, it couldn't be that." The thought brought him onto his back. "Because I caught hold of her?"

He stared upward again, remembering now the feel of her as his arms went around her and her face laughing into his, and he remembered thinking she could still be beautiful at that if she was happy. Her body had felt warm and soft and it trembled a bit, but he had done nothing, not even tightened his hold, he had let her go. Her face had been close enough to his to kiss. Not that he would have dreamed of doing that, but it had been.

When the front doorbell rang, he jumped as if he had been shot, and resting on his elbow, he stared across the darkened room. When it rang a second time, he scrambled out of bed and into his slippers and dressing gown and went out into the passage and across the hall. When he opened the door, there stood a policeman, and one that was known to him. Constable Tallow had been on market patrol when he first set up his stall.

It was the constable who spoke first. "Hello, Robbie," he said. "Sorry to get you up at this hour."

"It's all right, it's all right, but—but what's the matter?"

The constable paused for a moment, then said, "It's your shop. It's—it's been tarred."

"Tarred?" Robbie's cheeks moved up until they almost closed his eyes. "Tarred?" he repeated. "What do you mean, tarred?"

"Well, you know, there was a carnival on yesterday and that's a signal for some of them to go clean mad. They were at it in the town until two o'clock this morning. They get up to all kinds of things. They've stuck a joey on St. Stephen's steeple. Imagine that; one of them must have been a steeplejack."

"But my shop, how tarred? What do you mean tarred?"

"I think you'd better come along."

"Aye. Yes, I think I'd better," he said loudly. "But come in. Come on in a minute until I get me things on." As he closed the door and indicated to the constable to take a chair, Harry came into the hall, asking, "What is it? What's the matter? I heard the bell." Then he stopped dead as he saw the policeman. "Something, something wrong?" His

176

voice, his whole manner apprehensive, for policemen would always have an intimidating effect on him now.

Robbie, going quickly past him, said, "Shop's been tarred. Believe that?"

"What!"

As Robbie disappeared along the passage, Harry went slowly forward and if the policeman was surprised to see Mr. Blenheim apparently living with the Dunns he gave no sign of it, but he said courteously, "Good morning, Mr. Blenheim."

"Good morning," said Harry. "What is it, is it bad?"

"Well." The policeman jerked his head and said very softly, "Put a tarbrush into the hands of somebody who doesn't like a Jew and you know what to expect. Though why anyone should have their knife into him puzzles me; he's well liked and respected in most quarters if it's only for the guts he's got."

"Yes, yes." Harry nodded absently; then his tone quickening, he said, "I'll get dressed and come in with him." When he passed Robbie's room, the door was open and Janet was inside and she turned her face toward him, asking, "Who would do a thing like that, Harry?" He didn't answer her, but looking beyond her to Robbie, he said, "I'm coming in with you."

Robbie made no reply. He was pulling on his coat, now, and he said to Janet, "Don't worry; it mightn't be anything, just those mad hats letting off steam."

"Mad hats?" she repeated. "With a tarbrush!"

Within ten minutes Robbie drew the car up opposite his shop. He didn't get out immediately but sat looking through the window at what the headlights revealed. The writing started at the beginning of the wall three feet to the side of the window; it crossed the window and finished up on the shop door. The letters were two feet high and they said, "Dirty little Jew." The tar had run down the glass in streaks, and it appeared as if the words were crying black tears.

Then he opened the car door and stood on the pavement. Dirty little Jew. It was the word little that focused his attention. This writing was no insult to a race, this was a personal insult to a man, a little Jew. Twice as a boy, John Blenheim had called him just that to his face, "Dirty little Jew," and every time he had looked at him since his look had said, "Dirty little Jew." Since he could remember, he had hated John Blenheim; the feeling, he knew, was returned with equal force. At times he had wanted to lather

177

into him but, knowing how his mother felt, had checked his fists. The fact that Blenheim had for years been head and shoulders taller than him made no difference. He knew that given the chance, he could knock him out, and by God he would knock him out for this. He turned and looked at Harry, and for a moment he hated him as much as he did his son.

There were two policemen on the pavement now. One of them was saying, "It must have been done between three and four because we had them cleared from round here just after two, and at ten to three I drove past and all was quiet."

"We can't do much until tomorrow morning when the school opens," said Constable Tallow now. He paused, then ended, "This stuff takes some getting off."

Robbie had not spoken one word. He now moved toward the door, unlocked it, and stepping inside the shop, switched the lights on. He looked around him expecting to find the furniture all defaced, but it was just as he had left it last night.

The second policeman, stepping in behind him, asked, "Everything all right in here?"

When Robbie didn't speak but walked away down the shop, the policeman turned to Harry, who was within the door now, and said, "Enough to make a man mad when all's said and done. It's things like this that starts trouble off; this is how it started in London a few years ago. Some lunatic dabbed one place then others followed. Ten to one they're Nazis or"—his voice dropped—"somebody's got a grudge against him in the market; you can get on too quickly for some folks." He looked to where Robbie was standing at the end of the long room, his hand moving slowly back and forward over the top of a small table. Then looking at Harry again, he said, "I suppose you'll be around for some time, we'll be back later."

When Harry joined Robbie, he stood looking at his grim face for a moment before he said, "Don't take this to heart; as the constable said, you're highly respected in the town and—"

"Huh!" There was a slight pause after the exclamation; then again came the "Huh!" louder this time, and now Robbie's eyes were hard on Harry as he asked, "Have you any idea who could have done this? I mean, a vestige of an idea, can you think of anybody?"

Harry had to force himself to keep his gaze on the face

178

before him. Youth seemed to have left it; he had to look into the eyes in which he recognized a hate as deep as was in his own son, and it hurt him. He had never connected Robbie Dunn with hate. Hate and John, yes. He had recognized hate in his son at a very early age. Hate of everyone who opposed him. In the early days the hate had taken the form of sulks, but now it had matured and taken a tarbrush in its hand. And the reason for this was twofold: he wasn't only tarring a Jew, he was tarring his father, who was divorcing his mother to marry a Jewess. Gail's reaction to his connection with Janet was hurtful, and not quite understandable, but his son's attitude was frightening. Yet in a way he had been expecting it. The action had shocked him but not surprised him. What would have surprised him would have been John's acceptance of the situation.

"Well, do you?" Robbie asked again, his voice hard and the question pointed. And when Harry lowered his head and shook it, he once more emitted the telling syllable "Huh!" and looked at the man who was shortly to become his stepfather and whom up to a short while ago he had liked better than any other person in his life, except his mother. But now he wanted to yell at him, "Well! I'll tell you who it was, it was your son." But were he to do that, the relationship between the three of them would be severed for good. This was something he must accept, at least for the time being; but let him meet up with Master John Blenheim on the quiet, then by God there would be a settlement.

Dragging his coat off, he said, "Well, it's no use standing here. Petrol'll be the best thing; there's a can out in the back although I don't think that'll go very far."

And it didn't. It took four cans of petrol and five hours' work to clean off the three words. The hardest part was getting it off the brickwork, and during the whole process they hardly exchanged a word. It wasn't until they were cleaning themselves up in the back shop and the outer door opened and Sid came in that the conversation took on a lively note.

"What's this I'm hearing?" said Sid. "The shop's been tarred? I had just gone into The Stag when I heard. Bloody lot of mad bastards. What they want to go and do that to you for? You're well liked. Well, aren't you?"

Robbie looked at his assistant. Sid was a big individual, honest enough but without an overdose of intelligence, yet in a three-worded statement and a similar-worded question he had pointed out the difference between their nationalities.

179

They had both been born in this town, within a stone's throw of each other, but it was as if he and his kind were, at best, tolerated. "You're well liked." The inference was he was a tame wolf being singled out of a pack.

Around Bog's End there were Indians and Arabs, West Africans, Jamaicans, Chinese, and Greeks, and their businesses were not stamped with their nationality in tar, perhaps because, except for the Chinese and Greeks, none of the others had businesses. His was not the first shop that had had Jew written across it, and for a different reason from that which motivated John Blenheim. Jealousy was at the bottom of a lot of it, jealousy, because most Jews had the knack of surviving in the business world. They could build on a shilling; some had started on even less. Sid worked for him, but whether he was aware of it or not, he envied him, and yes, gormless as he was, dared to despise him.

He made himself say evenly, "It was the carnival spirit, I suppose, an' it's a pity you didn't hear of it two or three hours since, we could have done with a hand."

A few minutes later, as Robbie was locking up, Sid said, "What about the night? They might try it on again. Don't you think we should stay on watch, take our turns like?" And Robbie replied, "I don't think it'll be necessary." Then glancing over his shoulder at Harry, he asked, "What do you say?"

For the moment Harry made no reply; the look and the question certainly meant more than they said. He gulped before he answered, "The carnival's over, they'll have cooled down."

It was about eleven o'clock on the Monday morning when the three young men entered the shop. One had longish hair, one wore a brown tweed jacket over a purple pullover, the third one was in blue jeans and a windcheater; they could have been three lads from Bog's End, but Robbie knew immediately that these were the Technical wallahs.

"Mr. Dunn?" It was the one in the windcheater who spoke. He didn't say, "I want to see Mr. Dunn"; he seemed to know whom he was addressing and Robbie said abruptly, "That's me."

"We're from Technical College."

"Aye."

The young man hesitated then said, "We represent the Carnival Committee and I understand that we . . . I mean,

180

some member of the college has been blamed for disfiguring your shop window."

"That's right."

Again the young man hesitated, then said, "Well, sir, I want you to believe that all the fellows who were in the carnival have been up before the principal and they have sworn they had no hand in what was done; in fact, they are incensed that they are being blamed for it."

Robbie stared at the young man. He was a good six inches taller than himself. He had called him Mr. Dunn and sir. He could scarcely remember being called Mr. Dunn before, and never, never had he been addressed as sir. He liked this fellow in the windcheater and he wanted to say to him, "That's all right; I don't blame any of you," but he did blame one of them and he'd like to bet Mr. John Blenheim wasn't among the number who were indignant. What he said was "Well, there's one thing sure, it didn't get there by itself."

The young men stared at him, they were obviously embarrassed; even their spokesman didn't know what to say next until Robbie said, "Well, anyway, I appreciate you comin' along," then one of the boys who hadn't yet spoken said, "Well, we felt obliged to as it was a stigma on us an' all."

Stigma. They didn't like having a stigma put on them. It was a stigma on us an' all. The word "Jew" was a stigma.

Perhaps it was the look on Robbie's face that told the spokesman that his companion had made an unfortunate remark, for he said quickly, "I'm . . . I'm glad you understand, sir; I hope you won't have any more trouble."

Robbie nodded to this, and the three of them, speaking almost simultaneously, said, "Good-bye, sir."

Again he nodded. Then he watched them go out of the shop. He watched them until they were out of sight across the road, and he told himself not to let that remark turn the chip on his shoulder into a plank. The fellow hadn't meant it like that; they were decent blokes, else they wouldn't have come along and apologized.

Yet this moderate attitude did nothing to lessen the over-all feeling of rage that was seething in him. He felt burned up inside. If he could have talked to his mother about the matter, it might have helped, but if she even thought it was Harry's son who had done this to him she would immediately lay the cause at her own door. But there remained one person he could talk to; he could go to Miss Blenheim and give her a message for her bloody brother, a warning message. Yes, that's what he would do, and now. He'd catch her coming out at lunchtime; it wasn't likely that the family watchdogs would pick her up to take her to lunch.

It was just on twelve when he stopped the car some little distance from the shop and prepared himself to wait until one o'clock if need be; but it was only two minutes later when he saw Gail come out of the shop and walk rapidly down the street.

Abruptly he started the car and drove along the curb, but lost sight of her when he had to round a parked car, and when she came in view again, she was standing on the corner waiting to cross. In a second he had brought the car alongside the curb, and looking out of the window, he called, "Gail! Hi there, Gail! Get in."

She had been about to step into the road, and when she heard his voice and turned and saw him, she swayed a moment, then stepped back onto the pavement. Her head was shaking as she said, "No, no."

"Get in, I tell you. If you don't, I'll follow you. I'm holding up the traffic, get in."

"I can't . . . no."

He was leaning sideward, one hand on the handle of the part-open door, and he let it swing wide as he said, "Do as I tell you, get in."

He watched her look swiftly along the street from where was coming the impatient tooting of horns. He was on the corner of a narrow road at an angle that would make it a danger for anyone to pass him. He bawled now, "I'm stayin' until you get in."

When with a flounce of her body she entered the car, he started up almost before she had closed the door, and rounding the corner, he shot up the street, crossed an intersecting road, then made for the quiet outskirts of Jesmond.

It was she who spoke first. "Stop the car, I want to get out," she said.

"You'll get out when I say what I've come to say." He kept his eyes on the road ahead while he spoke. "What you frightened of? Catching something? Leprosy, say?"

"Robbie!" Her voice was pleading now. "Don't go any farther, please. I've got to be back in half an hour, Miss Frazer's got an appointment."

"Poor soul. Then I'm afraid she'll have to break it."

182

"Robbie, please, please stop."

"I'll stop when I'm good and ready and not afore. You can wave your hand out of the window; there's the police ahead. He'd have the squad car after me in no time. Go on and try it."

"Don't be silly." Her voice was no longer pleading, but harsh.

With a screeching of brakes and an abruptness that brought her brow almost in contact with the windscreen, the car came to a halt.

Her head was still bobbing when she said angrily, "What are you trying to do, kill us?"

"I shouldn't be a bit surprised."

"You're mad."

"Aye, I am." His face was thrust toward her now. "But not in the way you mean."

She turned her head away from him, and drooping it slightly, she said, "Look, I explained all I can explain."

"Oh, that's another matter altogether." His voice was airy now. "We'll come to that later. I'm not mad about you deciding not to condescend to visit us anymore; we should, I suppose, have been grateful for your previous visits."

She was staring at him now and he, ignoring her distressed look, went on, "Your retaliation to the fact that your father was going to marry me mother took the form of cutting us off, so to speak. But your brother's retaliation took a different form altogether. It's that I want to talk about."

"What!" Her head was poked forward. "What do you mean? Which—"

"Oh, you needn't say which one. Terry's no sneak in the night; Terry wouldn't hide behind a carnival to do his dirty work, then let other folk get the blame for it. No, you know which brother I'm referring to and it's ten to one you know what he was up to. You don't tar somebody's shop in a hurry without getting messed up, unless you wore overalls, and then you'd have to put them somewhere."

"Robbie." His name was just a whisper now and she repeated it again, slightly louder, trying to get him to stop talking. "Robbie, what—what are you saying?"

"Haven't you been listening?"

"You're inferring that John tarred your shop?"

"I'm not inferring any such thing. I'm damn well tellin' you straight out. He left a message on it in tar, the letters two foot high, and they said 'DIRTY LITTLE JEW.' "

Her hand moved slowly up to her cheek and her fingers cupped her ear as if in pain.

It seemed a long time before she said weakly, "No! He wouldn't."

"Wouldn't he? Well, he did."

"But—but have you proof?"

"Yes, yes, I've proof."

"How?"

He paused before he said "The word 'little.' DIRTY LITTLE JEW. Some other bloke would have just put 'Dirty Jew,' but your dear brother had used that term on me afore."

Her fingers were tapping nervously at her lips now and she looked away from him and down the road as she said, "I can't believe he would go to those lengths."

"No?" His voice was high. "But you do believe that he would be capable of doing somethin', don't you?"

She turned to him again and now she said quietly, "Yes."

"Oh, well, that's somethin'."

They stared at each other in silence for a full minute and then Robbie, suddenly turning from her, said, "Blasted bloody swine, that's what he is, a cowardly blasted swine; getting at me because he can't get at his father or me mother." And rounding on her again, he said, "I want you to go back and tell him that I know it was him an' that if he makes just one more move in my direction in any way I'll have the police on him so quickly he won't know what's happened till he's hanging on to his cell bars. You tell him that from me."

Again they were staring at each other in silence; and then, straining his neck out of his collar, he said, "Well now, I've had me say and you're free to go. I'll drive you back if you like or you can get off here, it's all the same to me."

When he saw her lips tremble, he thought, "Oh, my God. Let me get out of this." "Well, what's it to be?" His tone was thick and rasping, even ugly. "You getting out or am I to have the pleasure of your company for another few minutes."

"Robbie." Her eyes were lowered, focusing on a point on the car floor between their knees. "I—I just want to tell you that I'm not against Dad and Janet getting married, I'm glad. I said that in the first place and I meant it. I want them to be happy, but—but—" She swung her head and her lips opened and closed as if they were trying to find words. And then she ended rapidly, "It's my mother;

184

she's—she's very lonely. She's—she's cut herself off, she has no one, she has no friends; if—if I were to continue visiting Dad at your house under the present circumstances it would upset her. She's—she's so alone, you understand?"

He was looking straight into her eyes now. Yes, he understood; he had known all along it was her mother.

"It isn't that I don't want to come, Robbie."

He continued to stare at her. Then, his voice almost a whisper, now he said, "It's all right, don't upset yourself. I'm—I'm glad you told me."

But when she turned quickly from him and opened the door, he said flatly, "You're getting out then?"

"Yes." She was speaking from the pavement now. "I can get a bus."

"Please yourself." His voice, chin, and whole manner were cocky again.

"I'm—I'm very sorry about the shop, Robbie, really I am."

"Oh, don't let that trouble you. A mere detail that; just a mere detail." His heavy sarcasm made her close her eyes; then straightening up, she said, "Good-bye, Robbie." Her voice was cool now.

"Good-bye to you, Miss Blenheim." He inclined his head deeply toward her, then turned quickly to the wheel with the intention of starting up the car. But he didn't start it up; instead he watched her hurrying along the street toward a bus stop. He no longer felt anger concerning the defacing of his shop; what filled him now was a deep pain which was rising from its birthplace of resentment, bred in its turn from trials and purgatories of which he had no personal knowledge. Slowly he brought his face around to the car mirror and gazed at himself, and on a deep oath, he said, "Blast 'er! With you one minute 'It isn't that I don't want to come, Robbie' "—he mimicked her voice—"an' spitting on you the next. It isn't as if her mother or their John would see her around this quarter, an' at this time of the day. She doesn't want to be seen with me; it's as plain as that. She never did. The mother's a good excuse. Who does she think she is anyway? Workin' in a crummy bookshop and her dad done—" He pulled himself up. "Aw, to hell!" He started the car and drove away, passing her at the bus stop without a flick of an eye toward her. This was the end of him worrying about her; she could rot for all he cared.

185

BOOK THREE

THE OUTCOME

The dawn was just breaking as Harry stepped quietly out of the back door and, crossing the courtyard, went slowly up the hill. When he reached the top, he turned and looked back at the house. It was standing with its feet in mist, giving it an ethereal appearance, and for the first time he saw it, as Robbie had always seen it, as something beautiful. It was a year since he had first started on it. There was a lot still to be done, but what he had accomplished he could be proud of; he had in a way served his time on the house. As he stood looking down on it, he had a strong wish that it was his, that he owned it; but he would never own it, it was Robbie's house. Yet it was to be his home for the remainder of his life, his and Janet's. That was agreed. And today was his wedding day . . . and he was sad.

From the moment he had entered his room last night, his mind had been filled with thoughts of one person, and that person wasn't Janet but Esther, and how she had looked on that first wedding day over twenty years ago. He had risen early on that morning, too; too early to find the church open, and it was the church he had wanted to go into then. But he had walked to the river and sat on the bank and thought how lucky he was, and how he would love Esther until the day he died.

Last night he had said to Janet, "This is the last parting," and as she had pressed her lips to his, he had felt a deep sense of happiness at the thought that life ahead would revolve about her. But once alone, there had come over him a strange feeling; it was as if Esther was in the room telling him that it was wrong to take another wife when the first one was still alive. And he had paced up and down thinking, "She's right, it is." And the feeling had persisted and grown. And now as he watched the first rays of the sun breaking up the mist, he said to himself, "Don't be a blasted fool; if she had wanted you, you would have run back; there's nobody to blame for the present situation but herself . . . at least"—he qualified this thought—"for the continued separation and the divorce." Doubtless she had suffered. Of this he had been left in no doubt when Gail had said, "I'm not coming to the house, it's hurting Mother. And now the divorce is going through." And then she had added quickly, "I'm not blaming you. Don't think that. I want you to marry Janet, but the fact remains that Mother's upset."

Knowing his wife, he felt sure she was in some way putting a screw on Gail, and as time went on, he had become more convinced of this, for he sensed his daughter's hidden unhappiness.

Janet, however, said that she could see Esther's point of view, and if she was in the same boat and Robbie went visiting the other woman, she'd be torn in shreds.

He now walked to the other side of the hill and leaned against the rock. The mist on this side was covering the valley in great white waves; it was going to be another fine day; it had been beautiful for the last fortnight. Janet had said yesterday that she hoped it kept fine, yet she didn't mind if it poured. She had looked excited and young. It was odd but she seemed to have got younger over the past six months. She was happy as he had never seen her happy; it was good to know that he could do that for someone, make them happy. The thought came at this moment that there were other women he could have made happy. Betty Ray, for instance. God! Betty Ray. He was back to the bedroom. He was where he was at this minute because of that half hour of madness—how did other fellows get by for years on the same racket. He didn't know. He only knew that he himself was the type that could never get away with anything. It happened with all men like him, fundamentally nice blokes. Three women had wanted him. Not much of a record perhaps, yet he had been branded a Casanova. It was laughable, if you could laugh at it.

Thinking of happiness, what about himself? Was he happy? No! But he could be. Yes, yes, he knew he could be happy with Janet. And not just in placid acceptance, for she aroused in him a feeling that he thought had died for want of use. It was the transition from Janet Dunn to Mrs. Blenheim that seemed to be frightening him at the moment. If only it was this time tomorrow, and it was over, then he'd feel different; Esther would be irrevocably in the past . . . and John? Ever since the tarring episode he had gone in fear of his son's further reactions; and the nearer the day came, the deeper his fear had grown.

He started visibly when he saw Janet come out of the

190

mist. She didn't speak until she was close to him, and then she said, "I knew you'd come up here this morning. I wonder you didn't come out in the middle of the night. You haven't been to sleep, have you?"

He didn't answer but took her hand and made to draw her close to him, but she resisted. Yet still leaving her hand in his, she said, "You're not the only one who's been thinking, Harry."

"The time for thinking is past, Janet." He moved his head slowly. "It's deeds that are required now."

"Not necessarily." Her dark eyes were looking into his. "Harry, listen to me, and I mean every word I say. You don't have to marry me; I'm not demanding the final sacrifice. No! No!" She held up her free hand. "Listen. Listen. I'll be quite content to live with you. I'll be proud to live with you. I said as much on this very spot some months ago, but you didn't take me at my word. Well, now I repeat the offer, but I repeat it because I know you want me, whether it's as a wife or a mistress doesn't matter. In either case there's one thing I'm sure of: this is going to be our wedding day, Harry Blenheim."

"Oh, Janet. Janet." He was holding her tightly. This is what he wanted, what he needed, firm reassurance. When he kissed her, it was hard and long and loving. Then with her face cupped in his hands he said softly, "Roll on eleven o'clock."

They had a table booked at the Crown Hotel, and as the headwaiter ushered them to it, he guessed that it was a wedding party, and he hadn't to exert his powers of perception to gauge that it wasn't two of the three young people present who had been married, but the two older ones, for apart from the feeling that seemed to pervade the group was the fact that the girl was dressed very ordinarily, and one of the two young men looked as if he was rigged out for a tour on his bike.

And the waiter was exactly right in this, for Terry was dressed as he was most Saturday mornings since he had joined the motorcycling club, and Gail was wearing the same clothes as those she had worn yesterday for the shop.

No mention had been made at home about her father remarrying, but she knew that the thought was in the forefront of her mother's mind all the time. Yet this past week it hadn't been her mother's attitude that had worried her, but John's. He had been in one of his sulks again. She

191

called his mood sulking for want of a more correct definition of his withdrawal. Right up to this morning she felt that he might do something to prevent his father marrying Janet. She didn't ask herself how he knew it was the day; she only knew that both he and her mother were aware of it. Their knowledge emanated from them like a dark fog and filled the atmosphere of the house.

But now it was done. Her father had married Janet, and he looked happy; he looked as if he had been injected with new life, and all because of a dull and emotionless ceremony in a dusty office. Marriage was odd, when you came to think about it. A few words read out of a book, a couple of questions, and the signing of a name and that tied you to a man forever, or until such time as you wanted to get free, and then you sinned. Oh, she didn't want to think about it. Marrying, unmarrying, she hated it all.

She was grateful to Terry for having come, for he was making them laugh and that took some of the embarrassment away. Terry was a smoother of situations. He was telling them about his pal at the art school in Newcastle. "It's a fact," he was saying. "Everything happens to Jackie's mother. He has me rolling. But this is honest, and it happened because she's stone deaf. You know the Marsden line down Shields way. Well, whether you do or you don't, it's a little railway, not passenger, just for goods, and the engine driver sees this woman crossing the line, and he pulls his blower like mad. Honk, honk, honk, honk!" He demonstrated. "But she didn't seem to hear him and he couldn't pull up in time, so he hit her side on and she was dragged for twenty yards and broke about ten bones. Yes, it's true, honest it is. Jackie was in the hospital sitting by her bedside when she came round and she ups and yells. She always yells with being deaf; you should hear him imitate her. Mind, he likes her, oh, he likes her a lot, but he gets a lot of fun out of her. Anyway, there she was covered in bandages and she says, 'That you, our Jackie?' and he says, 'Aye, Mam, it's me.' 'Where am I?' she says. 'In hospital, Mam,' he says. 'Eeh,' she yells. 'I feel I've been kicked doon the street. Eeh, lad, have I had a stroke?' 'No, Mam,' he says; 'you were knocked down by a train.' 'Oh, was that it?' she yells. 'Well, thank God I didn't have a stroke.' "

They were trying in various ways to suppress their loud laughter. Janet had her hand held tightly across her mouth; Harry had his teeth clamped onto his bottom lip; Gail had her head down; and Robbie was bending over sideways hug-

192

ging himself. It was as he straightened up that Gail raised her head, and as he looked into her face, he thought, "It's nearly six months since I saw her. She's changed. It's right, after all, she's going to blossom out. She looks bonny the day, sort of sad, yet bonny."

And Gail, looking into the round black eyes, thought, "It's a new suit he's got on. Gray suits him. He looks nice." But when his gaze remained hard on her, she blinked and turned her eyes from him and to Janet. Janet looked nice, too, even pretty. No, Janet couldn't look pretty, she looked handsome. Her father was looking at her as if he were proud of her. Up to an hour ago her father had still been hers, solely hers because her mother had rejected him, but not anymore, for now he had Janet. The aloneness this thought engendered swamped her and she knew a moment of horror when she realized she was about to cry. But Terry was looking at her and saying, "Remember, Gail? Remember the time when I told you about Jackie being gone on that girl and taking her home to Bog's End, remember?"

Gail blinked rapidly and smiled and said, "Yes, yes. Tell them; that was funny, too."

Their attention was again focused on Terry, and he rose to the occasion and told them the tale of the refined shy girl meeting up with Jackie's eleven brothers and sisters in a small sitting room, the mother yelling her head off first at one and then the other, and Jackie's three married brothers scaring the daylights out of the girl by telling her what Jackie expected out of marriage, one small item being that he hoped to produce a larger family than his father.

There was more laughter at this, and altogether the wedding lunch could be said to have been a great success. And it was almost quarter of two when they left the hotel and went toward the car and the van parked on the driveway. But there, embarrassment seemed to envelop them, until Janet, offering her hand to Gail, said softly, "Thanks, Gail; thank you for coming. I'll—I'll never forget it."

For a moment Gail was about to make the polite reply, "Oh, that's all right, Janet, I wanted to come," but instead impulsively she put her arms around Janet and kissed her, and the gesture set a seal on the day. It took a weight from Janet's heart and a weight from Harry's mind. He held his daughter tightly for a moment before looking into her face and saying, "Remember what I said years ago? Well, it still holds. My love for you is a thing apart. Janet understands this."

193

The words were like warm oil on a sore. It was more difficult now to withhold the tears, so she merely nodded, then turned away.

Janet and Robbie did not embrace, they just looked at each other and he jerked his head at her, saying, "Well, I suppose I'll be seeing you the morrow night. Why the devil you can't make it a week is past me. All right, all right"— he wagged his hand at her—"I know. We've been through it and I'm not capable of lookin' after meself yet. Have it your way. Get in." He pushed her unceremoniously into the car, and there was more laughter.

But before Harry took his seat, he stood in front of Terry, and he said simply, "Thank you, son." And Terry, no longer laughing and lost for words now, flushed red to his ears.

There was no verbal exchange between Robbie and Harry, but they looked at each other and their glance, full of understanding, cemented the partnership that was already between them.

When Harry took his seat behind the wheel, not one of them could have guessed his thoughts, for behind his smiling face he was feeling weak with relief. All during the short ceremony, even during the lunch, he had expected something to happen. What, he didn't really know, but something instigated by John. But now it was over. If he had intended doing anything, he would have done it before this. He started up the car, then he and Janet called their final good-byes.

The three of them waved the car along the drive and out of sight; then Robbie, stretching his neck out of his collar and buttoning his coat, said briskly, "Well, that's that." Then looking directly at Terry, he added jocularly, "The van's at your disposal, me lord; I can drop you where you left your bike, right?"

"Right!" said Terry, laughing again. "Fine." Then he turned to Gail, and she said, "I've got some shopping to do, I'll get the bus."

At this Robbie almost groaned aloud. God Almighty! She was still going to keep it up. After a lunch like they'd had, all jolly good pals together, she was going back into her shell. Well then, let her. He hadn't pined because he hadn't seen her for months. He had been about to make some crack about her being his stepsister. God, it was just as well he hadn't, she would have swooned. Yet she had been all right with his mother, putting her arms around her and kissing her. It all went to prove what he had known all

194

along: it wasn't his mother marrying her dad that had brought on the Ice Age, it was him. She couldn't stand him. Well, to hell with her! The feeling was reciprocated. Aye, and with interest.

"O.K., let's get going." He jerked his head at Terry as he walked away adding, "The party's over. I've got a business so attend to."

Terry watched him go toward the van, then in an undertone to Gail, he muttered quickly, "Why can't you come? He can drop you off before you can get anywhere near home."

"And have our John see us?" Her tone was equally low, and when after a moment he nodded at her, she said, "Go on, don't keep him waiting."

Terry now made his way to the van and took his seat beside Robbie and within seconds they were flashing down the drive, passing Gail as if she was a stranger.

It was half-past two when Robbie returned to the shop. He felt in a vile mood, ready to go for the first one that crossed him, but he had to warn himself not to go for Sid because Sid had done him a favor in working through his dinner hour, and he was going to ask a further favor of him. He wanted him to stay on until six o'clock, or to such time when he returned from the house. There were a number of pieces he wanted to take out to finish off the long room, besides which he had an appointment to view some pieces at a private house around three-thirty.

He felt mad at himself for feeling mad. He shouldn't be feeling like this, he told himself, not with Monday before him. So much could happen on Monday; it could be the beginning of big things, real big things.

Some weeks ago an American had come to the shop and bought three pieces and paid well for them. They had got talking and the American seemed to take to him; anyway, he had put some business in his way. He said he was looking for an eighteenth-century lowboy and one or two Louis XVI pieces, a secretaire in particular, and a Louis XV commode. Did Mr. Dunn think it possible he could come by them? Robbie didn't think it was possible, not at short notice anyway, but he intended to have a damn good try.

He hadn't taken the man out to the house on that occasion, although he could have done so because he had some attractive pieces there already, but his alert mind was, as usual, giving him the completed picture and he could see

195

these French pieces lining the walls of the long room and the overall impression it would have on the American. Ten to one he wouln't only take the pieces he was after, but the lot.

He had, after much searching, managed to get hold of all the pieces except the commode, but he'd had to pay through the nose for them. Yet what he lost on the roundabouts he'd gain on the swings on this deal, he told himself, or his name wasn't Robbie Dunn.

The visit to the private house proved disappointing and he came out thinking, "They've got a nerve; I wouldn't put that stuff in the market." So his frame of mind hadn't lightened when he entered the lane and first smelled burning. He looked down toward the floor and sniffed. Perhaps it was his exhaust. He had reached the mine before he realized the smell of burning wasn't coming from inside the van but from outside. He put his head toward the open window and sniffed again. It was a strong smell now lying heavy on the air. He looked toward the old mind buildings at the back of the wheelhouse. Likely somebody was up to something in there. Kids, he'd bet. Yet there was no smoke to be seen.

He didn't see the smoke until he rounded the pithead. And there it was before him, spiraling up into the sky and spreading along the horizon, and filling the world, his world. He hadn't been conscious of bringing the car to a stop; he wasn't conscious of his hands gripping the wheel while his chest was pressed against it. One minute the car and he were still, the next minute they both seemed to be flying through the air.

When he tumbled out of the car in front of the house he became still again; not only his body now but his mind seemed incapable of movement. No thought penetrated the stupor as he gazed up at the flames licking out of the upper window; the floor of the house was a complete red glow that hissed and crackled. He didn't see the man in the T-shirt and the two policemen came toward him. When the constable said, "I'm sorry about this, Mr. Dunn," he turned a slow gaze toward him and his mind began to move again, but not around the enormity of the situation. What he thought was, "He's one of the fellows that was on patrol the night the shop was done; he's a Jonah."

"The fire brigade should be here any minute, but I'm afraid it's a bit late. You see, we knew nothing about it

196

until this"—he nodded to the man in the T-shirt—"this gentleman phoned in."

"Well, it wasn't me that phoned, it was me son, Tony." The man was gesticulating now. "He must have run a mile and a half along the road to the phone. And to think I saw the bloke do it. But it didn't dawn on me at the time. You see, mister." He was bending his head down from his six-foot-four to Robbie's level. "You see, mister, I'm from Wallsend and it just happened I had the feeling that I wanted to show me lad where I used to fish when I was a nipper, in the burn yon side of the sugar lump." He nodded toward the hill. "This house used to be empty in those days. We used to run in and out of it, build fires in that room there. Not as big as this one, though." He stopped on an embarrassed "Huh!" then went on, "Well, as we was passin' on our way down the burn, I stopped an' had a look. There seemed nobody about an' I was interested like, so we climbed on the wall round there just near the stables. I wasn't goin' to come over, just have a look, as I said. An' then, as I told the police here, up comes this car. Not right up; it stops along the road there"—he pointed back—"an' this fellow comes carrying a can, a petrol can. He passed us within two arms' length. Me and Tony saw him as plain as I'm seein' you, but you see at that time I thought he was the boss, the owner like. When he disappeared round yon side of the house we scarpered along by the wall, but as we was passin' the gate there, or the place where the gate was, I saw him opening the windows, so naturally I took him to be the owner. Well, we went on to the burn, but there wasn't any fish, not like there used to be—the chemicals have poisoned the pool down there—an' so we came back, 'cos I had a fancy to sit on the top of the hill there and eat me bait like I did as a nipper, as I said. An' then when we rounded the old mine, we saw the smoke, an' like lightning I put two and two together. That fellow was carryin' a petrol tin, I said to our Tony. God, did we run! But when we got here all the bottom was ablaze and even if I could have found the stopcock and a hose I couldn't have done anything, so I sent Tony flyin' for the police. But, mister, I'll pick that fellow from out of a million for you."

Robbie still hadn't moved. He didn't move even when the fire engine came jangling into the yard. When someone shouted, "Where's the stopcock?" he just pointed.

The man in the T-shirt was speaking again, he said, "I thought I'd be able to save some bits. I went round the

197

back, but that was worse than the front, everything was burnin' like matchwood. He must have set half-a-dozen places goin' at once. He knew what he was doin' leaving the windows open."

They all began to cough as a cloud of smoke enveloped them, and the policeman, taking Robbie by the arm, said, "Come over here, sir."

It was the contact of the hand on his arm that seemed to break through the shock and return him to life, for he startled both the policeman and the man by racing away from them and round to the back of the house, and there, dragging a coil of hose from a shed, he dashed with it to a tap on the side of the stable wall, and having attached the nozzle to it with hands that shook as if they had palsy, he ran with the end of the hose through the smoke toward his bedroom window.

Just that morning he had left three paintings stacked against the wall in there. He had learned a bit about paintings during the past three years, and about one of these paintings he had a feeling. He had picked them up from among the contents of an attic he had bought and the feeling told him he might have a find in the picture that showed the face of the Madonna and Child under the dirt and grime of years. On the back of the picture was a torn label with a few words discernible, indicating that it had at one time been hung in a gallery. Even when one of the firemen, coming up to him, shouted, "I don't think you can do much there, sir," he still kept the hose directed through the window.

Coughing and choking and almost overcome by the smoke, he staggered back across the yard and leaned against the wall and there standing sightless for a moment, he cried from deep within him, "Oh, God! Let me die. Let me die."

"Come away, sir; there's nothing you can do." When the man went to help him, he shrugged him off and picked his way over the tangle of pipes, through a patch of hissing steam and to the front of the house again, where the policeman met him, saying, "This gentleman's given me a full description of the man. Do you know anyone like this?" He looked at his notebook. "About six foot tall, fair. Very fair, you said?" He looked toward the man again, and the man nodded and said, "Yes, unusually fair, sort of silvery-like."

"About twenty to twenty-three years old," went on the policeman. "His clothes, I suppose, wouldn't be of much

198

help, but he was wearing a conventional suit and collar and tie. That's so, isn't it?"

"Aye," said the man. "He was dressed as if he was going into the town, Newcastle or some such place. That's why I thought he was the owner like."

Tall, six-foot, fair, silvery-like, twenty to twenty-three. He didn't need any description, he knew. He had known since he had smelled the smoke. Like a dam breaking, the rage swept through him, sundering the remaining stupor and the shock into fragments.

Once again he startled the policeman and the man by running, but now toward the van. Once inside, he threw the gear into reverse, but his backward move toward the gate was immediately impeded by the rear end of the fire engine. The policeman was shouting to him. "Where can we contact you, sir?"

"What?"

"I said, where can we get in touch with you?"

"I'll be back shortly. Yes"—he nodded to him—"I'll be back shortly."

"Very good, sir." The policeman continued to look at him, then he beckoned him forward and indicating to him to turn his wheel hard down right. This done, the road clear, the car shot backward and within seconds it was bounding over the road toward the mine, past it, then along the lane and onto the main road.

During the journey to Holt Avenue Robbie wasn't conscious of forming any plan as to his actions once having arrived there, yet when he drove the car to a grinding halt outside the gate, he didn't make for the front door but ran along the road and entered by the gate marked "Tradesmen." The lonicera-hedged path led to the square of cement outside the kitchen door, and it wasn't until he had his hand actually on the knob of the door that he paused. Lifting his hand gently off it again, he sidled toward the window and looked into the kitchen. It was empty. They'd be at a meal. The dining-room window looked onto the side of the house to his right, but he didn't make for it. Instead, he went back to the kitchen door, and slowly opening it, he stepped inside and stood taut as he looked about him. Everything was neat, clean, and prim—a portrait of Esther Blenheim. He wanted to see Esther Blenheim. Oh, yes, he wanted to see Esther Blenheim. But after he had seen her son. And he wanted to see her son now, when he was still feeling like this, mad, crazy, wanting to kill. This

199

feeling, once it had subsided, would never return. Never, he knew, as long as he lived would anything happen to make him feel like this again, for every fiber of his being demanded that he should get his fingers into the flesh of John Blenheim and tear that flesh, rend it, scar it, leave it so that the six-foot silvery-blond bastard would not be recognizable, even to his mother.

Swiftly and quietly he crossed the kitchen, and as he entered the hall, the thought came to him for the first time, "What if he isn't in?" Well then, he would wait until he came in, and neither Esther Blenheim nor a hundred like her would stop him.

The dining-room door lay along the passage to the right of him, and still on tiptoe, he was making for it when the sitting-room door opened and he froze to the spot and looked across at Gail, who was now standing staring at him as if at an apparition. Before she spoke his name, she glanced apprehensively to the side of her and up the stairs, and then she whispered, "Robbie!"

It was at this moment that a door banged overhead and now they both looked toward the stairs, to the head of it and to John Blenheim, who had come to a stop on the first step, one hand gripping the banister, the other flat against the wall. And there he stood for a space that seemed timeless.

"Well, aren't you coming down? I'm waiting for you."

Before her brother could make any reply, Gail cried, "What is it? What is it?"

Robbie didn't look at her, but he answered her. "I'll tell you what it is," he said in a slow, deliberate, frightening tone. "Your brother's burned me house down, right to the ground, and everything in it."

"No! No!" The two words were like a thin scream, and now Gail was at the bottom of the stairs staring up at her brother, shouting, "You didn't, John! You didn't!"

Again Robbie answered her, "He did."

"He's mad." John Blenheim's voice was cold, incisive, the tone scornful. "Always has been. He's potty."

Gail now turned and looked at Robbie, and her voice appealing, she said, "He couldn't, Robbie, he couldn't. Not that, not your house."

Robbie's eyes hadn't flinched a fraction from the tall figure poised above him, nor were his lids blinking. His stare fixed and fanatical never left the face that was now almost as pale as the hair above it.

200

When Gail stood in front of him, saying pleadingly, "He didn't, you heard him, Robbie. He wouldn't. Not that," he thrust her roughly away with his outstretched arm and she landed up against the wall to the side of the drawing-room door, and there she stood with both hands stretched across her mouth and watched her brother move slowly down the staircase.

When John Blenheim reached the last step, he paused, and from this added vantage point he looked down on to the dark, hate-filled countenance, and he spat at it, "Get out of here!"

The answer came in a spring that brought him from the stair and whirling into the middle of the hall. For a matter of seconds they faced each other like two judo combatants. Then they were locked together, struggling, tearing, clawing.

As if throwing off a small clinging animal, John Blenheim now tossed Robbie against the main balustrade of the stairs, and there he lay in a huddled heap until, like a cobra uncoiling, he slowly brought himself to his feet, and again he sprang. It wasn't the action of a man, it was more like some primitive beast, and it brought another high-pitched scream from Gail.

Robbie's hands this time made straight for John Blenheim's throat and by the sheer frenzy of his effort they found their target, and when he felt the flesh beneath his fingers he hung like a limpet to a rock. Although John Blenheim swayed and thrashed and grappled with the hands, he couldn't dislodge them. The next moment they were both on the floor, rolling and tossing, Robbie on top one second, John Blenheim the next. Both their faces were now covered in blood, but whereas a few moments before John Blenheim had been using his rugby tactics, now with the pressure tightening on his gullet, they were becoming ineffectual.

"Robbie! Robbie! Oh, Robbie, for God's sake, leave go. Leave go of him!" Gail tried pulling him off by his collar, then by tearing at both his hands with hers, but when she couldn't unloosen his grasp, she beat at him with her fists, yelling all the time, "Robbie! Robbie! Do you hear me? Do you hear? Please! Please!"

It was this scene that met Esther Blenheim as she came through the front door and heard her daughter scream at her, "Help me. Help me get him off."

Now it was as if another wild beast had joined the fray, for Esther Blenheim tore not only at Robbie's hands but at his face, and when at last her son was free, she fell on

201

her knees beside him, crying, "John! John!" When he didn't speak, she took him by the shoulders and lifted his limp head upward and shook him, all the time, crying, "John! John!" When his chest swelled and he drew in a deep intake of breath, she almost dropped him back on the floor with relief. Then, cradling him, she looked across at the madman her daughter was supporting and she cried, "You insane beast. Get out of here." And when Robbie made no move but continued to lean against Gail's supporting shoulder, she screamed in a voice that rang through the house, "You filthy, murdering little beast! Get out! Do you hear? Get out!"

It did not strike Esther Blenheim at the moment that her son was not only head and shoulders taller than his attacker but that he could also give him breadth all around. When she saw that Robbie Dunn neither moved nor made answer, she yelled at Gail, "Get away from him. Do you hear me, girl? Get away from him."

Shivering from head to head to foot, Gail stared at her mother holding John in her arms. It was like the picture of Christ taken down from the Cross; but John wasn't Christ and her mother wasn't Mary. And so she yelled back at her, "You know what he's done, our John? He's burned Robbie's house down. Do you hear me? He's burned Robbie's house down!"

Esther Blenheim now looked at her son, who was pulling himself from his knees to his feet, and her lips moved, but no sound came from them. And Gail was yelling at her again. "You could have stopped him, you could, you could. You knew he was up to something. All week he hasn't spoken. You knew what that meant, you knew he was up to something."

Esther Blenheim now rose from the floor, and following her son, who was shambling toward the drawing room, she touched his arm as she said, "Did you? Did you do this?"

Looking straight back into her face, he said, "No, of course I didn't. He's mad, insane. I'll have him for this."

"He's a liar, a dirty, stinking liar!" They both turned and watched Robbie stumble forward. They watched him wipe the blood from his mouth before saying, "He was seen by two people, they've given the police his description, but I wanted to deal with him in me own fashion afore they got their hands on him."

Now Esther Blenheim was cupping her face with both her

202

hands, and her voice, without strength now, muttered, "No, no! You're mistaken. You're mistaken."

"I'm not mistaken. Six foot, the men said, blond, silver blond, an' going into the house, my house, carrying a can of petrol. The man said he's only waiting to recognize him. No, Mrs. Blenheim, there's no mistake."

John Blenheim was now in the drawing room, and Esther, following him, cried, "John! Look at me. Do you hear? Look at me." And when he turned toward her, she demanded, "Did you do this, this thing?" And when he said slowly and bitterly, "Yes, I did it, and I'd do it again," she closed her eyes and bowed her head and held her hands over her ears as if to shut out his voice. After a moment she turned toward Robbie, who was still standing in the hall, and she said to him, "What are you going to do?"

"What do you think, Mrs. Blenheim, eh? What do you think? I'm going to leave it to the police. I don't know what the sentence is for arson and tarring a shop, but I should imagine it'll be more than his father got, an' if there's any justice it will be. An' without your permission, Mrs. Blenheim, I'm goin' to use your phone."

As he stepped toward the side table, Esther Blenheim came through the door. Her hands joined tightly against her breast, she pleaded, "Robbie! Please, please, wait. I've . . . I've lost everything and—"

"So have I, Mrs. Blenheim, so have I. An' not only me home but the best part of me business. That ground floor was full of antiques, specially got for a client who was comin' on Monday. I've lost everything an' all, Mrs. Blenheim."

"But . . . but you will have it all covered with insurance." She was gulping on each word and he smiled at her, a deadly smile, as he said, "Practical to the last, Mrs. Blenheim, aren't you? Now, aye, you would think a sharpshooting Jew like me would have the sense to cover the lot. Two thousand cover, that's all they would give me on the building when I took it. Six months ago they gave me four, but last week I put in to raise it to ten. An' that's what it was going to be, ten thousand, but it wasn't signed, so there I stand with four thousand cover, and the furniture in there was worth more than that. An' that's not covered, only when it was in the shop. So there you have it, Mrs. Blenheim. And to think, as Gail's just said, you could have stopped that maniac, but you didn't, because somehow you knew that the day your man was marrying me mother, an' you let

203

your retaliation have rip through him. Well, everything's got to be paid for, Mrs. Blenheim."

"I . . . I understand that, nobody better, everything's got to be paid for." Her voice was bitter, her manner haughty again, and now she said, "Give me a little time, please, time to think."

Robbie's hand was on the phone.

"I'll . . . I'll make up the difference, at least my father will. You won't be out of pocket, only please, I beg of you, don't take this any further."

"What! You're jokin'. Let him get off with this? Leave him free to do me down again? Oh, no."

"Robbie!"

He turned and looked at Gail; she was standing against the hall wardrobe as if she was afraid to leave its support. Her hands were pressed flat against the wood and she muttered, "Don't do it, please. She's—she's got to have something left, because I'm—I'm leaving."

Robbie stared at her. Her reasoning was beyond him at the moment. Why should she think that her leaving home would affect his decision? But before he could find an answer, his attention was drawn to Esther Blenheim; her manner no longer beseeching or persuasive, or even haughty, she was rounding on her daughter, crying, "You won't! You can't. You promised."

Now Gail brought her body stiffly from the wardrobe, and nodding toward her mother, she said slowly, "Yes, yes, I know what I promised, but I also know that if I stay here I'll likely go berserk and finish what Robbie attempted a minute ago."

"You promised, girl, you promised, you swore. Remember?" Her mother was almost screaming at her now. "I gave your father a divorce solely because you promised that you wouldn't marry him." She thrust her arm back, her thumb out toward Robbie. "You promised faithfully, you promised on your honor."

Robbie's hand moved from the top of the phone to the table and he leaned heavily on it as he stared first at Gail, then at Esther Blenheim, then back to Gail again What had she said? She had promised she wouldn't marry him and that was how Harry had got his divorce? But he had never asked her. Marry her? They'd hardly been civil to each other; they had never necked or courted, as it were. He had touched her that once when she had slipped on the ice. Marry her? His mouth was filling with blood from the

204

slit in his lip and he swallowed and blinked as Gail cried at her mother, "Promise or no promise, I'm leaving. And with him. And now. You can't do anything; Dad's married."

"Oh, yes, I can. Oh, yes, I can."

"Don't be silly, Mother." Gail's voice, although trembling now, was scornful, deriding. "Robbie has you in the hollow of his hand. You try to stop me leaving and he'll use that phone, won't you, Robbie?"

He stared at her. His mind was in a whirl, caught as it were in a strong current leading from the main stream of his hate. He looked at the hand now clutching his arm, and when she said pleadingly, "Come on, Robbie, let's go," he moved a step with her before pulling himself to a halt and saying, "Wait a minute. Hold on. Wait a minute." His body too had shrugged off her suggestion and he had turned half from her, only to turn quickly to her again and grab the hand that had left his arm, and he gripped it tightly and stared at her for a second before speaking to her mother again, saying, "That would be simple, wouldn't it, just to walk out, but it's not going to end like that, oh no." He slowly swung his head the width of his shoulders, and this action, more than further words, said plainly that he wasn't finished, not by a long chalk.

When, still holding Gail by the hand, he stepped toward the sitting-room door, Esther cried at him, "Don't go in there. Don't you dare go in there!" and he paused for a moment. Then ignoring both her and the restraining pressure that Gail was now putting on his hand, he stepped into the framework of the door. And once more he looked at John Blenheim, who was sitting now, his hands massaging his throat, and he said to him, "The greatest pleasure I can think up is to see you goin' out of this house atween a couple of policemen, but besides your dear mother"—he laid emphasis on the dear—"there'd be somebody else who'd feel guilty over you. And that's your father. But prison aside, you're not goin' to get off with it. By God, no, you're not. I want it down in writing, what you've done. Do you hear? IN WRITING. And signed."

"No, no. Don't, John." Esther was now standing near her son, and she looked down at him, saying, "Don't you do any such thing."

"He's got no choice, Mrs. Blenheim, an' you know it. So listen to me, both of you. Even as things stand, even if I don't phone for the police, there's still this man and his

205

son, an' they'll be on the lookout for you." His lips left his teeth as he paused and returned in full the baleful glare of John Blenheim before going on, "So I'd advise you not to run. D'you hear?"

Slowly now he turned his attention to Esther, saying, "Whatever's goin' to be done, it'll be done legal. You have him at the solicitor's on Monday morning. No"—he shook his head—"Monday afternoon, say three o'clock. These things've got to be arranged an' me solicitor, by the way, is a Jew. You won't be able to miss him; his name's Steen, three doors down below my shop. STEEN. Do you hear that, Mr. Blenheim?" He was bawling now. "His name is Steen. And if you're not there on time, then I'll do what I'm itching to do now, that is if you've not already been picked up, you dirty white-livered swob you!"

When John Blenheim, his face ashen, made to get up from his chair, Esther restrained him, and she glared at the pair standing hand in hand before her. Then her eyes focused on her daughter, boring into her until Gail, turning away, tugged once more at Robbie's hand, murmuring, "Come on, come on."

As Robbie looked at Gail, he was seeing her clearly for the first time since he had entered the house. He couldn't quite take it in that she meant what she had said, but she had said it. "I'm leaving with him." And now he said to her, more in the form of a command than a request, "Go and get your things."

"No, no." She shook her head. "I don't want any things." She knew that if she went up the stairs she would be trapped, and either by force or persuasion she'd be made to stay. "I'm going as I am. Come on."

"Gail!" Esther Blenheim made one last attempt. "Think, girl, think what you're letting yourself in for."

Gail turned and looked at her mother and she repeated, "Letting myself in for? Huh! That's really funny because whatever I was letting myself in for couldn't be any worse than the life I've been forced to lead over the last three years in this house. You're treated me like a prisoner."

Esther Blenheim remained silent for a moment, and her chin seemed to flatten itself out under the pressure of her jawbones. Then she said, "And where do you think you're going to stay if . . . if he no longer has a house? Give yourself time, girl, and—"

"That'll be my business from now on." Robbie's answer cut her off. "And that should be the least of your worries,

206

Mrs. Blenheim. What I would advise is you concentrating on Monday an' getting your son to Mr. Steen's, together with—an' let's not forget this—the difference in the money, and that should be around six thousand pounds. No, don't let's forget the money, Mrs. Blenheim, the money's very important to me. Come on." He went to turn away, then looked back and into the staring eyes of John Blenheim, and he said, "As for you. You can remember for the rest of your days that you were nearly finished off by somebody half your size, a dirty little Jew." He paused, then ended, with a threat in his tone now, "Until Monday, you swob, or else."

When they went through the front door Gail attempted to run, but he pulled her to a walking pace, saying, "Steady on, what's your hurry?" And that was all he said until they were on the main road and nearing the lane leading to the mine. And then he glanced at her and asked softly, "You all right?" And in reply she lowered her head but didn't speak.

When he entered the yard, the house was still blazing. As he got out of the van, the policeman came up to him, but didn't speak. Instead, his eyes ranged over him from the long deep nail scratch down his cheek to his split and swelling lower lip over his bloodstained shirt and torn coat, the pocket ripped away exposing the lining. An hour ago the little fellow had looked spruce. He'd heard he had just been to a wedding, his mother's wedding; now he looked as if he had come out of the wrong end of a wrestling match. He said to him pointedly, "Did you find who you were looking for?" and Robbie, returning his look, was about to say, "What do you think?" but aware of Gail standing by his side, he said nothing. When he looked at her she was staring at the house and her face was awash with tears. They were silent tears, flowing from pain, and he took her by the arm and led her over the tangled hoses, around the side of the house, across the smoke-filled yard, where the firemen were still fighting the flames, and into the stables that Harry had turned into a workshop; and guiding her to a wooden form near a long bench, he pressed her gently downward, then sat beside her, but looked at her dumbly as her crying became audible. At the height of her sobbing she gasped, "Oh, Robbie, Robbie, I'm s-sorry."

"It's all right, it's all right." He made to take her hands, but they were covering her face, so he pressed his own between his knees and bent his head deeply over them, his

207

teeth gritting against each other to prevent himself now from crying with her.

After a while her sobbing eased and he looked up at her, to find her eyes on him. She was still gasping as she said, "It's dreadful, Robbie, dreadful. I can't believe any—anybody could be so cruel, so vindictive."

It was some time before he answered her; then to his own amazement he found his stiff lips moving into a smile, and he said, "It doesn't seem so bad, nothing seems so bad now." He was holding her gaze. "Back there you said that—that you had promised not to marry me—"

"Oh, Robbie." Her chin was on her chest now, and her voice was a mumble. "She—she forbade me to see you. John had been spying on me coming here. I don't know what possessed me, it just came out. I—I said I would marry you. It was just something to say in defiance. It was then she made the bargain with me. If—if I stopped seeing you, she would give Dad his divorce. It was fantastic. It seemed an easy way out at the time, I mean to get Dad his divorce, but—but as time went on it got harder, I mean not seeing you." Slowly she lifted her eyes to his again and she saw in them a strange expression, for Robbie Dunn and humility didn't go together; but that was the expression on his face, a soft humility.

He now caught hold of her hands and his voice was gruff as he asked, "Do you really mean it, Gail? You're not just sorry for me, or anything like that?"

"Sorry! Oh, no, no. I admire you, Robbie."

"You admire me?" The phrase was a question, a soft doubtful question, but she nodded quick confirmation. "Yes, oh, yes. I know now, I always have."

"I'm a Jew, Gail. As your John so aptly put it, a little Jew, not dirty, no, I won't have that word attached to me, but still a little Jew. Some Jews don't look like Jews, except that their noses might give them away, but every bit of me looks a Jew. Mind"—his voice now became a tone higher—"I'm not makin' excuses for meself, I'm not ashamed of being a Jew, but if a girl like you married me, some people might say you must be hard up for a man."

"Oh, Robbie, don't. Don't." She pulled his hands toward her breast.

"It's true, because you've only got to look in the mirror. I thought a while back that you'd gone off, gone sort of plain, but now you're just like you promised to be, you're bonny beautiful, an' you'll get more beautiful."

208

"Robbie!" She gathered his hands so tightly to her that his face was only a few inches from hers, and her eyes moved over each prominent race-translated feature before she said, "If I don't marry you, I'll marry nobody. I thought after that business with Grandfather that I couldn't bear a boy . . . a man near me, ever, but from that day I saw you in the bookshop I knew I could you, but only you."

When their mouths touched, the pain from his cut lip stabbed through him, but it was as nothing because he was holding Gail Blenheim in his arms, he was kissing Gail Blenheim. Gail Blenheim had said that if she didn't have him she'd have nobody. She was beautiful, lovely, and she wanted him, him, Robbie Dunn. The aching secret that he had pressed deep down into himself over the past years, refusing to recognize it, even to acknowledge its existence, surged upward and filled his body with power.

When at last he released his hold on her, she still remained leaning against him, and he held her gently now and they were both silent. After a while he said, with a catch in his voice, "It's getting on, we'll have to find some place for you to stay the night. There's a little hotel near—"

She raised her head from his shoulder and asked "Where are you going to sleep?"

He thought for a moment, then said, "The back shop will do me; there's a studio bed in there. It only came in last week, it must have known. I'll kip there tonight, and we'll have to think up something before they come back the morrow. An' that's another thing, they're going to be shocked to the core, especially your dad, because he'll blame himself . . . still, he'll have you near him now and that should make up for—"

"Robbie."

"Yes, love." Even using the ordinary endearment brought a slight flush up under his dark skin.

Her lips were trembling and her eyes half veiled as she said, "I don't want to go to a hotel, I—I don't want to be separated from you, ever, ever. I'm—I'm frightened, Robbie. I'm frightened that if ever I lose sight of you something will come between us."

For what seemed a long while he stared into her eyes, then gently took her face between his hands, and his voice scarcely above a whisper, he said, "This time next week we'll be married; we can do it by special license; in the meantime, I'm not goin' to take anything from you that you'll regret later on. Understand? All right? All right?" He shook

209

her face gently. "We'll be together, nothing or nobody will put more than a few yards atween us until we're married."

The tears were in her eyes again and her voice cracked as she whispered, "I love you more every minute, Robbie." Then after a moment, she added, "Do you love me, really?"

He stroked her cheeks now and brought his hands down her neck, around her shoulders, and up through her hair before he muttered thickly, "What I feel for you, Gail, couldn't be said with just 'I love you.' Adore, worship, all kinds of words aren't big enough, they don't fit. I can only say this, that the feeling that's in me now has made that out there"—he jerked his head toward the door—"of little importance, an' if you knew me like I know meself, then you'd know that all me life I've been workin' toward building that house, owning that house. It was what you would call a kind of lodestar, the pinnacle of all my dreams, and, and now it doesn't seem to matter much. So that's what you mean to me, Gail. You understand?"

When she moved her head slowly, he said, "No, you can't, you can't, an' it'll take a lifetime to prove it to you. But I'll work at it, you'll see. An' I'll tell you another thing. By the time I'm finished you won't be seeing me as five-foot-five Robbie Dunn but as I see meself inside, big, capable of achieving anything I set me mind to . . . aye, an' capable of loving you like you never dreamed of being loved. An' by that time we'll have a family an' you'll be mistress of a fine house. Aye, I promise you that an' all, for it'll be rebuilt." He again thumbed toward the door. "But above all else—" His face now underwent a change. The natural arrogance went out of it and the bumptiousness out of his tone, and his head dropping to her shoulder, he murmured, "Above all else, and although I may never mention it again, I want you to know now I'll always be grateful to you for having me."

"Oh, Robbie! Robbie Dunn!"

About the Author

CATHERINE COOKSON was born at Tyne Dock, part of the Tyneside scene she re-creates so vividly in her novels, and most of her early years were spent in what was then the small hamlet of East Jarrow. After leaving school she followed a variety of occupations, finally moving south to Hastings where she met and married a local grammar school master, and has lived there ever since. Over the past twenty years she has firmly established herself as one of the most popular of contemporary English regional novelists.

HANDY FILES AND CASES FOR STORING MAGAZINES, CASSETTES, & 8-TRACK CARTRIDGES

CASSETTE STORAGE CASES

Decorative cases, custom-made of heavy bookbinder's board, bound in Kid-Grain Leatherette, a gold-embossed design. Individual storage slots slightly tilted back to prevent handling spillage. Choice of: Black, brown, green.

#JC-30—30 unit size (13½x5½x6½") $11.95 ea.
3 for $33.00

#JC-60—60 unit size (13½x5½x12⅝") $16.95 ea.
3 for $48.00

MAGAZINE VOLUME FILES

Keep your favorite magazines in mint condition. Heavy bookbinder's board is covered with scuff-resistant Kivar. Specify the title of the magazine and we'll send the right size case. If the title is well-known it will appear on the spine in gold letters. For society journals, a brass-rimmed window is attached and gold foil included—you type the title.

#J-MV—Magazine Volume Files $4.95 ea.
3 for $14.00
6 for $24.00

8-TRACK CARTRIDGE STORAGE CASE

This attractive unit measures 13¾ inches high, 6½ inches deep, 4½ inches wide, has individual storage slots for 12 cartridges and is of the same sturdy construction and decorative appearance as the Cassette Case.

#J-8T12—4½" wide (holds 12 cartridges)
$8.50 ea.
3 for $23.50

#J-8T24—8½" wide (holds 24 cartridges)
$10.95 ea.
3 for $28.00

#J-8T36—12¾" wide (holds 36 cartridges)
$14.25 ea.
3 for $37.00

Please send:

ITEM NO	COLOR (IF CHOICE)	DESCRIPTION	QUANTITY	UNIT PRICE	TOTAL COST

Postage and handling charges (up to $10 add $1.50) ($10.01 to $20 add $2.50) ($20.01 to $40 add $3.50) (over $40 postage FREE)

I enclose ☐ check ☐ money order in amount of $_____ Total _____

The New American Library, Inc.
P.O. Box 999
Bergenfield, New Jersey 07621

Name_____

Address_____

City_____State_____Zip_____

Offer valid only in the United States of America.   (Allow 5 weeks for delivery.)